COME FIND ME,
SAGE PARKER

ALIZA LATTA

Kaitlyn!
I hope this book
takes you on a
journey of
hope!
Aliza

Come Find Me, Sage Parker © 2017 Aliza Latta

ISBN 10: 1775018407 (Paperback)
ISBN 13: 978-1-7750184-0-7

This is a work of fiction. Names, characters, places, and incidents are a product of the author's imagination. Any resemblance to actual people, living or dead, or to businesses, companies, events, institutions, or locales is completely coincidental.

Cover design by Brendon Downey
Hand lettering by Aliza Latta
Editing by Mary Carver

Visit the author's website at www.alizanaomi.com

For the incandescent dreamer
(May you grab yours with both hands and run)

ONE

"WHERE THERE ARE PEOPLE THERE are no limits," my mother once said to me. "We are unbounded—capable of magnificent and excruciating possibilities. Just look up and you'll see the stars and constellations that prove our immensity. We are limitless, Maeve. Don't listen if they tell you otherwise."

I remember when Sage said this. She was braiding my hair like she frequently did, and I sat at the foot of her bed, my gangly legs tangled up together. She brushed my hair and told me stories, brushing until her knuckles ached and the strands were velveteen, and then the braiding commenced, her fingers flying, crisscrossing the locks into intricate and complicated weaves. She braided herself right into me, our fibers knit like the cross-stitch that hung on the wall.

Sol used to tell me I looked just like her. "I'm not saying that's a good thing," he added.

We did look alike; our hair light, especially, for me, after a day beneath the sun. Sage wore brimmed floppy hats to prevent wrinkles. She wore them even while the sun wasn't shining, but I preferred to feel the sun's warmth on my face. My eyes held a mixture of blue and green, like those marbles that shift color depending on how the light shines through. Sage had those eyes, too, but hers were flecked with tiny speckles of hazel and gold. Often I tried to count the specks that capered in her eyes, but they were limitless. As was she.

Sage found two bicycles in the junkyard and brought them home for us. She believed everything had a use, and when that use was fulfilled, she'd find another purpose. Sol teased her, calling her a hoarder, but Sage just laughed.

She brought the bikes home and found me playing in the front yard. She ran up to me, one bike in each hand, an excited smile stretched across her cheeks. "Maeve!" she called out. "Can you believe this? I found these bicycles in the dump. Who in their right mind would throw out two perfectly good bicycles?"

It turned out the bicycles weren't perfectly good. Their brakes didn't work, and whenever I rode mine, I prayed there was a soft landing I could crash into. I pointed this out to Sage, but she smiled and said, "They aren't broken, Maeve. They're just not perfect. Now tell me, who would want something that's perfect, anyway? Perfection is awfully boring."

This is how I remembered her: a sun hat perched on her head with a flowing braid down the side of her body, her fingernails long and painted soft pink, her lips turned out in a half smile. When I closed my eyes, I saw her this way. She was mystical; her thoughts a thousand impossible secrets, a human mystery with daisies in her hair. She asked me not to call her Mom. It made her feel old, she said, or perhaps simply responsible.

On cold nights Sage wrapped her arms around my body like a flannel blanket, whispering to me the story of my father. They were very young, she said. Sage was just seventeen when she had me. My father was only seventeen and a half—on the brink of adulthood with a future seemingly filled with possibilities. Sage told me he wasn't sure if he was ready for a baby. It was tantalizing, I suppose, to dream up a life that didn't dare include me. But Sage was a firm believer in everything happening for a reason.

My father loved Sage something fierce. He asked her to marry him three weeks after I was born, proposing with a simple silver band he had spent four months saving for. She told him yes, but wore the ring on her thumb because she was never much into tradition.

Sage didn't put me in school. She believed I could learn much better in God's nature than I could in some stuffy classroom with teachers who thought they knew more than her. Together we studied butterflies and caught frogs, painted with brushes and our fingers, learned harmonies to songs. She'd sing high and I'd sing low. We'd never be able to finish the song because we'd end up laughing like our guts were going to burst. Sage loved art, and some days we would paint and sculpt and draw. We would hang paintings throughout the house, covering every inch of our walls and she'd make Sol pretend to buy a ticket to our art gallery. Sage especially loved to dance. She'd play classical music and we would dance with one another, swinging our bodies from one corner of the room to the next.

It was always Sage and me, never my father. He died before I turned three, killed in a drunk driving accident, and Sage cried so hard I thought the ocean was erupting from inside of her. At the funeral she pressed her silver ring onto the casket, settling it among the roses that a few people had placed there. She took my chubby hand and said it was time to move on. We moved from that house a month later. With the small amount of money my father abruptly left behind, we rented another one in the town of Sycamore.

Sage told me we didn't need a man in our lives; we could get by just fine. We were "strong, independent women," she would say. Over the years, Sage grew bored of her strong, independent life, and the year I was seven a man named Sol ambled into our little peach home. Sage never told me where she'd met him. She had brought back other men before, a few times, but Sol was the only one who continued to return. Gradually, he became a permanent resident in our two bedroom abode, and in some way or another took the place of my father. Everything seemed okay for awhile. But then The Day happened.

It was March 13. I woke up the morning of The Day, finding my room damp and dewy. It had rained the night before and Sage must've forgotten to close my window. I loved sleeping with the windows open, the way the breeze would flutter through, forcing you to slip deep beneath the covers in order to stay warm. I slid off my mattress, my small body disheveled and bedraggled from a night of dreams. I could hear Sage and Sol arguing downstairs.

"I'm done, Sol. Done!"

"Sage, don't be ridiculous. You have responsibilities here. You have a daughter. Think about Maeve. We can make this work. I know we can."

"She'll be fine."

"She's seven! She won't be fine."

"I never wanted a family!" Sage yelled.

"Then you shouldn't have had a baby!"

I could hear Sage sobbing. "I couldn't do that, Sol. How could I live with myself knowing I killed my baby? She's the best thing I've had."

There was silence for a long moment.

"The best thing?" he asked quietly.

"This is rich. You think you're the best thing?" She snorted. "I did you a favor by letting you live with us. Had I wanted, I could've found someone a little better than you." I heard a dish smash and Sage yelled, "Oh, Sol, please! You can't even have a reasonable conversation!"

"Nothing is reasonable with you, Sage. It always has to be your way. You flit around, changing your mind about everything every two seconds! You're impossible to keep happy!"

She laughed, but it didn't seem amused or kind. "You're

right, Sol. I've changed my mind about a lot of things—the most recent one being you."

I crept to the top of the stairs, spotted the broken plate, heard Sol begging, "Please, Sage, please don't leave me. We can make this work, I promise," and saw my mother throwing things in a floral bag. I think I whimpered or made some sort of noise because Sage looked up at me. She cocked her head, moved up the stairs like the graceful long-legged woman she was, and scooped me in her arms.

She looked at me for a long moment, then tucked me in close against her. "Oh, my darling," she whispered. "I'm not sure how to part with you." She put her face in front of mine and her eyes looked directly at me. "You're safe, Maeve." Her eyes were large, begging me to try and understand her. "You'll remember that, won't you? You're a special and important girl."

She hugged me hard and pressed a kiss from her fingertips to my lips. Then she looked at me for a long moment. "Someday you'll understand why I'm doing what I'm doing. I don't know who I am, Maeve girl. How can I possibly care for someone else when I don't have a clue how to care for myself?" She gave me a sad smile and plopped a floppy hat on her head. Before she went out the door she looked back at me and said, "I'll be back soon, my darling. Don't you worry. I just need to go find myself."

I watched the screen door slam and Sage Parker was gone.

Sage told me we were limitless. If what she said was true, she could be anywhere.

I DIDN'T EAT FOR THREE days after Sage left—not by choice, mind you. I didn't eat because Sol had forgotten since he was now my unofficial guardian, he needed to go buy groceries. Sol spent those three days sitting in his chair by the window, drinking from a glass bottle the color of burnt auburn. I finally got the nerve to talk to him. (I was a little nervous after seeing the smashed plate.) I tiptoed up to his chair and tapped his shoulder.

"Sol, I have a question."

It took him a moment, but he finally turned to me, his eyes glassy. He blinked a few times before focusing on me. "I forgot you were still here. I assumed she would've taken you with her. Figures."

"I'm hungry."

"Go get yourself something to eat."

"I can't find any food."

Sol sighed and got up to go to the kitchen. He pulled out a half empty bottle of ketchup and some crackers that had probably been sitting in the cupboard for at least a year.

"Here you go. Dinner." He pushed the food toward me, but I stared at him. He glared at me then squirted some ketchup onto each cracker. "Is that better?"

I nodded and bit into a cracker. It was awful and hard to chew, but the pains in my stomach prevented me from complaining.

He got up to leave but I said, "Wait, Sol!"

"What?"

"Why did Sage leave?"

He leaned against the doorpost and stared at me for a long time. "She doesn't like us anymore, kid."

I thought about this for a moment. "Do you still like me?"

"Sure."

"Okay."

He turned to go once more, but I said, "Where did Sage go?"

Sol sighed. "I wish I knew."

"She told me she's coming back soon."

He nodded. "That's right. We'll hang in there and she'll be back soon."

We did not speak to each other for the rest of the night. By that point, the ketchup and crackers had long since worn off, and I was feeling very hungry.

I went to the room where Sol had been living and asked him for more food. There were bottles and crushed cans scattered across the room. He got up and smiled in a way that sent shivers up my spine.

"Look who it is. My little Maeve." He came over to me and grabbed my arm quite hard. "You know something, girl? Your mother's gone forever. And now you're mine."

In that instant, I felt scared.

He looked at me, disgusted. "You look just like her." A pause. "Do you know why she didn't take you with her?"

I shook my head. Sol was staring so intently at me, it seemed as though he was memorizing my face.

"As a reminder that she left me. She doesn't care about you, Maeve. She would have taken you with her if she cared."

"You're lying! She loves me!"

"She doesn't!" he yelled. "She doesn't love you," his voice softened and he looked out the window, "and she doesn't care about me."

"Sol, are you okay?" I quietly asked.

His eyes hardened as he turned, his hand slapping me directly across my face. "Do you think I'm okay, Maeve?"

I shook my head, bewildered that he had hit me. My face stung. I reached up to touch it when he grabbed my arm again.

His eyes were wild and wretched—all at once. His fingers wrapped around my forearm as he crushed me against him, whimpering, "I'm sorry, Maeve, I'm sorry. What did I do? I'm sorry. I didn't mean to hurt you—"

Tears sprang to my eyes because my face was burning, and I wanted to get out of the house and find Sage. *Sage, where are you and why did Sol hurt me?*

Sol released me and stepped back, taking a swig from his auburn bottle. "It's going to be different around here, Maeve." His voice was hoarse and scratchy, his face lined with a deep shadow, his bulky frame cocooning the room. "You're not a baby anymore, all right? It's you and me now. I don't want you crying or screaming, and I don't want you bothering me. You got that?"

I was terrified he might hit me again, so I pleaded, "Yes! Yes, I got that, Sol! I got that!"

Sage, Sage, Sage, come home. Please, come home.

"Good. Quit crying. You're fine, Maeve. You're just fine. It'll be all right. We're going to be okay."

I ran to my room and pushed my small body against the door so he couldn't come in. Even though Sol had apologized, I was worried he might change his mind and slap me again. I crawled underneath my bed and with heaving sobs tried to fall asleep.

Please come home, Sage. Please, please come home.

SOL PUT ME IN REAL school because unlike Sage he wasn't thrilled with the idea of homeschooling.

"Sometimes you have to stretch the truth in order to get what you want," he told me the first day we pulled up to the school. He spun a tall tale to the principal, a young woman who appeared to be easily charmed by his rugged features. Sol told her he was my uncle, my only relative left living in the world. The principal didn't question him, simply taking my hand and stroking it, murmuring what a poor, poor girl I was. She stroked Sol's hand, too, and told him he was nothing short of a saint for taking me in. Sol told me afterward: we live in a world of fools.

I fell in love with school. First grade was a haven of structure and routine. Miss Fitz became everything to me, and I began to think of her as my mother. Miss Fitz was kind and compassionate and put on different voices during story time. When she would ask the class to do something ("Class, please be quiet," or "Class, please make sure to put away all the toys"), I would do it quickly and quietly and think to myself, *yes Mommy*.

One day, I made the huge mistake of saying it out loud.

When Miss Fitz asked the class if someone knew any words that rhymed with cat, my hand shot in the air and I yelled, "I do, Mommy! I do, I do!"

A boy yelled, "Stupid Maeve thinks the teacher is her mommy!" The class laughed and laughed, and I wanted to cry. But instead of crying, I looked at the boy and punched him square in the face. That shocked him and he promptly burst into tears.

Pride swelled up inside me. Miss Fitz said I needed to stay with her after school. I said, "That's fine," and was excited because I thought she wanted to spend time with me. Maybe she always wanted a little girl; maybe we were going to go to the park, or ride bicycles, or paint our nails. Or maybe she was going to braid my hair!

I was forced to apologize to the boy, even though I wasn't terribly apologetic. Fortunately, he was forced to apologize for calling me stupid even though I had the sneaking suspicion he wasn't that sorry either.

Miss Fitz gave me a cookie that afternoon as we talked. "Maeve, can I ask you a question?"

Part of me wanted to point out that she already had asked me a question, but I just stared at the fat chocolate chips and nodded my head.

"Do you know why you called me Mommy?" She asked kindly.

No answer, mostly because I didn't know if I should lie or tell the truth. I was concerned if I didn't follow the same story Sol had told the principal, I would get hit again. But Miss Fitz didn't seem to know what Sol had told the principal months earlier.

She lifted my chin with her hand and forced me to look into her eyes. "Maeve, honey, why did you call me mommy? Is your mommy at home?"

I shook my head.

"She's not, huh. Do you have a mommy?"

I nodded.

"Okay. Do you sometimes go to your mommy's house?"

I shook my head again.

"Does Mommy sometimes come over to your house?"

I didn't quite know how to answer that question, so I didn't do anything.

"Maeve, why don't you tell me all about your mommy?"

"She is really pretty and we used to ride bicycles together and she would paint my nails yellow. One time she let me paint her nails, but I wasn't very good at it so she said I should wait 'til I'm a little older to paint my nails by myself."

"She sounds like a very smart lady."

I nodded. "But then one day she left and now it's just me and Sol. I don't really know where she went, and I don't think Sol does either. She told me she was coming home but she hasn't been home in a long time."

"I see. Is Sol your daddy?"

"Kinda."

"Kind of?"

"Well Daddy died a long time ago, and now Sol lives with me."

Miss Fitz was quiet for a moment so I said, "I'm sorry, Miss Fitz. I promise I won't call you Mommy anymore."

She smiled sadly at me and gave me a quick hug. I hadn't been hugged since Sage left and I didn't want the warm feeling to end.

"You're a very special girl, Maeve. You're very sweet, and I'm honored that you would think of me like your mom. But," she said as she took my hands, "I'm not your Mommy." I nodded and she hugged me again. "You're a good girl, Maeve." She raised an eyebrow, "But you are not allowed to punch anybody. Ever."

I looked down and finished off my cookie. "Yes ma'am," I said, my mouth full, and she looked at me and laughed.

I never called her Mommy again, but I basked in the warmth of Miss Fitz's kindness and grace—that is until first grade was over. I entered the rest of my life, leaving chocolate chip cookies and Miss Fitz behind.

AS I GOT OLDER, I stole away into the school library whenever I could.

The truth was, I couldn't read very well. I'm stubborn and I wasn't about to allow my uneducated childhood hinder me from surviving middle school. It wasn't that I wanted to excel in every class. I just didn't want to fail and be held back and thought of as stupid.

Even though it didn't come easily, I loved reading. When I read, I felt as though I was transported into someone else's world for awhile. It came as a sweet relief for me. It took me a long time to figure out how to read, but the more books I read, the more words I learned, and the easier it was to escape my reality.

I read books like *The Diary of a Young Girl* and *To Kill A Mockingbird* because the school had assigned them for us to study. I decided I wanted to be like Scout. To me, she was incredibly brave. I liked the idea of bravery. I wanted to be strong and bold and wildly courageous.

I just had no idea how.

So instead, I hid in that library and escaped into written worlds, and as I acquainted myself with the characters I pretended I was one of them. My favorite part in *To Kill A Mockingbird* was,

"Atticus, he was real nice."
"Most people are, Scout, when you finally see them."

And I wondered if I had ever really finally seen anyone. I thought of Sol. Had I ever finally seen him? Underneath the layers of vulgar words and whiskey bottles, was there something more to the man with whom I lived under the same roof? Some days he was kind, days where he didn't drink and didn't get mean, days where it felt like he and I were a family.

I thought of Sage.

I'll be back soon, my darling. Don't you worry. I just need to go find myself.

Those words echoed through my mind almost daily. During the first few years after she had left, I ran to the door every day to see if she had found herself yet. But she was never there. A car never pulled into the driveway. A woman with a floppy hat didn't show up at the door. My mother never came back for me.

Do you have to run away in order to find yourself? And when, exactly, do you know when that self you were so desperately looking for is found?

I hated Sage. And I loved her. But mostly I felt hate.

I hated how she left me with Sol. I hated how she didn't keep her promise. I hated how she wore those stupid floppy hats, and didn't allow me to call her Mom because it made her feel old. I hated how she left me. I hated how she left me. I hated how she left me.

But more than anything, I hated how she didn't come back.

TWO

THE SWEETNESS MISS FITZ SAW in me when I was seven was all but untraceable by the time I entered high school. I didn't know who I was, but more than that, I didn't know who I wanted to be. I wanted to be the girl hidden away in the library, the one camouflaged with books and stories. But I also wanted bravery; I wanted to be seen. Except the more I thought about it, the more being seen seemed too much like walking around naked—stark and bare, on display for everyone to gape at. So I shoved my dreams of courage and visibility down as far as I could, and I began to add layers. I spent hours combing through magazines, staring at photos of glamorous women, mesmerized by their dark makeup and big hair. I tried to teach myself their techniques, investing in cans of hairspray and sticks of eyeliner.

The year I turned sixteen, Sol got fired from the car dealership he was working at. The only job he could find was at a steel mill a few hours away. So in the middle of the summer, we moved from the peach house in Sycamore, the house where I grew up, the last place I saw my mother. We moved two and a half hours away to the town of Rutherford: a new school, a fresh start. Or at least that's what Sol said it would be. I didn't believe him.

I painted on my makeup the first day of my new high school. Rutherford wasn't a huge town—it wasn't minuscule either, but I felt like I could make a real impression if I wanted. Sol told me I should try to make new friends, and get involved in school activities or something. He told me these were supposed to be some of the best days of my life.

He drove me to school in his truck. "Have a good day, okay, Maeve?" Sol said as I hopped out.

"Yeah," I said flatly, "It's going to be life changing."

I threw my backpack over my shoulder and started making my way through the parking lot toward the east entrance. A few picnic tables were scattered outside the school. They were forsaken, and so was I. Each of us was abandoned. With twenty-five minutes before class officially started, I wasn't in a rush. I tossed my backpack down beside me and sat.

A girl was leaning against a tree a few yards away, curls of smoke coiling around her, a cigarette pressed between her pursed red lips. She was dressed similarly to me, heavy make-up and clothes void of any color.

I watched her as she smoked. She caught me looking and glared. I pretended to urgently need something from my bag.

"It's rude to stare. Didn't your mother tell you that?"

I looked up. She was standing in front of me. "I wasn't staring," I mumbled.

"Sure looked like it to me." She took another drag then dropped the cigarette on the grass, crushing it beneath the sole of her army boot. "Are you new here?"

I gave a stiff nod.

"Where are you from?"

"Sycamore."

"Never heard of it."

"It's about two hours north of here."

"You've got one shot in this town, baby. If you blow it, it's kaput. Freaking Rutherford. Take my advice: don't screw yourself over." She studied me. "I'm Ky McNeil."

"Maeve Parker."

"Interesting name."

"I could say the same about yours."

"A valid point." She slipped her bag off her shoulder and set it on the table. She sat beside me. "What grade are you in?"

"Eleventh."

"Me too."

"Have you lived here long?"

"All my life. Someday I'm gonna get out of this place and go to Iceland."

"Iceland? Why?"

"It's pretty far. Kind of weird. Not popular. Sort of mysterious."

"Like you." I meant it as a question, but it left my mouth accusatory.

She laughed. "Yeah, I guess so."

"Are you going to do anything in particular there?"

"Finally live. Rutherford is stifling. It smothers you. Like my mother."

"Your mom smothers you?"

Ky sighed. "Yeah. I tried to kill myself this summer, but I didn't do a very good job at it. Ever since then, she's been impossible to live with."

I was startled by her blunt confession. "Maybe she's just worried about you."

"No. She feels guilty. Plus she thinks her constant coddling makes up for the years of bad boyfriends."

"Lots of bad ones?"

"Too many to count. The current one's the worst though. Treats her like crap, but she just takes it, you know? Which means I have to take it, too."

I looked out across from where we were sitting, staring at the red brick walls of the high school. "Why did you try to kill yourself?"

"Apparently I'm clinically depressed. They actually give me drugs." Ky smirked. "My mom spent years lecturing me about the dangers of drugs, and now she's checking in on me every night to make sure I'm taking mine. The irony," she said dryly. "My mom put me in the hospital, said I was 'mentally unstable'. Now I'm not even allowed to shave my freaking legs."

"So you want to go to Iceland and erase all of this?"

"That's what I tried telling them. It's not like I wanted to kill myself permanently. That sounds stupid when I say it out loud. I just... I wanted to somehow become someone else. Figure out a different life or something. But killing myself was all I could think of at the time."

We were silent for a long moment. She asked, "Have you ever thought about it?"

"Killing myself?"

"Yeah."

I shook my head. "No. Not really."

She laughed. "I guess you're not depressed. Not clinically, anyway."

"I guess not. But I would like to disappear. Become someone else. Do something new."

I couldn't understand why she was telling me this, a girl she didn't know. Maybe she wanted to see if she could scare me away — but she didn't scare me. In fact, she made me feel safer than I'd felt in a long time. It was rare for someone to tell you exactly what they thought.

Ky let out a held breath and looked at the kids walking into the school, with their haircuts and backpacks and brand-new, freshly bought clothes. The seemingly normal ones. "Maybe everyone does."

I HADN'T PLANNED ON MEETING Levi.

Maybe that's a stupid thing to say because I suppose you never truly plan on meeting people in general—unless they're some sort of celebrity or something, but going to a new school I was content to not meet anyone. I'd already failed that plan by meeting and somehow becoming friends with Ky, but I didn't feel like I needed anyone else. I was doing okay on my own.

But a week and a half after I met Ky, I met Levi. On the way to the bathroom.

I didn't actually have to use the bathroom. I just thought I was literally going to die if I heard my math teacher talk about his weird dreams again. He had a habit of talking about his strange dreams in between math lessons.

So I raised my hand and got a pass for the bathroom.

I took a long time to get there, meandering through the graffiti-filled hallways that caused the principal to constantly be threatening expulsion, and yet there was consistently more graffiti each day.

A boy was sitting against a locker, across from the bathrooms. His hand was bleeding.

"What happened to you?" I blurted out before I realized what I was asking.

He looked up at me. The first thing I noticed was the black-blue bruise already forming around his right eye socket. The second was the color of his eyes. Oceanic, tidal wave blue. You could drown in that ocean if you weren't careful.

I sighed. Every knuckle on both of his hands was scraped and bleeding. I went into the bathroom and got him some damp paper towels. When I came out to give them to him, he was still sitting there.

"Here. Take these."

He mumbled a thank you and took them, pressing them against his eye. I stared at him for a moment, then sat down. I left a good chunk of room between us.

We were quiet for a long time. I half-wondered if my math teacher, Mr. Herman, was still talking about his dreams. Last week he'd dreamed about one of the girls in our class, and then of course told the class all about it. Honestly, there must be laws against that.

"You can't tell my parents, okay?"

I looked at the boy. "I don't even know who you are, let alone your parents. Don't worry about it."

He seemed relieved. I was going to point out to him that they were bound to find out by the looks of his face, but decided against it.

"Does your eye feel better?"

"It never really hurt."

I raised my eyebrow.

"What?"

"I'm not in the mood for a guy to pretend to be macho."

He looked wounded. "Thanks."

"Are you going to tell me what happened? Or should I go back to Mr. Herman's class? I'll probably fall asleep — it's so boring."

"That dude's the worst."

I grimaced. "Tell me about it. I don't know how I'm going to survive the semester."

"Yeah, I'm glad I don't have him." We were quiet for a moment. "I got into a fight. It's not a big deal."

"I'm assuming you lost?"

He narrowed his eyes. "You're exceptionally good at building up people's pride."

I smirked. "It's called honesty."

"Right."

"But you did lose, right?"

"Yeah." He pressed the paper towels harder against his eye. "Yeah, I guess I lost."

"Why'd you fight him in the first place?"

"Do you want to guess? Assuming you don't want to go back to class."

I laughed. "Uhh, sure. Okay." I repositioned myself against the locker, stretching my legs out in front of me. "Let me see. You seem, to me, to have some sort of heroic pride, some sort of savior complex. You want to rescue people, but you're not the strongest, so you lose. I'm guessing you've done this a few times and your parents aren't pleased about it. Maybe they feel like it stains their reputation or something. So I'm going to guess you got into a fight to save a girl. To be the knight in shining armor. How romantic."

"Wrong," he said flatly. "I was not trying to save a girl."

"Was the rest of it at least close?"

"Are you normally this cynical?"

"Depends on my mood."

"It does make my parents mad, but they don't care that much about their reputation."

"So if it wasn't for a girl, then who was it for? Wait—are you one of those weird, misogynistic guys who spend their entire lives playing video games in their mom's basement and then, when absolutely forced to have human contact, it's revealed that you have zero social skills and feel like your only means of survival is to fight people?"

"No."

He smiled then.

"Good," I said, pretending to be relieved.

"It does hurt," he said after a moment.

"Want more paper towel?"

He nodded, so I stood up and got him some more from the bathroom.

"Why are you being nice to me?" he asked when I handed him the next batch.

I sat down again. "I think there are two possible theories. One, I could simply be a nice person. Or the second, I could be exceptionally bored and positively dreading going back to math and hearing a mix of Herman's dreams and the Pythagorean theorem."

"Definitely the first."

I laughed. "So, if it wasn't a mystery girl, and you're not an antisocial video game lunatic, who were you trying to save?"

He didn't speak for a while. "Me."

I tilted my head and looked straight into his eyes. "You?"

"Is that strange?" he asked.

"No," I told him quietly. "Not strange. I can't begin to count the number of times I've tried to save myself."

"Have you lost?"

"Every time."

"Me too."

"But I don't think it means you stop trying."

He looked at me for a long time. "You're new here, aren't you?"

I nodded.

The intercom crackled and *Levi Fisher, please come to the office* played loud over it.

He grimaced.

"Levi Fisher, huh?" I asked.

"Just Levi," he said as he got up. "You?"

"Just Maeve."

Levi sighed. "Thanks for being kind to me. Or being bored. Either way, thank you."

I smiled. "Good luck down there."

"Thanks." He turned to walk down the hall and then looked back at me. "Hey, Maeve?"

"Yeah?"

"I hope you figure out how to save yourself."

Me too, Levi Fisher. Me too.

"And when you do," he continued, "will you let me know how?"

"Of course," I told him. "Could be a long time though."

"Don't worry. I'm sure I'll still be here."

I hadn't planned on meeting Levi, and yet now that I had, it suddenly seemed up to me to figure out some way to save him.

THREE

SAGE PAINTED THE HOUSE PEACH.

It was before Sol moved in, only a few weeks after my father had passed away. It was a rental house, so she didn't even know if she was allowed to paint it—but she was a risk taker, she said—and decided to paint it anyway. She came home with buckets of paint and all sorts and sizes of paint brushes. The house was a silvery-grey, with a tint of deep green. The color of dried sage, in fact. But Sage decided she hated the color, despised it with all of her being. She'd been saying it for a while, every time we would bring in the groceries or come home from the park.

"The house is a terrible color, Maeve. Don't you agree?" She never actually gave me the chance to answer. "Yes, I think so, too. It's very sad. Very sad indeed." Then she heaved a vintage sigh and walked into the house, wondering aloud what she could possibly do to make our home appear happier.

The solution, she figured, was to paint the house bright peach.

"We're starting an art project," Sage explained to me the day she brought home the paint. "Well, I suppose it's a mix of art and home decor. Either way, it's good experience."

"Am I gonna paint the house too, Sage?"

"That's right. You and me. Other people might hire painters—some people paint houses for an actual living, you know—but we're going to paint it ourselves. We're regular do-it-yourself-er's."

I nodded as if I understood precisely what she was talking about.

"It's important to do things in life that seem hard," Sage continued as she handed me a paintbrush and my own tiny bucket of peach. "And we might not do the job perfectly like a professional would, but you know how I feel about perfection, don't you, Maeve?"

I did.

We painted our home rather imperfectly that weekend. I was in charge of the bottom and Sage the top and middle. It was a one-story house, so she was able to reach the top with a ladder.

"Why are we painting it this color, Sage?" I asked her halfway through the first day. Had she wanted my opinion, the obvious choice would have been yellow.

"It's a beautiful color, Maeve. Not quite orange, but not pink either. And it's bright. Vivacious!" She hummed loudly to herself and I listened to her song, slapping coats of paint on the side of the house.

When we finally finished, we stood across the street and proudly admired our handiwork. There was no contest. It was by far the ugliest house on the block, but Sage didn't care.

"I love it," she said.

"It's different from the other homes," I told her, looking at the other houses that were painted gray or brown, or a mix of gray and brown. They looked dismal in comparison.

"That's the point, my darling. Us Parkers will really stand out now."

"Why do you want us to stand out?"

She squeezed me against her hip. "There's no point in trying to be like everybody else, Maeve, because everybody else isn't the type of people we should ever hope to be like."

FOUR

"YOO-HOO!" A VOICE, SHRILL AS anything, pierced through my head, interrupting my Saturday morning sleep.

"Sol," I called. "Sol, someone's at the door."

He didn't answer.

I rolled over, but the incessant tapping at the door kept me from finding sleep again.

"Sol!" I called louder. "Get the door!"

I rolled out of bed and found Sol lying on the sofa, a bottle dangling from his fingers. I shook him hard. He groaned. "Get up. Someone's at the door."

His eyes slowly opened. "You get it, Maeve. I don't like people."

"I don't either. Do you want them to see you like this?"

Sol closed his eyes again but found his way to a sitting position.

I sighed.

"Hello?" A female voice called. "Is anyone home? Helloooooo?"

Sol swore under his breath.

"We could just ignore her," I whispered. "She doesn't know

we're home."

Sol nodded. "Okay. Be quiet."

We waited silently as she continued to tap, her voice singsongy, "Hello in there! I see your car! I know you're home!"

Sol and I stared at one another.

"We have to get it," he whispered.

"What kind of crazy person is this? She's standing there waiting for us?" I whispered back.

"Maybe something happened."

"Maybe she's a stalker and is planning on kidnapping us. Maybe she's going to cut off our fingers and make us eat them!"

He rolled his eyes. "You watch too much T.V."

"Fine. But we get her to leave as soon as possible."

He nodded.

I opened the door.

She couldn't have been more than five feet tall. Curly red hair spilled over her shoulders, lending her a wild, frenzied look. I guessed she was in her early thirties. She began to shake my hand vigorously. So vigorously, in fact, I briefly wondered if I might end up with whiplash.

"Hi!" she said excitedly, her voice impossibly high. That came as no surprise to me. "I'm Francine Sinclair! I'm your new landlord!"

"Hi there…" I said slowly, trying to subtly extricate my hand from her grasp. No luck. She had stopped pumping it up and down, but continued to hold on tight.

She looked at me, expectant. "And… you are?"

"Oh," I sputtered. "I'm Maeve."

"Maeve!" She exclaimed. "What a beautiful name!"

At that point, I assumed everything Francine said ended with an exclamation mark. I was weary already and wishing we had stuck to the original plan of ignoring her.

"Thank you…"

"Do you live here alone?" she asked. I contemplated how

much caffeine she needed to consume per day in order to make her so chipper. She looked at me, blinking quickly. I pulled my hand away slowly, and—finally—she released me.

I shook my head and opened the door wider so she could see Sol. "With my stepdad." I had come to call him that. It was easier than people asking questions like Miss Fitz, and the principal from first grade was long gone so I didn't need to refer to Sol as my uncle.

"Hello!" She said to him. "And your name is?"

"Sol," he croaked. At least his eyes were open.

"He… isn't feeling well," I told her, wondering why I still covered for him.

"Oh, you poor dear. Are you nauseous?"

Sol nodded and Francine made her way toward him. She sat beside him on the couch. I remained at the doorway.

"Do you have any anti-nausea medication? If you don't, I can go run to the store and get you some." Francine turned her head toward me and smiled. "I don't want to simply be your landlord. I want to be your friend."

She was a walking infomercial. "Don't they say not to mix business with pleasure?" I muttered and closed the door. It was cold out and Francine clearly wasn't leaving anytime soon.

Sol laughed. Francine didn't.

"If you want my opinion, I think that's a ridiculous notion. It would be so fun if we were all friends. Don't you think, Solomon?"

"It's Sol," he said. "And sure—fun. Loads."

Francine patted his leg but removed her hand quite quickly. I didn't blame her; he desperately needed a shower. "It's simply terrible that you're under the weather."

Sol coughed. "Something must be going around."

"So what do you do for a living? Let's play a quick round of twenty questions. I love getting to know my tenants. That's one of my favorite parts of this job!"

"You know, Francine," I told her as I went back toward the door, "It's very nice of you to drop by unannounced like this on a Saturday morning, but we have a lot to do today."

"Maeve, don't be rude," Sol told me. I glared at the little traitor. Francine smiled at me, oblivious. My head hurt. I wanted my bed.

"I work at the steel mill." He told her.

"You must be a hard worker. I've heard that's draining."

"Nothing I can't handle."

It was more like he couldn't find anything else, but I didn't say that. I flopped myself down on a chair and sighed dramatically.

Francine smiled and asked, "What about you, Maeve?"

"Umm… I'm just a student. A junior."

"How exciting! Are you loving it so far?"

"Sure…"

She sighed. "I loved high school. Such good days. I hope you find some people you love dearly."

"That'd be the dream, wouldn't it?"

Francine nodded. "We need other people. All of us do. That's one of the reasons why I want to get to know my tenants, to get to know you. I want you to know you can count on me."

"Is our rent going up?" Sol asked suspiciously.

"Oh, gosh, no. I would hate to do that to you."

"Right." He looked at me. "Aren't you going to offer our guest a drink?"

I was annoyed he was finding reasons for her to stay.

"We have juice, water, milk…"

"And wine," Sol suggested.

Francine giggled then flushed. "Oh, I don't think I should be having wine at eight o'clock in the morning. Water, please. Thank you, Maeve."

"My pleasure," I muttered and went into the kitchen to get her a glass of water.

"I'll have one too!" Sol called. I grabbed another glass.

I handed them each their beverage then moved back into the kitchen to do some homework. Look at me, spending my Saturday with math and my new crazy landlord.

I was jealous of my own life.

DURING HERMAN'S CLASS, I WENT to the bathroom again.

Levi Fisher was there. His eye looked even worse than it had the first time I saw him.

"You look terrible," I said, lingering at the mouth of the hallway, a dozen feet away from him.

"I appreciate the honesty."

"Suspension from school?"

"Actually, no. Not this time."

"How'd the parental units take it?"

"Yeah… not so great."

"Lecture?"

"Long one."

"Brutal."

"T'was brutal," he agreed.

Levi slumped down against the lockers. I walked over and sat beside him.

"You want to know what was more brutal? The fact that they decided since I clearly cannot handle myself, I am in desperate need of being put into anger management classes. Again."

I turned to him. "Really?"

"Yup. Brutal."

"Wow."

"How was your night? Probably better than mine."

"For sure," I laughed. "Although my stepdad can be a little crazy, so it's never boring."

"What makes him crazy?"

29

I shrugged. "He drinks pretty often. He's fine when he's sober."

Levi nodded as if he understood, and I wondered if he did. "Does he get drunk a lot?"

"Not a lot. Sometimes."

"Does he hurt your mom?"

I shook my head. "She left a long time ago, so it's just him and me. Been that way for most of my life, it seems."

"What about your dad?"

"He died when I was three. I don't really remember him."

"I'm sorry."

I looked at him. "Why? It's not your fault. It is what it is."

"But you deserve a mom."

"A lot of people deserve a lot of things. That doesn't mean you get them."

"That's true."

"Does he hurt you?"

"Third degree over here, eh?"

He smiled. "Sorry."

"Yeah, he has before, but not in a long time. It's not that bad. Nothing I can't handle."

Levi rolled his eyes. "Maeve, I'm not in the mood for you to pretend to be macho."

I looked at him quickly. Realizing he was joking, I smiled. "Funny."

"People tell me that all the time."

"That you're funny?"

He nodded.

"They must tell you you're humble, too."

"Of course."

I groaned. "I don't want to go back to Herman's class."

"Do you hate math or do you just hate Herman?"

"Both? I'm no good at math. Where are you supposed to be right now?"

He grinned. "Construction with Miller."

I pretended to gag.

"Yeah, tell me about it. Though I'd rather be there than Herman's."

"Good point."

A teacher walked down the hall and glared at us. "When on a study period," she said without stopping, "we expect you to be studying."

"Yes ma'am," Levi said.

I giggled. She shot me another look and walked away.

"I'm no good at math, but I want to go to college," I explained.

"Don't you have another year before you have to worry about that?"

"I guess so. But I've got to keep up good marks so colleges will hopefully be more willing to accept me. You know?"

He nodded. "Yeah. I'm sure you'll do fine."

"I don't think so—at least not in math. I can blame it on Herman, but I honestly don't get it. I care more about English, anyway."

"You like all that?"

"Yeah. Do you?"

"I don't know what I like yet." He turned his head to face me. "If I had my way, I would get away from here and go live on the beach."

I laughed. "Wouldn't that be nice."

"I'm serious."

"And what would you do there?"

Levi shrugged. "I don't know. I don't like this city—not the forest or the pollution from the stupid mill or the way the buildings in town feel crammed together. I want to live on the ocean, where it's wide and open and you can be by yourself. I don't particularly like people all that much."

"Won't there be a ton of people at the beach?"

"Only during vacation. And not if I got one that's private."

"You won't get lonely, living by yourself?"

"I don't really get lonely."

"Do you have friends?"

Levi scratched a piece of graffiti off the locker with his fingernail. "Sure. But they like me more than I like them. Besides this is high school. People hardly stay friends with the people they went to high school with."

"Is that so?"

He nodded.

"Then I guess I'll go now. We probably don't have much chance at staying friends according to your little philosophy."

Levi laughed and looked at me for a long moment. "But you're different than other people."

I felt embarrassed and turned away. "What's that supposed to mean?"

"You didn't ask me what my name was when you first saw me. I was a person and you were a person, and that was all that mattered."

I didn't have anything to say to that. After a long moment, I asked, "Why do you get angry?"

He sighed. "I don't know."

"What does it feel like when it happens?"

"You ask personal questions."

"So do you."

He gave me a coy smile and shifted his feet beneath him. "I've gone to anger management classes before. I hate them. My mom let me drop out because I was pretty much making her life a living hell, but after yesterday they'll definitely make me complete it." He sighed. "It feels like… like there's pressure inside of me. Like a pressure cooker is embedded inside of my stomach, and it boils and boils and boils until one day it explodes. I want to save myself and stop the anger but I don't know how."

"Do the classes help?"

Levi shrugged. "I guess. The first thing they tell you is to find an outlet. Okay wait, that's not true. The actual first thing they tell you is that you must admit you have a problem. Like you're a drug addict or an alcoholic or something. The next thing they tell you is to find an outlet. We have to calm down, but not suppress it, but also not express it in a way that will hurt someone. Therefore find an outlet." Levi smiled, his teeth white against his lips. "They suggest running or painting or something. But I hate those ideas."

"So you need to find some way to cope?"

"Yeah." He hesitated for a moment, the start of a shy, rosy blush painting the edge of his cheeks. "You help me cope."

"Me?"

He nodded.

"We hardly know each other."

"I know, but I feel calm around you."

"Oh." I blinked.

"Is that weird?"

"No, just surprising. I don't normally have that effect on people."

"You could be my outlet until I find an actual way of coping."

"What does that entail?"

"Well, you can ask me anything about my problem and I have to be honest." He started speaking with a British accent, "'Honesty is the key. You must express your anger in an assertive, but not aggressive, manner. You must clearly communicate what your needs are, and how they should be met. And you must always, always be honest.'"

"So you can never lie?"

"I can. But I'm not supposed to. Is anyone supposed to?"

I laughed. "I don't think so. Golden rule and all that."

"The golden rule is not Do Not Lie."

"Then what is it, Intellectual Genius?"

"'Do to others as you would have them do to you.'"

"Really."

"You didn't know that?"

I shook my head.

"My mom quoted it to me and my brother every time we fought."

"How old is your brother?"

"A year younger than us. Fifteen. Do you have any siblings?"

"Not that I know of," I joked. "So if you can't lie: what's the trigger that makes you get angry?"

Levi blew air from his lips. "Loaded question. I'm still trying to figure it out."

"Fair enough."

We were quiet for a few moments.

"We all have our problems, don't we, Maeve?"

I nodded. "Sure we do. All of us."

"What are some of yours?"

I laughed. "You're the one that has to be honest, not me."

He smiled. "Touché. But someday you'll answer as many personal questions as you ask me."

"Maybe. But that's not today."

I STARTED TO DREAM OF paradise.

Paradise included Levi Fisher, a long stretch of Levi's ocean, and the sweet scent of freedom.

I dreamed of a day when I would stand in the water. It would be salty, of course, and blue, and it would swirl around my ankles. I would wade in, one step at a time, and the sand under my toes would melt away with every step I would take. A wave would come and force my body gently to ride along with it, and my hair would get flung into the sea and I would arise out of the water bold and beautiful.

The fragrance of freedom would waft underneath my nose.

And I would linger there for a lifetime.
In paradise.

FIVE

"YOU'RE GOING TO THE SADIE Hawkins Dance, right, Maeve?"
Ky asked me one morning in the bathroom before the first
period started. I was washing my hands and she was reapplying
her makeup.

I turned to her, incredulous. "You really think I'd want to go
to some stupid school dance?"

"Maybe." She shrugged her shoulders.

I waited for a moment. "Are you going to the Sadie Hawkins
dance?" I was expecting an automatic no since Ky thought all
school events were ridiculous.

She pursed her lips, gazing into the mirror. "I'd like to, yes,"
she said nonchalantly.

"You're kidding me. I thought you hated dances."

"I hate normal dances. This time we can choose any boy we
want." She applied some more red lipstick. "This time," she
winked, "we have all the power." She started to laugh evilly.

"Quit laughing like that. It's creepy."

"So if I go to the dance, will you go too?"

"I'm going to go with a no on that one."

"Please, Maeve? It could be fun."

"This is freaking me out. You hate dances, you hate boys, and you hate dresses."

She gave me a look. "Stop being so dramatic. I do not hate boys."

"You've made fun of every boy in this school."

"That's how I show affection. You have a problem with that?"

I looked at her. "I'm pretty sure that's not a legitimate way to show affection, Ky." I felt her forehead. "Are you sick?"

She scowled. "No. I'm perfectly fine." Sighing, Ky took my hand. "Maeve."

"Yes, Ky?"

"We are becoming women. We're not immature little girls anymore. We need to recognize who we're becoming and go after it."

I stared at her. "What magazines have you been reading?"

She smiled sheepishly. "My older sisters'. She left them at my house when she left for college. That's not the point. The point is that we are going to this dance. We are going to choose boys to go with us. We are going to look very, very good, and we are going to be remembered. C'mon Maeve, we have to make some lasting impressions."

"You actually want to do this?"

Ky hesitated. "Fine. No, I don't—at all. But my mom said I have to choose at least one school event to go to so she knows that I'm making an effort to be more involved in activities."

"Couldn't you choose… a football game? Basketball? Something that doesn't involve me or getting dressed up?"

She bit her nail. "There's a possibility it might be fun."

"Convincing."

"You might meet your one true love."

I rolled my eyes.

"Jared the Boyfriend dumped my mom, so I'm all she thinks about now. Plus she said I'll have to go back to the doctor if I don't start showing her some changes. Please, Maeve? Please? I wouldn't ask you to endure this with me if it wasn't really, really important. I don't want to go back to the doctor."

I looked at her, her dark hair framing her skinny, serious face. "Fine."

Ky almost squealed, wrapping her arms around my body. "Maeve Parker, I owe you big time."

"You can say that again."

THE NEXT WEEK AFTER SCHOOL, Ky and I bussed to the next town over. It had more shops, therefore more options for dresses. We walked down the streets, window shopping, and as we passed a boutique I saw a dress I didn't despise. Please indulge me for a moment: why is it that it's the female gender who's forced to wear moronic fabric which prohibits her from doing quite a vast amount of things? While boys can still do a fair bit in a suit—though I must admit, those ties look lethal—girls are stuck in either tight, skimpy dresses that prevent her from breathing, or flouncy ones that resemble that of a six-year-old on Easter Sunday. And please, don't get me started on high heels.

But this dress seemed different to me. It was bright yellow with little straps and a few tiny buttons that decorated the top of it. It was fitted to the waist, then puffed out in complete taffeta glory. It may have been on the closer end of resembling something a child would wear, but it was yellow. And yellow was everything I wanted to be.

I pressed my hands against the glass and looked at the beautiful dress.

"I want that," I told Ky. "That's my dress. I want that."

"It's yellow," She said sourly.

"So? I don't care." I stared at it again. "You don't like it?"

"It's kind of… bright."

"Like you said, we'll make a lasting impression."

The little bell jingled as I walked through the door.

"Excuse me." I asked the lady at the counter politely, "What does that yellow dress in the window cost?"

Her glasses slid down her nose as she looked me over.

"That yellow dress in the window?" She pointed to my dress and I nodded. It was the only yellow dress in the window, and I knew she was being rude.

"Yes, that one."

"Sixty-nine dollars," she said crisply.

I tried not to appear as shocked as I felt. "All right. Thank you."

"That thing is almost seventy bucks!" I exclaimed to Ky as soon as I heard the front door shut.

"How much do you have?" She asked.

"Only thirty." I sighed sadly. "The dance is next week. There's no way I can make enough to buy that dress. It doesn't matter. I hate dresses anyway."

Ky was quiet for a moment. "We'll get you your dress. Tomorrow."

"I won't have enough money by tomorrow!"

"Would you hush?" she demanded. "Don't worry about it."

The next day we bussed back over. We walked by the boutique, and to my delight, my dress was still hanging in the window.

"I'm going to go in and ask to try on the dress. While I'm in the change room, you have to go in and start talking to the lady. Make sure to get her full attention. Once you see me leaving, run out of the store," Ky said to me.

"We're going to steal it?" I blurted out.

"Shut up, Maeve. Do what I told you and it will be fine." She walked into the store. I could see through the glass that she was talking to the same rude lady from the day before. The lady came up to the window and took the dress off the mannequin. I watched her hand the dress to Ky, who darted off into the change room. I took a couple of deep breaths and entered the store.

"Hello, ma'am," I said cheerily.

She looked up at me, her glasses once again sliding down her nose.

"How are you today?" I asked her, smiling.

"Fine."

"That's great!"

"Is there anything I can help you with?"

"Um, yeah, I just wondered," I went and touched a blue satin dress, "I wondered what this was made of. You see I'm doing a project for school and—"

"Satin."

She looked back down at the book she was reading.

"Okay. Great. Thank you." I went to a different one. "And this?"

"Satin with toile overlay."

"Great. You know, uh, I'm interested in someday owning my own shop. Do you like working here?"

"I suppose so," she said, still reading.

"Is it a dream come true for you?"

She breathed a sardonic laugh. "Hardly."

I drummed my fingers on the counter. "So, whatcha reading?"

"A book." She replied.

"What's it about?"

"Poor, young girls who don't know how to leave someone alone."

"Sounds riveting," I told her flatly. "You want to know something?"

She didn't answer.

"I'm not a young girl. I'm practically a woman. I'm beginning to recognize who I'm becoming and I'm going after it," I said dramatically, quoting Ky's sisters' magazine.

She looked up, stared at me for a moment, then went back to her book.

"Well," I huffed, quite agitated with the woman for calling me young and poor, as well as with Ky for taking so long. "Let me tell you something, lady. Your finest skill is not customer service."

I heard steps behind me and the bell from the door rang.

"Lovely talking to you. Enjoy your day! And that stupid book!" I flashed her a smile and took off.

I ran behind Ky, hearing the woman yell after us, but Ky and I were too fast. We were practically flying with adrenaline coursing through our veins.

When we had gone a safe distance, we collapsed on the grass in a fit of laughter.

"That," I tried to catch a breath, "was amazing!"

"I told you we would get it!" Ky threw the dress at me.

I rolled over to her and gave her a huge hug. "Thank you! Thank you! Thank you!" I squealed as I held the beautiful dress in my hands. I smelled it and sighed. "It's perfect."

Ky laughed and said, "And this is coming from the girl who hates dresses. It's still not the greatest color, but whatever makes you happy."

"It's stunning." I declared. "I can't believe how easy that was."

We got up and started walking toward the bus stop.

She nodded. "I don't normally make such a scene but there weren't any other customers in the shop. It's much easier when it's a busier place. Plus, that lady isn't the manager. She could easily get into trouble if she tells her boss because she wasn't paying enough attention to the store. We should be in the clear. Besides, they have no idea we live in Rutherford."

"You've done that before?"

She snorted. "I do that all the time. It's such a rush."

I agreed with her there. "It is a rush. I've never felt that way before."

She raised her eyebrows. "Someone's turning into a bit of a rebel," she teased.

I laughed. "You're a bad influence on me."

We pulled out our passes and climbed on the bus heading to Rutherford. We found seats beside each other near the back. Ky asked, "What guy are you going to ask to the dance?"

I groaned. "I have no idea. Maybe Levi. He's the nicest one I know."

Ky shook her head. "Don't ask him."

"Why not?"

"You should take a risk and ask somebody you don't know very well. I've heard some boys are renting hotel rooms for after the dance."

"I don't know if Levi would do that. He and I are just friends."

Ky snickered. "He wouldn't. He's kind of weird, don't you think? Very reclusive. I doubt he'll even go. Which is the exact reason you should choose someone else. Levi is boring—"

"He's not!"

"He's dull. You need someone who will show you how to have a good time."

I rolled my eyes. "He's a good friend to me. You should give him more of a chance. You hardly know him."

"We've gone to school together our whole lives. I know him."

"He's a good person, and you could use another friend."

She made a face at me. "Do what you want, but you're not a little girl anymore. We're women, remember?"

"We're sixteen. I feel like we're not exactly classified as women."

"Whatever." Her eyes grew wide. "I have an idea."

"What?" I wasn't sure if I wanted to hear it.

"Well, I was thinking of asking Brett."

"Brett Meyers? The same Brett Meyers you're consistently

making fun of because you consider him a dumb jock?"

Ky nodded smugly. "And I was thinking you should ask Cade Samson."

"I don't think Cade Samson even knows I exist," I told her.

"Of course he does! Everyone notices us, Maeve. We're wanted."

I giggled. "No, we're not! Amanda Wright is wanted."

"You know why?"

I shook my head.

"Because she carries herself with confidence."

"I thought it was because she throws herself at guys."

"Well, that too. But confidence—that's what's crucial." Ky was very serious. "We are wanted, Maeve. But we have to believe that." She tossed her hair back. "I'm going to ask out Brett Meyers, and I don't care if he's a dumb jock or not. He'll say yes to me. I hope you ask out Cade Samson because he'll say yes to you too. Mark my words, Maeve Parker. He'll say yes if you're confident."

I let out a breath. "But what about Levi?"

"I'm sure some nice girl will ask him. We're not nice girls, Maeve. We belong with boys like Brett and Cade. Those are the type of girls we are."

I looked down at the yellow dress we had stolen and knew Ky was undeniably right.

LET ME TELL YOU ABOUT Cade Samson.

He was my age and keen on impressing girls as if it were his life's mission to always be seen with a female. He was an interesting creature, I'll give him that. I often pondered how many bottles of hair gel he went through in a month. I pictured his mom ordering the bottles in a bulk shipment, where a big truck would come and drop them off on the twenty-seventh of each month. I think he'd keep them stacked up in cardboard boxes in his room. A giant hair gel collection. Revolting, if you asked me.

Cade had blonde hair—at least what I thought to be blonde. It was hard to know the color beneath the crusty gel. His eyes were dark, and not dark in the mysterious, you-could-drown-in-them kind of way, but instead in the way where they simply resembled mud. Strangely enough, it seemed as though every girl in the entire school wanted to swim in those mud-colored eyes, so I kept those thoughts to myself.

As a surprise to no one, Ky marched right up to Brett Meyers and being her volatile and authoritative self, told him she had decided they would go to the dance together. "Have some confidence," she had whispered to me beforehand. Rumors were spreading that many girls had asked Brett and Cade, which made me nervous they had already agreed to go with someone else. But Brett told Ky yes.

Therefore I held a sliver of hope that Cade might tell me yes, too.

On a seemingly normal day to anyone else but me, I walked up to Cade and prepared myself to politely ask him if he might want to go the dance with me. He sort of whipped his head back, and I think his hair was supposed to swish in an aren't-I-irresistible sort of way, but his hair was so gelled to his head that not even a strand of hair moved.

"Would you like to come to the dance with me? Ky McNeil had this grand scheme that the four of us might go together."

"Sure, Maeve. I was hoping you'd ask me. I'm tired of the other girls."

"Tired?"

He nodded. "Amanda and Brittany and Dylan... we've grown up with those girls. You're new. And Ky's gotten weirder, so she feels new."

"You were hoping I'd ask you?"

"Yeah."

"Okay."

A long pause.

He cleared his throat. "I think I'm supposed to ask you what color you're wearing?"

"Oh. Right. Yellow."

"I only have a black suit."

I sort of laughed and said, "That's fine. Together we'll look like a bumble bee."

Cade sort of laughed, too. I thought to myself: this may be going downhill quickly.

THE DANCE CAME, AND WE took photos at Ky's house beforehand. I was surprised she wanted to have pictures taken. She quickly informed me it was her mother's doing. Her mother was concerned Ky was lying and wasn't actually going to the dance. Somehow by having a mini photo shoot at her house, we were proving her otherwise.

Ky and her mother could have been identical twins, aside from the black eyeliner Ky wore. I had started wearing more natural-looking makeup—ever since Amanda Wright told me I looked like a Goth in front of all the girls in the gym locker room. Ky told me not to let it bother me, but no matter what Ky said, it had. I stopped wearing all that makeup.

Ky's mother, Alice, was much more enthusiastic than her daughter, which drove Ky crazy. Put those two pairs of ruby lips pursed together, and you swore you were seeing double. Alice loved photographs. I think she was reveling in a night of normalcy for her clinically depressed daughter. For an hour we smiled, stuck our tongues out, and fake laughed, posing for Alice who, after each shot, sighed and told us, "That one was definitely scrapbook worthy!" Ky rolled her eyes after every picture, and almost didn't complain. Meanwhile, I began to notice Cade's hand creep lower and lower down my back.

45

He winked at me, and I removed his hand.

When we got to the dance, Ky and Brett immediately ran off together. I couldn't tell if she was leading him on, or if she genuinely liked him.

"What are we supposed to do?" Cade asked.

I shrugged. "I dunno. Ky forced me to come."

Cade looked at me. "Brett made me come."

I laughed. "Really?"

"Yeah."

"Looks like we have more in common than I thought."

He put his hands in the air as if he were surrendering. "Hey, I wasn't opposed to being with a gorgeous girl all night."

I stared at him. "You think I'm gorgeous?"

"Everyone does."

As soon as he said that, I knew he was lying. Although I had to admit, I did feel pretty good in that bright yellow taffeta dress. It swished around my knees whenever I took a step. Maybe that was why dresses were invented—that nice sort of feeling they gave you.

"We don't even look that much like a bumble bee," I joked, changing the subject.

He smiled at me. "You want to dance? I think that's what we're supposed to do."

"Sure. But I've never danced before."

We joined the other clumsy couples on the dance floor. I didn't think I was that bad of a dancer—at least not in comparison to how terrible Cade was. It was downright laughable, but I didn't want him to feel embarrassed.

A couple of songs into the night, just after Cade had gone to fetch some punch, I felt a tap on my shoulder. I knew exactly who it was even before I turned.

"Hey, Maeve. You look beautiful."

I laughed nervously.

Levi shrugged and said, "I'm supposed to be honest, remember?"

"Well then, thank you. So do you. Handsome, I mean."

He laughed, grinning at me. "Want to dance?"

"Okay. Where's your girl?"

"The bathroom."

I nodded. So a girl had asked him. A nice girl, probably. A girl who might not know about his bruised knuckles or anger management classes. A girl who would go to his beach with him.

It happened to be a slow song as Levi took my hand in his. He was a pretty good dancer, and oddly, that didn't surprise me.

"I didn't think you'd come tonight," I told him.

"Why not?"

I shrugged, embarrassed. "Your aversion to people and all that."

"I'm trying to participate more in life."

"You sound like Ky. Although she's being forced, and yours is by choice."

"Who's forcing her?"

I laughed. "The big bad mom. She doesn't want Ky to be sad anymore."

"What makes Ky sad?"

"I'm not sure, to be honest. The world, I guess. I think she sees the world differently than us. A little bit grayer."

"Is the world gray to you, Maeve?"

"Parts of it."

He nodded. "Why did you ask Cade Samson?"

I studied his shoulder blade. "I don't know. Ky wanted me to, I guess."

"Do you always do what people want you to do?"

"Of course not."

He didn't reply. Instead, he started to hum the song that was playing over the loudspeaker.

"Why didn't you ask me?"

I looked at him.

"Honesty…" He singsonged.

"I'm not…" I hesitated and looked down at my shoes. I forced myself to glance back up at him. "I'm not the type of girl who should ask you. I'm the outlet for boys like you, you know?"

"Maeve, I didn't mean anything by that, all I wanted—"

"No, it's okay. I wasn't offended by it. I'm glad we can be friends… and that you feel like you can be honest with me. I really am glad for that. Truthfully. I am. But I know that's all I'll ever be to someone like you."

"Someone like me?"

I nodded.

"I don't understand what you're saying."

"I'm not the type of girl you'd want to be with," I sighed.

"You can't say that."

"I can. I'm just, I'm not who you think I am."

The song ended and I walked away from him. I could feel him watching me, but I kept on walking. Ky came over and grabbed me by the arm. "Come with me."

"What's the matter with you?" I asked harshly as she yanked me to the back of the gym.

"Maeve Parker, what are you doing?" She hissed.

"What do you mean?"

"Dancing with him. After you asked Cade out!" Ky was furiously tapping her foot on the ground, her arms crossed over her tight purple dress.

"Cade was getting punch. Levi asked me to dance, so I said yes. It was nothing. Trust me."

"We were all watching and it sure looked like something to us!"

"Who's us?" I asked her.

"Who do you think, dummy? Cade, Brett and I. Cade feels manipulated."

"Nice big word, Ky," I quipped.

"This isn't funny, Maeve."

"It's not like Cade and I are a thing."

"He wants to be!"

"No, he doesn't." I shook my head.

Her red lips were pursed. "Yes, he does. He was going to ask you tonight. Looks like you ruined that."

"I didn't want to come to this. I only did it for you!"

Ky looked at me with disgust. "You are such a child. I'm surprised Cade liked you in the first place."

I felt like I had been slapped. Tears sprang into my eyes.

Immediately, Ky grabbed my arm. "I didn't mean that, Maeve. Honest! I'm sorry. Of course he would like you. What's not to like about a girl like you..."

My head was spinning and the room had gotten foggy. I wanted to get out of there. I could see Levi dancing with some blonde girl from my English class. I ran outside, sat on the curb, and gulped three big breaths. I sat there for a long time, breathing slowly. It was the end of September and the evenings had started to get chilly. I began to shiver and wished I had brought a jacket. I contemplated how to get home and wondered if Sol would be drunk or sober.

I heard steps on the pave way beside me. They slowed when they came close to me, and I knew it was Cade. I focused on memorizing a crack in the pavement.

"Hey," he said.

"Hi."

"Are you okay?"

"Fine." I turned to him. "Just so you know, I was only dancing with Levi. Nothing was going on. I don't like him like that. We're friends. That's all, I swear. I didn't mean to hurt you."

Cade laughed. "Levi Fisher is the least of my worries." He sat next to me. "What I'm really worried about... is you."

"Why?"

"I like you. I wanted you to have fun tonight."

I tried my best to smile at him. "I did have fun. Dances just aren't my thing."

He looked at me, his eyes soft and brown, less like mud and more like chocolate. "I like you, Maeve."

"Thank you, Cade. I like you, too."

"No," his eyes grew even softer. "I *like* you, Maeve."

My cheeks burned.

"Maeve," he said, his mouth forming my name like butter, his face coming closer.

And then he was kissing me.

His lips were chapped against mine, and his arms hurt the way they held me. But I let him kiss me. The autumn air was crisp and cold in between our bodies, but I let him kiss me. It felt awkward and after a few moments I wanted him to stop, but still, I let him kiss me.

"I'm sorry about what it looked like inside," I told him afterward.

"No, no, no, that's okay, Maeve." He nestled his nose near my ear. "You want to get out of here?"

I said sure because I did not want to go back inside and face Ky, nor did I want to see Levi. Cade took my hand and led me to his car.

I was tired. Weary right to the bone. I wanted to go home, fall into bed and sleep for a year. Or forever.

When we arrived at our destination, I realized it was not my home, but the hotel Ky had told me about. Except it wasn't a hotel—it was a cheap, repulsive motel, the pay-by-the-hour kind. When we got to the room and Cade opened the door, I saw the bed and relief swelled inside of me.

I ran and jumped on it. Cade jumped on me.

He kissed me soundly on the lips, and I felt his tongue in my mouth. I immediately pulled back.

"No, Cade," I whispered as he came closer to me. "Too fast."

He ignored me and put his hand up my yellow dress, trying to pull off my underwear. I kicked his chest and he yelped.

"Why did you do that?" he asked me angrily.

I backed up against the headboard. "Why are you trying to take off my underwear?" I retorted, though I full well knew the reason.

"Ky warned me you might be like this."

"Ky knows nothing," I shot back at him.

"C'mon, Maeve," he said, crawling onto the bed. "Let's have some fun. Wasn't it fun back there, outside of the school? You seemed to like it. Or are you just a tease?"

I felt perplexed and mystified and unsure of what to do. I slid off the bed and stood with my arms crossed.

He pouted. "You danced with a different boy, and now you don't want to have any fun with me. I'm hurt."

"How can you afford this place?" I asked him.

"My brother let me use his credit card. He told me this is the first step to becoming a real man. We have two hours."

"You should have told him that's bull."

"I like you a lot," Cade told me. "You're funny and gorgeous and you look amazing in that dress." He whistled.

I blushed and hated myself for it.

He leaned forward and kissed me. He kissed me for a long time. He began to fumble for the zipper at the side of my dress and in one quick motion, my taffeta gown was in a puddle on the floor. He paused and stared at me. Heat flushed through my body.

"Do you love me?" I asked him as he touched the front of my bra.

"What?"

"Do you love me?" I repeated to him, slower.

He was trying to figure out how to undo the clasp. I could feel his fingers on my skin, and I turned to him when he didn't answer. I wanted to look him in the eyes, and I tried to, but he was too busy pulling his arm around me to slip off the straps. I reached my hand to feel my cheek. It was burning, searing hot to the touch, a volcano churning inside of me. He didn't love me, wouldn't even look at my eyes. The lava spilled into my lungs and my breath felt damp and warm.

"Cade..."

His fingers were pulling the clasp.

"I don't want this." I wriggled from his grasp.

"What do you mean?"

I stepped into my dress, pulling the comforting fabric up against me. I zipped it and was concealed once again.

"You can't leave, Maeve."

"I can. I am."

"No! You can't leave, Maeve. You can't do this!"

I was at the door. I wondered if he might grab me, but he didn't. I looked at him once more. "Just so you know," I said calmly. "You're not nearly as attractive as everyone says."

I opened the door and went outside.

And then I began the long walk home.

SIX

THAT MONDAY, I WENT TO school and found the kids staring at me everywhere I went. I figured it was because I was hobbling slightly as I walked. Huge blisters covered my feet from walking home from the stupid motel. It had taken me at least two hours to get back to the house. I swore off wearing those strappy high-heeled sandals again.

I wasn't sure if I wanted to talk to Ky. I'd never been in a fight with a girl, and I wasn't sure if I was supposed to forgive or ignore her. But I knew that she had hurt me.

Amanda Wright came up to me after our first class. "Wow, Maeve Parker. Turns out you're exactly what I thought you were. Poor trash."

"Excuse me?"

She laughed sharply and walked away. I sent daggers through the back of her flouncy head.

I was getting a binder out of my locker when two boys came up to me. One leaned against the locker beside mine, and the other stood behind me.

"Hey, Maeve." The one leaning on the locker said.

I looked at him. "Hi…"

"I'm available tonight if you are."

"What?"

The boy behind me flaunted two twenty-dollar bills, flashing a smile. Acne covered the majority of his face. "Yeah, I'm free tonight, too."

"What are you guys talking about? We don't even know each other."

The one leaning on the locker rolled his eyes. "Stop pretending. You don't have to be shy with us, Maeve. It's okay."

"We can meet in the forest around ten o'clock if you're embarrassed," the one behind me said.

"I have no idea what you're talking about, but I'm not going anywhere with you guys. You're disgusting and you need to leave me alone."

The boys looked at each other and the one pulled out another five-dollar bill. "Forty-five dollars, Maeve. How can you turn that down?"

"Why are you offering me money?"

The one behind me started to push me closer to my locker. "Stop it!" I yelled at him. "Quit touching me."

He ignored me and leaned in closer, placing the bills into the back pocket of my jeans. "We'll see you tonight, Maeve Parker. Meet at ten, on the north side of the forest. You better be there."

The other one laughed and said, "Wear something pretty. Maybe like that yellow dress?"

Both the boys snickered.

"What are you talking about?" I took the money out of my pocket and threw it on the ground in front of them. "I don't want your stupid money. Leave me alone!"

"Maeve, Maeve, Maeve," the one who was leaning against the locker touched both my arms with the tips of his fingers. "There's no need to be ashamed. We'll keep it a secret. No one will have to know."

"Know what?" I shrieked at him. "I have no clue what you're talking about!"

"Get your hands off of her."

The boys started laughing, and the one who was touching me squeezed my arms stronger.

"I said," he repeated slowly, "get your hands off of her. Now."

Levi.

The boys laughed harder and one of them taunted, "Oh yeah, Levi Fisher? What are you going to do?"

"Conrad, get your hands off of her."

I tried to kick the boy, but his grip on me strengthened and I couldn't move.

Ky appeared and was screeching, "You get your hands off her this minute or so help me I will rip your heads off! The both of you!"

"Get your hands off Maeve," Levi told them. "I'm serious, Conrad."

The one holding me—Conrad—laughed. "Right. I'm terrified."

Levi's blue eyes glowered and I wondered if the pressure cooker inside of him had begun to boil.

"Don't fight them, Levi," I warned.

He ignored me.

Conrad's grasp tightened on my arms. Levi reached over and grabbed him, wrenching his fingers off of me. Levi was fast and clever and actually seemed pretty strong. He punched Conrad hard, right in the face.

I groaned. "Levi..."

Conrad stumbled back, holding his hands over his face, and the second boy took a swing at Levi. Levi pinned him to the ground and punched him hard as well. Both boys had blood seeping from their faces. Conrad's nose was slightly crooked.

"Don't touch her again," Levi said quietly.

Ky snickered. She took the money off the ground and whipped it at them. "Take your money. We don't want it."

"You better meet us there tonight, Maeve." The second one taunted, albeit with less confidence than before.

Ky shrieked at him, "You even think about looking at her, let alone talking to her and you'll be dead so fast you won't even have time to say goodbye to your mother!"

Levi stared at them for a long moment before the two boys slunk away.

"I am beyond serious!" Ky yelled after them.

"Are you all right?" Levi asked me.

"Yeah." I gave him a small smile. "Thank you. Is your hand okay?"

His knuckles had already begun bruising. He smiled coyly. "It will be fine."

I shook my head. "Your parents are going to be so mad at you."

He nodded. "Yeah, they are."

"You didn't have to hit them... I'm sure I would have been fine..."

"I couldn't just stand here."

Ky came and wrapped her tiny arms around me. "I'm sorry, Maeve. For Friday night... for right now. I'm sorry I made you go out with that stupid, worthless..."

"It's okay." And I meant it. It felt good to have her back. I still didn't know why she had acted the way she did, but I had missed her immensely.

"Everyone thinks you slept with Cade," Ky informed me in a somber tone. "He's has been telling everyone that after the dance you two went to a fancy hotel and you slept with him. For free. But he said you told him you'd do it with others if they paid you. He told everyone that you're very desperate for money."

"Are you kidding me?" I asked, stunned.

"No. What a little..." She began muttering things under her

breath.

"You know that's not true. Right?"

"Obviously," Ky said. "Levi went up to Cade and told him he's a big, fat liar and someday he'll grow up and everyone will realize the type of person he actually is."

"You did?" I turned to Levi.

He shrugged, embarrassed. "Not one of my finer moments."

I laughed. "Did you punch Cade, too?"

"Almost. I probably should've."

"No," I said quickly. "No more punching."

Ky grinned at Levi, and I could see that she was giving him a chance. "I hated this school before," Ky said. "But I hate it more now."

"This will blow over," Levi assured us. "These things always do."

"Not soon enough," I muttered.

"Oh, I have news!" Ky announced suddenly. "I dumped Brett."

"That lasted long."

"His best friend can't go around saying trashy things about *my* best friend. It doesn't work that way. I broke it off with Brett in front of the entire cafeteria this morning." She smiled with satisfaction. "It was hilarious. He looked like a lost puppy. He's not used to being dumped, I guess. He prefers to be the person doing the breaking up, and that's what made it all the more satisfying."

I looked at Levi.

"At least she didn't punch him."

I laughed.

"It was like Cade and Brett think you and I are..." Ky was still talking, searching for the right word. "...Like they think we're easy. Like they think you and I are the type of girls to sleep with them for *money*. And we're not, Maeve. We have real standards." She rolled her eyes. "Those boys are jerks, and now, everybody knows it."

I leaned in and hugged Ky and Levi. "Thank you," I whispered.

I hugged them and held on tight; afraid to let go, afraid to lose them, afraid if I released my hold they would drift from me and I would be unable to find them again.

THAT AFTERNOON, LEVI AND KY met up with me in the forest. Levi brought us candy. He was fully at fault for my newly developed sweet tooth. We sat there on some tree stumps, and Ky began carving our initials into each of them with a pocket knife.

L. F.

M. P.

K. M.

"There," she said, dusting off her hands. "Now we each have a place." She turned to me. "I'm still sorry about earlier. I shouldn't have said that to you. I can't believe I was so mean."

"That's done, Ky. It doesn't matter anymore."

She seemed almost shy, which was rare when it came to Ky. "Maeve," she said softly. "I don't know what I was thinking. Those boys are stupid. I don't know why I thought going out with them would make a difference."

"Make a difference?" I asked.

She nodded slightly. "I thought..." she sighed. "I feel stupid. I thought if we went out with them, I would *feel* different. More normal, maybe. Less of a crumpled up thing. I didn't. I just felt like a fraud."

"You want to be normal?"

She lifted her shoulders and lowered them gently. "I don't know what I want."

I laughed. "Neither do I."

"You have friends, Ky," Levi said. "People who like you for who you are."

"Are you saying that you're my friend, Levi?"

Levi blushed. "If you want me to be."

Ky snickered, her moment of vulnerability vanished. "That's fine, but don't be surprised if I keep pointing out when you're acting like a loser."

"I wouldn't expect anything less."

Levi wanted us to play what he had casually dubbed The Levi Game, which I was almost positive already existed. I kept that thought to myself. The Levi Game consisted of choosing between two things—both of which you didn't like.

"If you had to eat one thing for the rest of your life, and your only choices were monumentally cold leftover spaghetti or two-year-old broccoli casserole, what would you choose?"

I poured some M&M's into my hand and popped them in my mouth. I ate them all at one time. Ky and Levi were savorers and sucked them individually, relishing each piece. I didn't understand how they had the patience.

"Both of those are disgusting."

"That's the point of the game, Maeve," Ky said.

"You have to choose between two equally disgusting things?"

Levi sighed. "You have to choose what you would want to eat for the rest of your life."

"Yes, but why couldn't I choose… chocolate milkshakes? Or ice cream?"

Laughing, he said, "Those are both ice cream."

I shrugged. "Exactly."

"I would choose broccoli casserole," he decided, putting a red candy into his mouth. "But only if it was my mom's homemade kind."

"It's good?"

"Better than the alternative."

I nodded. "I guess I would choose the broccoli casserole too. At least it would be hot. But," I grinned, one eyebrow raised, "ice cream for dessert?"

Levi laughed. "What would you choose, Ky?"

"The spaghetti. Broccoli is nasty." She popped another piece of candy into her mouth. "My turn to ask a question. What do you hate most about yourself?"

"That question isn't valid according to The Levi Game," I teased.

Ky rolled her eyes. "I didn't like that game anyway. No offense, Levi." She smiled. "So, what's your answer? What do you hate most about yourself?"

I thought for a moment.

"I hate how anger is always my first reaction. It's the easiest, most comfortable thing for me to feel," Levi said, staring out at a tree.

Ky nodded and looked at me.

"Um…"

"There has to be something, Maeve."

"There are lots of things," I told her. "That's the problem."

"What tops the list?"

"I'm weak."

Levi looked at me. "What do you mean?"

I shrugged helplessly. "I'm weak. I'm not strong. I hate how I'm not strong. If I were strong I could do so many things."

"Like what?" Ky asked.

"Like…" *Try and find Sage.* I cleared my throat. "Like actually become someone. Like… tell my stepdad to screw off. What about you, Ky?"

"I hate my name."

Levi laughed and Ky glared at him.

"Don't laugh at me, Levi."

His eyes widened. "Sorry… I thought you were kidding."

"No," Ky said. "I'm not."

"Why do you hate your name?" I asked her quietly.

She pulled out her package of cigarettes and lit one. She silently offered it to Levi and I, but we both shook our heads, awaiting her response.

"My father always wanted a son. He dreamed of having a little boy. He's one of those masculine dudes that think girls are lesser humans than guys. It's charming. He also wanted to keep the McNeil name going. My mom got pregnant, and my dad thought that was it, that was his time. In a mere few months he would be introduced to his precious little boy. But he wasn't. Instead, my older sister was born. And he was okay. Slightly disappointed, but okay. Two years later, Alice gets pregnant again. At this point, my mom and dad were starting to have some problems, but Alice felt like this baby would seal the deal of their marriage—that this angel baby would be a boy, and that he would miraculously mend all of their problems. Of course, out pops me." She cast us a sardonic grin. "I'm going to assume that you've both figured out that I am actually—and surprisingly!—not a boy. My dear dad was more disappointed this time. It went beyond disappointment actually, more toward anger, and possibly a sprinkle of loathing. He took me from the arms of Alice, christening me Kyle Aspen McNeil. Because if he could not literally have a son, he would make one."

Levi and I stared at her.

"That is why," Ky softened her voice, "I despise my name."

Levi was the first to break the spell. "Where is he now?"

"My father?"

Levi nodded.

"He and my mom divorced shortly after my third birthday. He got remarried a couple of years ago and now he and his new wife have three sons. They live in Florida. The happy little clan."

"Do you see him?" My voice sounded timid to my ears.

"The sister and I get shipped down there every other Christmas, but that's about the extent of it. I prefer not to see him. Your turn, Maeve."

I could have asked a lighter question, I should have really, but Ky had unlocked a door where our secrets now seemed too big to hold onto by only ourselves.

"What are you most afraid of?"

"Death," Ky answered. She didn't offer anything after that.

Levi said cancer.

I nodded, because sometimes there are moments where that's all that you can do.

"My nana died of cancer, and my mom has always been a bit worried she might one day get it too." Levi looked out, his thoughts lost amongst the trees that surrounded us. "It's a horrible thing; cancer. I hate how they say 'you're fighting' it. You know? How everyone says cancer is a battle? I understand that, I do. And I do believe that you are 'fighting the battle' but what happens when someone dies because of it? Does that make them any less of a fighter? I don't think so." He paused. "My mom tells me about it sometimes. About the chemotherapy, and the radiation, and the nurse visits to their house everyday to give my nana the needles. About my nana losing her hair, and then slowly losing her spirit, because the cancer just seemed to drain everything from her. Even the strongest person in the world."

He turned back to us. "But I guess it's inevitable, right? If it happens, it happens…"

I said the only words I could think of. "If that happens, we'll be there for you." I hesitated and looked out at Ky. She smiled reassuringly. "If… anything happens, we'll be there for you."

It was his turn to nod. "You know I'll do the same for you, right?"

Ky said yes. I didn't. I didn't know that, but I earnestly wanted to believe it. So I simply smiled, instead of saying anything that might possibly make him want to change his mind.

"What are you afraid of?" Levi asked me.

"I don't know," I said quietly, fiddling with the candy that sat in my hands. After a moment of silence I whispered, "I'm scared I'm going to be alone, I guess."

They sat there, still, allowing me to process the thoughts that terrified me.

I inhaled softly. "My mother left me when I was seven. I'm sure you've both wondered why I don't have one."

Levi gave a nod. Ky simply looked at me.

"Well, when I was seven, I woke up one day and went down the stairs to find Sage and Sol fighting. Sage came over and kissed me, said she needed to go find herself and that she was going away for a while. She never came back."

"How does that make you feel?" Levi asked.

I laughed out loud. "Please stop. You sound like a therapist or something."

He laughed too, but then grew serious. "No really. How does that make you feel?"

"Unwanted, I guess." I kept looking at Ky. She knew what I meant. She knew exactly what I meant.

"I just think sometimes, you know, why hasn't she come back for me? Hasn't she ever wondered what I'm like or how I'm doing?" I hadn't thought like that for a long time, and I could feel the rage start to bubble from my insides. "Didn't she ever want to throw me a birthday party? Or know when I had a crush on someone? Or want to help me with my homework? And what about all the stuff you learn about in health class? They tell you to go talk about it with your mom, and instead, I couldn't talk about it with anyone. I've always had to figure out everything on my own. Everything! How could she ever be so selfish that in order to find herself she had to leave me behind?" I gulped a deep breath, suddenly exhausted and embarrassed. Sighing, I looked at them. "I know you don't have the answers. I'm sorry. Sometimes I need to vent."

Levi spoke. "I wish I did have the answers. I so badly wish I had the answers to give you."

We were silent for a long time.

"I don't know why your mom left," Levi said after a while. "But it makes me angry. It honestly does."

"Why?" I asked him.

"Because," he stood up. "You didn't do anything wrong. You were just a little girl."

"She wasn't very old either." I murmured.

Levi started to pace back and forth. "It ticks me off that she didn't care enough about you to stay. Or to take you with her! You know what it is, Maeve?" He answered his own question. "It's selfishness. Pure selfishness."

"There are a lot of selfish people in this world, Levi," Ky said.

"Mothers aren't supposed to be selfish."

Ky laughed but it was hollow. "We're all selfish."

"I don't agree with that," Levi insisted.

"Of course you don't."

"What's that supposed to mean?"

"You live in an idealistic world, Levi Fisher."

"I live in a good world, Ky. Not idealistic, but good. Bad things happen to good people, yes, I know, and that's terrible, but the world is still good."

"I hope you never lose that," I told him.

"Lose what?"

"Your hopeful living."

"I don't know what else we'd have if we didn't have hope that things would get better."

Ky laughed softly. "You're a good guy, Levi Fisher. I'll always think you're a tad on the idealistic side, but I'd like to think someday the world will be made up of more people like you."

"Thanks, Ky."

"Maeve." Ky turned to me. "Promise me something."

"What's that?"

"Find your mother. Promise me someday you'll go out there and try and find Sage."

The sun had started to set, casting shadows against the trees, casting a kind of light onto Ky that made her look remarkably older than the sixteen short years that pressed in.

"Promise me."

She was iridescent, in a way. Mystical.

"Promise."

"Okay," I told her. "I promise."

SEVEN

LEVI DIDN'T SHOW UP TO school the next day. But he was waiting for me after school, right at the north end of the forest which marked my entrance to head home. I was surprised to see him.

"What are you doing here? And why weren't you at school today?" I demanded.

"Nice to see you, too."

I stuck my tongue out at him. "Hi. Now what are you doing here and why weren't you at school?"

"Are you busy tonight?"

The question caught me off guard. "No…"

"Good. Come over." He started walking away.

"Like tonight? Or right now?"

"Sure," he tossed over his shoulder.

I sighed, exasperated. But I followed him anyway. I caught up to him and asked, "Why am I coming over?"

"You don't have to come if you don't want to."

"I assumed that, this being a free country and all."

Levi laughed and continued walking.

"Why weren't you at school today?"

He looked at me. "You're inquisitive."

"Could you stop being frustrating for like half a second? Answer me."

He kicked a stone out of the way, ignoring my jab. "Questions are good, Maeve. Don't stop asking them. They help you learn."

"Thanks for the tip. So are you sick?"

"Sick? No…"

"Oh, I understand. Trying to be a rebel by cutting all of your classes, huh?"

He smirked at me. "*Moi?* Rebellious?"

I feigned surprise. "I know, what a concept."

We were silent for a minute.

"Seriously, Levi, why weren't you there today? Ky and I were looking for you at lunch."

He gazed at me, sort of pensive. His head tipped slowly to the side, a sheepish smile whispering across his lips. "I got suspended. I'm not allowed to go back to school until Monday."

"Suspended?" I yelled.

Levi's slow gait was relaxed and at ease. Mine was not.

"Punching those kids. It all happened yesterday afternoon when we were in the forest. I guess Conrad went to the nurse because his nose was bloody and kind of banged up." He paused. "Actually, I'm pretty sure they said something about it being broken…"

I groaned.

"So anyway, the principal called my parents last night and told them I was suspended."

"This is all my fault."

"What?" He looked at me, surprised. "No, it's not. Why would any of this be your fault?"

"Because! The whole reason you clocked him in the first

place was because of me!"

"It was my choice, Maeve. Last time I checked they were my fists. Not yours."

I shook my head. "I am so sorry. I should be the one getting suspended—"

He halted in his tracks. "Stop."

I looked at him.

"Why are you blaming yourself for this? When it was never your fault?" Levi sighed. He seemed older than he was.

I stayed quiet.

"Stop doing that, okay? Stop blaming yourself for other people's stupid actions. Those guys are jerks. They were trying to pay you to have sex with them, Maeve. Don't you get that?" He wasn't being unkind.

I nodded. "I figured that out…" I said slowly.

"He deserves a lot more than a broken nose if you want my opinion. But he's Conrad so he'll manage to get away with it."

"You're angry," I realized.

He raised his eyebrow and continued walking. "Are you kidding? Anger would be an understatement."

"Because of the suspension?"

He sighed again, shaking his head. "I couldn't care less about the suspension. I'm angry because they had the nerve to treat you like that." His exhale rang hollow. "It's ridiculous how they think it's okay to treat anyone that way."

"I still feel bad you got suspended for me."

"We're friends, Maeve. That's the kind of thing friends do for one another."

He said it simply, as if it were an assumed thing, as if it were something every person in the world was already aware of.

By that point, we were trekking across his driveway, heading towards his front door.

"So what are we doing here?" I asked.

Levi grinned. "Did I forget to tell you? My mom and dad

wanted you to come over for supper."

"What? Why? Levi, that's so awkward—" But the door was opening and there we were, in his home, Levi's mother in a busy motion of swirling activity.

"Well, hello there!" His mom said when she spotted Levi and me. She was wearing a coral shirt with big yellow flowers, paired with red gingham oven mitts that decorated her hands. Her ears were adorned with long, green, dangling earrings that should have looked strange with her pulled back dark hair and vibrant outfit, but somehow the whole ensemble worked. I decided she could probably wear anything and pull it off. Her eyes were bright blue, and I knew exactly where Levi got his from.

"It's good to meet you, Maeve." She threw the oven mitts on the counter and went to shake my hand, then changed her mind and enveloped me in an exuberant hug, her long earrings swishing against my cheek.

Everything about her was happy. I reminded myself I wasn't there to make friends. I had caused her son's suspension.

"It's nice to meet you too, Mrs. Fisher."

She laughed, "Oh please! If I can call you Maeve, you can call me Nora. I'm not that old." She winked. I had a feeling some people may have found her overwhelming, but I didn't. She was everything I wasn't: colorful, vivacious, kind beyond reason. Her laugh was like music and she hummed as she worked away in the kitchen.

"Please come in," she told me. "Make yourself at home. We have lots to talk about!"

Nora Fisher was the epitome of a homemaker. As we walked through her house, I saw that the table was set and ready. A huge vase of purple flowers and six or seven flickering candles sat in the center.

"Wow." I was looking at the table.

"She can be a little extravagant," Levi said.

"I heard that!" Nora hollered. The smell coming from the

kitchen was delectable.

"This smells amazing," I told her as we sat at the kitchen table. "Is there anything I can do to help?"

"Levi and Simon should take a cue from you!" Levi made a face while she giggled to herself, switching a pot from one burner to the next. "But I'm fine, thank you. Almost finished!"

It looked like chaos. It was chaos. But it was her chaos—entirely hers. She was in her element.

"And Levi, regarding your little comment about me being extravagant," she turned to us, her gingham oven mitts back on her hands. "I want to celebrate each day. Every day is worth having home-cooked food, a big bouquet of flowers, and of course the china and good silverware. I don't care if it's a holiday or not! Every day is worth celebrating." She punctuated the last sentence, nodding as she said this as if she were reassuring herself as well as us. She went back to the food, pulling something from the oven.

The front door opened and Levi's father appeared. I briefly wondered if he ever hit Levi, if maybe that was a thing all men do, but when he came over and placed a tender hand on Levi's shoulder, I instantly knew he was not the hitting kind.

He turned to me. His eyes smiled when his lips didn't. I liked him immediately. "So you're the girl our son got suspended for."

Nora swatted him, laughing nervously. "Oh, honey, be gentle on her."

Levi's dad held his hand out to me. "It's good to meet you."

I shook his hand. "Nice to meet you as well. I'm Maeve."

"Jonas."

Nora smiled at me. "Levi told us he had made a friend. We're very happy to hear that."

"Mom," Levi said. "It's not like I don't have friends."

"Oh honey, that's not what I meant…"

Levi looked at her.

Nora sat beside me at the kitchen table. "Maeve, we need to

talk to you."

"Mom, you promised you wouldn't bring this up—"

"We understand that Levi got into a fight yesterday."

"It was my fault," I told her.

Levi sighed. "No, it wasn't."

"Did Levi need to get involved?"

"Mom, you can talk to me, too. I'm in the room."

Nora glanced at him but spoke to me. "We're concerned."

Levi sighed again. Jonas put a hand on Nora's shoulder.

"It wasn't Levi's fault. He was helping me. He was... being a good friend."

"We're really happy that you two have become friends. However—and granted, I don't know your family—but our family does not condone fighting."

"Mom," Levi said, "please stop."

I looked at him but said to Nora, "I'm really sorry."

"It's not Maeve's fault. You promised me you wouldn't talk about this."

Nora looked out the window. I think she had tears in her eyes. "I'm worried about you."

Levi pounded his fist on the table. "I get that, Mom! You've made that more than clear!"

Nora's head whipped around. "Levi—"

He sighed and lowered his voice. "I'm sorry I yelled. But you need to leave Maeve out of this."

"Levi, you broke a boy's nose!" Nora was definitely crying. "This is serious!"

"I know, Mom, I'm sorry—"

"Sorry? You're sorry? His parents could press *charges* against you—"

"Nora," Jonas said calmly, "Let's talk about this later."

"Without Maeve," Levi said.

Nora looked at me, her blue eyes even more vibrant with the red rims that surrounded them. "What happened, Maeve?"

"He was trying to help me," I said quietly.

Levi huffed, "Mom, please—"

"What happened, Maeve?" Nora asked again.

I looked down at the table. There was evidence of scuffmarks and scratches, presumably from years of homework and passed potatoes and hot coffee in the morning. "Some boys were trying to… get me to do things… that I didn't want to do." My cheeks burned hard.

"I'm sorry," Nora said. "They should never have done that."

"I know," I said.

"But Levi shouldn't have punched them."

Levi didn't say anything. I repeated myself. "I know."

Nora got up abruptly and went to the stove, stirring something in a boiling pot.

"Simon! Food!" she called.

Jonas looked at me with his kind eyes. "We're sorry if this is awkward, Maeve."

I tried to laugh, but it left my lips as a spurted cough. "It's okay." Although it was awkward. Sincerely awkward, indeed.

A boy, who was the miniature of Jonas, came into the kitchen. I had seen him around school before.

"We're going to eat now," Nora announced, her voice a strange mix of weariness and sorrow. She draped an arm around the boy's shoulders, squeezing him tight, even though he was almost as tall as her. Maybe she needed to hold onto something steady. "Will you boys carry the food to the table?" Before they had the opportunity, she raised her hand and said, "I don't want to hear a word of complaint."

I watched the three of them silently gather the food and head to the dining room.

Nora smiled at me, but it was forced. "You do what you have to do when you're the only girl in the house."

She had no idea the depth in which I understood those words. She began to wipe the counter down.

"Mrs. Fish—Nora?"

"Yes, honey?"

"I'm sorry. I didn't mean to involve Levi. I should have stopped them myself."

Nora turned to me. "It's not your fault, Maeve. Not at all. You didn't ask for those boys to do that to you. What they did was wrong, and they should be held accountable for that." I thought she might cry again. "But a mother doesn't want her son going around punching kids and breaking their noses, even if it is for a sweet girl like you. It's not right, Maeve. The whole situation isn't right. I'm a worrier, I admit. Levi has a lot of anger and sometimes I get so worried to think what might happen." She sniffed. "I shouldn't have involved you though. That was wrong."

I nodded. "If it's any consolation, he's been a good friend to me."

She smiled again but still, it seemed sad. "C'mon," she told me, "let's go eat. We won't talk about this anymore."

We walked side by side into the dining room. I sat at the table next to Levi. There was a place card at the edge of my plate, my name written in swirly letters. That was my spot at their table. That was my place. The aroma of fried chicken, buttery mashed potatoes, and sweet corn filled my nostrils as I inhaled. I was in a family. For the first time in my life, I was a part of a real, live family. Even if only for one night.

Nora's eyes sparkled against the candlelight, and she looked at Jonas who sat at the end of the table. He smiled at her, as if he were comforting her without words. There was something special between them; you could feel it. I wanted what they had—that love, that structure, that reason to come home.

"Time to say grace," Nora announced, and reached out to Simon and me who sat on either side of her.

I looked at Levi, unsure of what grace was.

"We're thanking God for our food," he whispered, sliding his fingers into mine. "I'm sorry about how awkward that was for you."

I shook my head and whispered back. "Don't be."

"They worry a lot."

I nodded. "They love you."

He had my one hand, and Nora held my other, and Jonas thanked God for our day. Each of us a link on a chain, hands clasped together, a united force no one could possibly rip apart.

SAGE KEPT A LIST.

She didn't think I knew, but one time when she was showering I snuck into her bedroom and found it. Her list was kept in a black moleskin notebook—the small kind you could tuck quiet into the back pocket of your blue jeans.

It was sacred, she told me, when I asked her what her notebook contained. And according to Sage, sacred things were not meant to be played with—I suppose, particularly, by me. But when someone tells you specifically not to think about a purple spotted elephant, I guarantee there's nothing else you can think of.

I formed a plan to find the sacred notebook.

It wasn't hard. It was one of the nights where Sol had passed out from drinking, and Sage went to shower off the whiskey stench. It didn't seem to matter how many showers she took, if it had been a drinking night, the alcohol would permeate deep inside our little peach home.

It was only a few months before The Day. I slipped out of bed when I heard the water beginning to run and slipped into Sage and Sol's bedroom. There it was: her black moleskin waiting for me beneath her cardigans in the second dresser drawer. I had timed her showers, so I knew I had around seven minutes and forty-two seconds before she would find me. I was well equipped, bringing along my own paper and pen in order to copy down what Sage kept so preciously hidden away.

It was a list, I realized when I leafed through the pages. Certain words were circled and marked and starred.

Sage Parker's List To Stay Living

- *Go to a butterfly conservatory*
- *Have my own apartment*
- *Swim in an ocean*
- *Learn Mandarin*
- *Fly first class*
- *Plant one tree*
- *Plant a forest*
- *Throw a huge party*
- *Let go of one hundred and one RED balloons at the same time*
- *Go to a winery*
- *Paint a mural*
- *Fold nine hundred and ninety-nine origami cranes*
- *Take a road trip—a long one*
- *Fall in love*
- *Dance*
- *Dance*
- *Dance*
- *Go back to Aubrey*

I didn't know who Aubrey was, and I traced my finger against her name as if the pressure of my fingerprint would reveal more information. I never figured it out. All I knew was that I was holding Sage's list to stay living, or maybe to start. It wasn't a bucket list because Sage Parker didn't believe in dying. Instead, she believed in living.

She just believed in living without me.

EIGHT

KY'S MOTHER, ALICE, STARTED DATING Jared again. Ky hated him.

We were in her living room, studying for English. Well, I was studying. Ky was smoking.

"She's such an idiot."

"Why did she take him back?"

She took a long drag from her cigarette. "Because she's an idiot."

That was Ky's answer to most things regarding Alice.

"He came over last night, at like three am. I mean, who in their right mind goes to anyone's house at three in the morning? Freaking Jared, that's who. And he knocked incessantly. Like there was no way we could ignore him, though let me tell you, that's obviously what I voted for. But Mom got all giddy when she saw him and she opened the door, even though I told her not to. Well, lo and behold, there was Freaking Jared the Boyfriend with *flowers*. But it's not like he was giving her a little bouquet, no, Freaking Jared had flowers everywhere. I mean everywhere. All over our porch. Down the steps, on the driveway. He was standing in flowers. It literally looked like he had stolen an entire field because obviously, he didn't buy them. He would never actually spend money on my mom." Ky took another drag. "So Alice is freaking out and crying hysterically, and Jared is crying, and they're both having this sob-fest and Jared is telling her that there isn't any way he can possibly live without her—blah, blah, blah—so of course my mom is falling for it hook, line, and sinker." She looks at me. "He's lying. He doesn't love her."

I leaned back on the couch. "What if he does? What if he's telling the truth?"

Ky glared at me. "He's not. He's a dirtbag. He's cheated on my mom—from what I know—at least six times. That's just what I know. Who knows how many actual times?"

"How do you know that?"

"I follow him."

"You follow him?"

Ky nodded.

"When have you followed him?"

She shrugged. "A bunch of different times. He always leaves at night which makes my mom sad because he tells her he'll sleep over and have breakfast with us the next day, but never does. I can't fall asleep knowing he's in the next room so I stay up until I hear him leave. I wondered for a long time where he went. I figured I might as well follow him."

"Where did he go?"

"A couple of places. He'll go to the liquor store first, and then the 24-hour grocery place, and then *Billy's*, the bar down on Mayfield."

"You followed him to each of these places?"

Ky nodded.

"How did you get into the bar?"

She looked at me. "It's not hard to get a fake ID, Maeve."

"Does Jared see you?"

"No. He's pretty busy."

"What does he do there?"

"Hits on any woman who's breathing."

I grimaced. "Really?"

She rolled her eyes. "I know. I was pissed the first time. He has this routine. He'll play pool or something with four or five girls, and then he narrows it down throughout the night and finally chooses one. The lucky winner. Then the two of them go to this old house that's been empty for years." She stubbed her cigarette in the ashtray on the coffee table. "I always go home then."

"That's terrible, Ky. I hate him."

"Me too. My mom won't listen to me either. That's the worst part of this whole thing."

"You've told her?"

"Not in so many words…"

"Are you going to?"

Ky sighed and flopped herself against the couch. "I've told her I think she deserves more than him, told her I hate him, told her he's literally one of the creepiest people on the planet, but I have yet to tell her that he's off with another woman as soon as he's done with her."

"That's not an easy conversation to have."

"You're telling me."

Ky flipped the television on to her guilty pleasure: a show featuring people's weird addictions.

I groaned. "I can't handle watching another one of these."

"Shut up, I haven't seen this one yet."

"Yeah right." I leaned down and tried to do my homework while Ky watched a woman eat cat litter. "I don't get why you watch this. That's so disgusting."

"What do you think makes someone that desperate?"

"Desperate enough to eat kitty litter?"

"Yeah."

"They're probably crazy. Crazy people do crazy things. Don't you think?"

Ky looked distant.

"Ky?"

"What?"

"Are you okay?"

"Don't be dumb, of course I am." She turned the volume up on the television. "Thinking about desperation, that's all."

"What do you think makes someone that desperate?" I asked her quietly.

She shrugged. "Don't know. I think that's why it's so intriguing."

"Ky!" Alice called out. "I'm home!"

"Great!" Ky hollered back. "I'm thrilled!"

Alice came into the room with her hands on her hips. "Don't talk to me that way, Ky. Have you taken your pills yet? Oh, hi, Maeve."

"Hey, Alice."

"So, have you taken your pills yet?"

Ky pressed mute and said, "Nope. I'm planning on killing myself later this week, so I figured why bother?"

Alice's hand flew up to her mouth in horror. "Kyle Aspen McNeil, don't you dare say that to me again."

"Don't call me that. It was a joke, Mom. Chill."

Alice leaned back against the doorpost and I thought she might faint or keel over. "Go," she said, albeit weakly, "and take your pills."

"It's not even the right time to take—"

"I don't care." Alice pinched the bridge of her nose. "Just do it."

Ky rolled off the couch and disappeared into another room.

Alice sank into a chair by the window. She closed her eyes for a long time.

"You okay, Alice?"

After a few long moments, she looked at me. "What did you say, Maeve?"

"I asked if you were okay."

"No." She closed her eyes again. "I'm not okay. I'm the furthest thing."

"Long day?"

"It was good until now."

"What was good?"

Alice looked at me again. She actually smiled. "Jared took me out for lunch. He's a good man, Maeve. He's the kind of man I hope for Ky. He really loves me."

I wondered if Levi were here if he would tell Alice the truth. I wondered if telling someone the truth was worth the hurt it would evoke inside of them. I didn't say anything.

Ky came in, shaking the bottle of pills as if it were a maraca. "Mother dear, I brought them down so you could watch me take it."

With dramatic flair, she swallowed the pill.

"Thank you," Alice said. "I'll go make us some dinner. Maeve, you staying?"

I shook my head. "I need to go home and finish my English project."

"All right. Ky, Jared's coming over later so it will be the three of us for supper."

Ky's eyes flashed. "Why is he coming?"

Alice laughed. "Because, honey, he wants to spend time with me. With us."

"I'm not hungry," Ky said.

"Ky, please, don't be dramatic."

"I'm not being dramatic, I'm just not hungry. I'll go with Maeve to her house. We need to finish our homework anyway."

"Fine." Alice got up. "But I wish you'd make more of an effort with him. He likes you."

Ky's face went gray. "Come on, Maeve," she told me. "Let's go."

THE FOREST HELD A LOT of secrets.

Sometimes I would write them down, scratch the memories permanently onto paper. And then I'd rip them. Rip them into pieces, hundreds of pieces, scattering them across the wooded, leafy floor. They'd fall down like rain, or maybe more like hail because those memories hurt as they pelted down upon me.

"Forest?" I whispered, and maybe you'd think me crazy, but that was my haven, my refuge among those trees. "Will you keep my secrets safe for me?"

A breeze rustled the trees a bit, and it was like they were whispering back to me, whispering that my secrets were retained safely within their walls. I suspected the trees had seen a lot of secrets, long before mine.

There's a specific spot in that forest, a place where if you lay down, you can see an opening in the trees, like a picture with a chunk cut out. As you lie on the ground, there's a perfect view of the sky directly above you, even through all of those trees.

I often went there and lay down. The clouds would move quickly, hurrying along as if they had some other important place to get to. I would watch them float further down their path, and they felt close and yet so far away, and I wanted to grasp onto them and float away, too. I felt very small lying there, but never scared. I liked that feeling of being small. I felt protected, looking at the large sky and trees looming above me. I felt small and young and as if I had a world of possibilities ahead of me.

I sighed, watching the rolling clouds against the endless blue sky. The clouds moved so quickly, I almost felt like the ground below could swallow me into the earth.

And I don't think I would have minded it if it had.

NINE

I WAS WORKING ON A piece of poetry for my English class when Sol and another man stumbled in through the doorway. It was late on a Friday night and they were both on the teetering edge of drunk.

"Where have you two been?" I asked Sol flatly.

"At *Billy's*," he replied.

"Great choice. I see you're setting your standards real high."

"Good day at school?"

"Living the dream."

"Sol," the other man said. "Are you trying to hide this beautiful woman from me? You never told me about her." He came up behind Sol and stood next to my chair, his fingers resting gently against the table.

I looked at him. "Who are you?"

He was handsome in a rugged way. I would have guessed he was in his late twenties or so, and he had wavy hair and a bit of stubble on his cheeks and chin.

"The name's Grayson, but most people call me Gray." He stuck his hand out. I didn't accept the handshake. He laughed. "And you?"

"Maeve."

"Maeve," he smiled. "The pleasure's all mine."

"She's my daughter," Sol explained.

"Not really," I told him. "Only sort of."

"Sort of?" Gray asked.

"Long story."

Sol rummaged through the cupboards. "I'm starving. Maeve, will you make us something?"

"Not only beautiful, but also handy in the kitchen? Does it get any better than that?" Gray asked, laughing. Sol laughed, too.

I rolled my eyes. "You two should become comedians. I mean really, you're hilarious." I got up to make them some food as Sol popped the tops of two beers.

"You want a beer, Maeve?"

"No thanks." I cracked open a few eggs and whisked them along with some milk. I heated a pan and poured in the egg mixture, chopping up a few vegetables and adding some cheese.

"Here you go," I said, handing them each a plate when it had finished cooking. "Omelets. Very gourmet, I know."

They thanked me and took them. Beer and eggs seemed like a disgusting combination in my opinion, but they didn't seem to mind. I started to clean the pan, and Gray took my notebook from the table and began reading it out loud.

"Well, would you look at this," He said. "She's a chef and a poet. Multi-talented, Maeve. I'm impressed."

I flew around. "Give that back to me."

"'And I have learned how diving's done,'" he read mockingly. "'The shoreline is not a place for me. A laugh is unleashed beneath'—"

"I said, give that back to me!"

Gray held the paper higher above me, far beyond my reach.

"—'Beneath the sun,'" Gray continued, "'And then under again. The silence is pure and loud'—"

"I'm serious!" I screamed at him. "Give that back!"

"You're quite the little writer," he said and handed back the poem.

I ripped the notebook from his hands. "Don't take what isn't yours. Didn't your mother ever teach you that?"

"What's the poem about?"

"None of your business."

"A feisty one, aren't you?"

I glared at him and he laughed as if I were amusing. A moment later, I tilted my head in towards him, purposefully growing a smile large across my cheeks. "I have an idea," I said, lowering my voice.

"What's that?" Gray asked, bending in.

I kept my large grin and batted my eyelashes a few times. "C'mere," I said. "I'll tell you."

He leaned in closer.

I brought my lips within reach of his, and I could see him looking at them. Tilting in even more, I told him, "Eat your food, drink your beer, and get out of my house." I spun on my heel and stalked up to my bedroom, holding the notebook tight in my hands. I closed the door and sank onto my bed.

And I have learned how diving's done
The shoreline is not a place for me
A laugh is unleashed beneath the sun
And then under again

The silence is pure and loud

It's pounding
My head with a distant thud

The shoreline is not a place for me
I cannot spend a day on the sand
Freedom exposed
Underneath the sea

Do not tell me what to feel
I'll dive till diving can't be done
I'll laugh till laughter fades forever
Feelings fade
Choices are made

Dive with me

"MAEVE," MY ENGLISH TEACHER SAID after the bell had rung at the end of class. "Can I talk to you for a second?"

Nodding, I wrapped my arms around my notebook and binders. Ky made her eyes wide and mouthed good luck. I narrowed my eyes jokingly at her and she gave a small cackle, leaving the room.

"Am I in trouble?" I asked when I walked up to the desk.

Miss Meyers shook her head. She had a smile like she had graduated from college yesterday. "I wanted to tell you you're a good writer. I read your poems over the weekend, and you have a different style of writing than the students I've taught before. Are you interested in pursuing it?"

"Pursuing it?"

"For college."

I bit my lip, hesitant. "I enjoy writing. I like it a lot."

Miss Meyers bobbed her head. "I can tell. It's all very natural. I encourage you to continue, Maeve. You'll have to work for it, of course. Writing is hard work, let me tell you. But if you love it, it's more than worth it."

"You think I could get into college?"

She smiled. "I do. Keep working hard and we'll talk again. Start to write a variety of things—more poetry, but also some short stories and even longer fiction. You still have this year and all of next, but it's good to start determining your writerly voice."

"All right," I said. "Thank you."

"No need to thank me, Maeve. I just hope you'll keep writing."

"I will."

TEN

"WE HAVE TO TALK," I told Sol one night as I was clearing the dishes away from the table.

He looked at me. "About what?"

Keeping my gaze steady, I asked, "Do you ever think about Sage?"

Sol's eyes flashed. "Why are you bringing her up?"

I began to fill the sink with hot water, squirting in some soap. "She's my mother."

"I realize that."

"I want to find her."

"No."

I turned to him, drying my hands on a cloth. "What?"

"I said no."

"You can't tell me no. She's my mother."

Sol swore and got up from the table, pushing his chair hard away from him. "I've looked after you for your entire life! I haven't asked for one thing in return. Not a thing, Maeve. But I'm asking for this."

"You're not asking. You're telling me. There's a big

difference!"

"I'm trying to protect you!" he exploded and threw his glass of water against the wall. It shattered. I stared at him. His chest was heaving. A mix of water and shards of glass covered the floor.

"Very mature," I muttered. He didn't look at me, simply left the room. A few minutes later I heard the door slam shut and the sound of his car turn on and speed away. I knelt to the ground, beginning to mop up the water and pick up the remains. One of the pieces cut me, and I rested my hand on my pants—the cut dripping deep and bloody, the scarlet soaking into my jeans.

I cradled my sliced finger, holding it close to me, trying to stop the bleeding.

I wished he hadn't left.

I wished people would stop leaving.

There was a knock at the door. I figured it must have locked behind Sol, so I got up and went to unlatch it. When I swung it open, it wasn't Sol.

"Maeve! Hi!" Francine said cheerfully.

"Oh!" I was surprised to see her. "Hi, Francine."

"Sorry to pop in unexpected, especially on a Saturday night, but I just wanted to check in—oh my heavens, your *finger*!" She shrieked, and I took a step back. I looked down and saw it was still bleeding immensely. I clutched it closer against me.

"I cut myself. Don't worry, I'm fine—"

"Fine? That's fine?" She stepped past me and went into the house.

"Francine," I called after her, not wanting her to go in any further. "Please, really, everything is fine. I promise it looks worse than it is."

She ignored me. I sighed, annoyed, and shut the door, following her into the kitchen. "Be careful!" I cautioned.

I heard her gasp, and I assumed she was seeing the shattered remains of what was once the glass. I refrained from rolling my eyes. "I dropped a glass of water," I told her. "…accidentally."

She started rummaging through drawers, and I sat down on a chair at the table.

"Now, where do you keep your dishcloths?"

Dizziness flooded my head. "Um, the left drawer. Down one."

"Aha!" She said, victorious, beginning to run the newly found cloth beneath some water, pushing aside a stack of dirty dishes. I stuck my face between my knees, indistinctly recalling someone once saying that was supposed to help lightheadedness.

"Are you okay?" Francine called out to me.

I pushed my face down harder, further, closer to the floor. I focused on the tiles, but they were shaking and swirling; back and forth, around in circles. The patterns they made were impossible to comprehend, and nothing was steady or certain or concrete anymore.

"Maeve? Are you going to faint?" Her voice sounded far away and distant, and I wanted to ask her where she was going and why she wasn't staying with me.

"Francine?" I whispered.

I tried to look up, but suddenly I was in a tunnel, unable to escape. Black dots danced in front of me and I couldn't find Francine anymore, and I remember feeling sad because I thought that like everyone else, she too, had left me.

I AWOKE TO FRANCINE'S GIANT eyes staring down at me.

"You're alive!" she squealed. Her tone would've been the same had someone handed her an ice cream cone.

I closed my eyes again. She began to blow air through her lips onto my face.

"Stop it."

"You need air—"

"No. Stop it."

She stopped.

"I'm exhausted," I told her. I opened my eyes to view her face directly above mine.

"Of course you're exhausted. Your body has been through an incredibly traumatic experience!"

"I fainted, Francine. I highly doubt that would be considered traumatic."

"You were unconscious, Maeve. You were passed out. You were not here with me. You—"

"Okay." I stopped her. "Yes, I understand. Thank you."

"Here, drink this." She shoved a glass of orange juice in my face. After much too long of a gulp, I pushed it away.

"I think I'm doing okay." I tried to sit up.

"No!" She put her hands on my shoulders, not allowing me to move. "You need sugar, and you need to lie down. Drink the orange juice and stay on the floor."

"Has anyone told you how bossy you are?"

Francine actually laughed. "That's what makes me such a good landlord. Besides, I'm the oldest in my family. Someone had to be bossy."

"Your poor siblings," I muttered and took another sip of the juice. I didn't tell her, but it actually felt pretty good sliding down my sandpapered throat.

I could feel her wrapping something around my finger, but I didn't care. I was so tired. I wanted to close my eyes and find some sleep, preferably for a fairly long amount of time.

"I've been calling Sol over and over," she was saying. "Does he ever answer his phone?"

My eyes flew open. "You've been calling Sol?"

Francine looked at me with a funny expression. "Of course I have! I'm still debating taking you to the hospital. He's your father—"

"Stepfather and only sort of—"

"—he should know you lost so much blood you fell unconscious!"

Realizing Francine had a slight tendency to over exaggerate, I chose not to remark on the latter comment. Through gritted teeth, I informed her, "I do not need to go to the hospital."

"You might need stitches."

"I'll be fine."

"You might scar."

"I'll be fine."

"You might—"

"I will be fine," I said this slowly, coolly, hoping it might sink in. My head started to ache, matching the throb of my finger.

I made my way to a sitting position, albeit still on the floor. I was wondering what Sol would think when he saw approximately forty-seven missed calls from Francine. She had swaddled my finger in a washcloth and it was tight and pressured, seeming fairly secure.

"You can go now," I told her.

"Oh," Francine said, sort of chewing on her bottom lip. "You want me... to leave?" She looked almost sad as if the evening had been a planned party with confetti, balloons, and birthday cake, and I was forcing her to go home early.

"I think I'm going to go to bed," I lied. I wanted to clean up the glass, finish the dishes, and contemplate why Sol suddenly and viciously wanted to protect me from the only flesh and blood I still had.

"Let me help you!" she said, scrambling to take my arm and assist me up.

I looked at her. Her red hair had come out of the clip, and she had dried blood on her pants and hands. She was standing there, waiting for me to give her some sort of direction. A pang went through me.

"Um…" I hesitated. "Thank you. For everything."

"Oh! Of course! I couldn't leave you on the ground bleeding out."

I smiled. "You could've, but thank you for deciding not to."

She turned to face the kitchen. "Who's going to clean up all this glass? I can do it."

For the first time, instead of feeling exasperation, I wondered why she was so eager to help. "I'll clean it in the morning," I said.

"Your finger's going to hurt in the morning, mark my words. You're going to need to take quite a few painkillers for that."

"Are you a nurse, too?"

She smiled, softly. "My mom was. Before she passed away."

I wasn't expecting that from her. But everyone experiences pain, don't they? Everyone knows some form of brokenness. "I'm sorry," I told her. "I didn't mean to bring that up."

Francine flashed a large, overcompensated grin. "Don't worry about it! She died when I was ten. That was a long time ago. It doesn't hurt anymore."

But I knew that wasn't true. Because the hole that's created with the departure of a mother never truly heals. Maybe it scabs over, maybe some days it's even forgotten about. But it's never truly whole again.

"Well, this was kind of you. Thank you, Francine."

She tilted her head to the side and asked, "Can I take you to lunch?"

"Lunch? Right now? It's nine o'clock at night."

She giggled. "Not now. But maybe this week? Or next week. Or whenever you're free. It would have to be on the weekend because of your schooling, of course."

I mentally kicked myself. Obviously, this is what happens when you let your crazy landlord into your home for the evening.

"Oh! I have the best idea! We could make it a girls day! We

could get our nails done and have lunch!" Francine actually clapped her hands together as she said this. I was overwhelmed already.

I started to motion her towards the door. "I'll have to check with Sol. You know, just to see if he'll need me or something…"

"Of course!" She was nodding her head, excited. Too excited. I needed sleep.

"How about," she said as she gathered her purse, and I was relieved to know she might actually leave, "I'll call you. We'll go out later this week. That way you'll be able to talk it out with Sol."

"Great."

She touched my hand gently. "Thank you, Maeve. I can't tell you how glad I am that you and I have become friends."

And then she was out the door, that whirlwind of a woman, and I was left thinking how in the world I had somehow gained a friend.

"SO MAEVE," FRANCINE SAID AS she plopped a lemon wedge deep into her water. I watched it sink to the bottom, and a few seeds disentangled themselves, floating away free. "What are your dreams?"

We were out on our aforementioned girls day, and Francine was treating me to lunch at a ritzy café forty-five minutes outside of town. She had offered to buy me a glass of wine, but I politely reminded her of my age. She smacked her head and said she'd forgotten, which didn't actually surprise me because she was scattered like that. I stuck with water. She was switching back and forth, her lemon water on one side of her plate, the glass of merlot on the other.

"My dreams?" I echoed.

I tried to focus on the menu in front of me. The lighting in the restaurant was dim—you would never have known it was only one o'clock in the afternoon—and the font on the menu was a fancy but minuscule script, and I squinted hard to read it. I finally saw that the simplest salad was seventeen dollars. Yikes. And it was beets, mozzarella, and mandarin oranges. I hated beets.

"Yes, your dreams. Like… if you could do anything, or have anything, or start anything, what would that be?" Francine closed her menu, setting it next to her plate.

My finger was still sore from the two days earlier. Sol had actually been fairly panicked when he came home. He had seen all of the missed calls from Francine and was worried something detrimental had happened. I assured him it was just my finger—and I was fine. But it still hurt. And it surprised me that he seemed to care.

The waiter came over, an extremely good-looking guy around my age who had smiled at me when we first walked in. "Are you ready, ladies?" He asked.

Francine flushed as she looked up at him. "Why, yes, I think I am. Are you, Maeve?"

"Um," I stammered, trying unsuccessfully to read what else was on the menu. "Yeah. Sure."

The boy, whose gold embossed nametag read *Luca*, turned to Francine. "For you?"

"I'm going to have the salmon. With… rice and the mango salad." She smacked her lips together and I wondered if she might skip lunch and take a bite out of Luca instead.

He scribbled her order down on his tiny notebook and looked at me. I felt self-conscious and wrapped my maroon cardigan tighter around my shoulders.

"And, for you? What can I have the pleasure of bringing you?" His teeth were uncommonly white. The left front one was crooked.

"Um," I looked at the menu again. "I guess I'll have this salad." I pointed to the first one. "Um, could I have it without the beets?"

A funny look passed across his face, but he simply wrote it down and gathered our menus, his fingers faintly brushing against mine as he took the menu from me.

"Does he seem weird to you?" I asked Francine after he walked away.

"Weird?" She tipped her head to the side.

I could feel my cheeks going pink. Maybe I was overreacting. "Like... I don't know. Forget it."

She took a small sip of wine. "He probably thinks you're pretty. Boys don't generally know how to act around girls they think are pretty." She smiled, placing her hand over her heart. "Oh, to be young again."

I pressed the cold glass against my cheek to try and cool myself. I tossed her a small smile, but I knew he didn't think that. "You are young."

Francine rolled her eyes. "You never answered my question. Tell me about your dreams, Maeve, your dreams."

"Right." I thought for a minute. No one had asked me about my dreams before. "I'm not sure if I have any," I told her honestly.

Her mouth flew open. "That's not true. Everyone has dreams. Some people might just have to dig a little deeper to find them."

I pondered this. "What are your dreams, Francine?"

She sighed wistfully and twisted her straw in between her fingertips. She said it so softly I almost didn't hear. "To be a mother."

"You want a baby?"

"I do. I really do. My husband—well, my ex-husband now— he left me because I can't have a baby." Tears filled her eyes. "He didn't say it in so many words, but... I know that's why he left. The doctors told me it was out of the question." She took her napkin, dabbing at the corners of her eyes. "I wanted to adopt, you know, once I finally realized that becoming pregnant was an impossibility. But Jack wouldn't have it. Said the baby would never be his. Said he didn't want it if it wasn't his own flesh and blood. Truth is, I don't think Jack wanted me either. Not anymore."

I reached my hand slowly across the table and rested it slightly upon hers. I didn't know what else to do.

"Was this recent?"

"The divorce?"

I nodded. Or the sinking understanding of no baby?

"About two years ago. He got remarried in March." A tear slipped down her cheek. "His wife is due in December."

"She's pregnant?"

Francine nodded slowly. I wanted to find wherever this Jack lived and kill him. How dare he.

"I'm so sorry, Francine." It was all I could manage.

"You shouldn't be the one apologizing!" She blew her nose into her napkin. "I feel very foolish, crying over here. This is not why we got together for lunch." She smiled weakly.

"Don't feel foolish. We're friends." I stole Levi's line. "This is the kind of thing friends do for one another."

Luca came, two plates in hand. "Now for you," he set a plate in front of Francine. "The salmon with rice and mango salad. And for you," he turned to me, "A beet salad without... the beets." He set my plate down.

Francine giggled.

"Um," I looked at him. "No lettuce?" My 'salad' was mozzarella cheese and mandarin oranges. No beets as I had asked, but no lettuce either. The mozzarella and oranges were placed artistically on the plate, creating what I think was supposed to resemble the sunshine. Honestly. "So where's the lettuce?" What kind of salad comes without lettuce?

"There's no lettuce," Luca confirmed. "The beet salad is made with oranges and mozzarella stuffed inside of the beets.

Without beets, there would be only oranges and cheese."

I felt my face redden. Francine was giggling uncontrollably on the other side of the table, and though I was grateful her tears had vanished, I wanted to die.

"I can... bring you some lettuce?" Luca offered.

I sucked my cheeks in. "Sure," I muttered. "Thank you."

He took my salad away and Francine laughed out loud. "Oh, Maeve!" She gasped. "I needed that!"

I smiled at her. "I'm glad you find my stupidity entertaining."

"Not stupidity on your end." She giggled again, trying to catch a breath. "I also assumed salad came with lettuce."

I laughed, too. It was humorous, albeit mortifying. "The font was so small on the menu I couldn't read what was underneath it."

"It was tiny. Gosh, I thought that was just me. Thank goodness! I was thinking I might have to go to the store and get glasses, and I don't want those."

"You'd rock glasses."

She scrunched her face hopefully. "Do you think so?"

"Absolutely. You could get pretty ones to match your hair."

Luca set the newly created salad, with lettuce this time, on the table. He looked at me. "Better?"

Laughing, I told him, "Yes, thank you. I'm sorry about that."

He smiled again. I wondered if he used whitening strips or only a toothbrush. "Don't worry about it. It wasn't a problem. I still don't understand the whole stuffed beets thing."

Francine started giggling again. When he walked away, she was dabbing her eyes again—this time from laughter.

"Are you sure there's not even a small dream that pops into your head?" she asked me.

"Well..."

"Tell me."

"I love to write. Poetry. I really like writing poetry."

A smile broke out wide across her face.

"Is that so?"

I nodded.

"Have you thought about getting any of your work published?"

"Oh no, never. I don't think it's good enough—"

"Maeve!" Francine clapped her hands together. "We must think about this." She quickly took a bite of salmon. "I know a man—Maurice Morris is his name." She rolled her eyes. "Who knows what his mother was thinking. Any-who, he's an editor at a newspaper. *The Dish*? You heard of it? It's not very big by any means—hardly anyone reads it—but I think they're currently looking for a few writers of some sort. It might be a good option to look into. I realize it's not exactly poetry, but you never know what could happen!"

I took a forkful of my salad.

"What do you think?" she asked.

Taking a breath I said, "I'm only in high school."

Francine waved her hand. "Let me talk to Maurice. He's a crusty old coot, but he's my friend and he might understand."

I raised my eyebrow doubtfully.

"Don't look that way."

"What way?"

"Like you've given up already when we haven't even tried."

I liked how she said "we," as if she and I were a team. We talked for a little longer, about lighter things, and then I excused myself to go to the restroom. The lighting in the washroom was considerably worse than the rest of the café. I washed my hands, having to actually search for the soap dispenser.

I left the washroom and started walking down the dimly lit deserted hallway, back to our table. But then a voice called out, "Hey. What's your name?"

I kept walking because I assumed the voice was not directed at me. But it called out again, "It's Maeve, right? That's what the lady called you?"

I turned, and there he was. Luca. He was walking down the hallway with a stack of dirty dishes in his hands.

"That's right," I said after a while. "It's Maeve."

"Mine's Luca."

"That's right," I said again. I pointed to his gold embossed badge. "I never would have guessed."

He laughed, his teeth bright even in the poorly lit hallway.

"If the power went out," I informed him, "People would always be able to find you."

"What?"

"Your teeth."

He blinked.

"People could use them as a flashlight. Because they're bright. You have very white teeth. So if the power went out…" I stopped talking.

"Thank you," Luca finally said. "I think."

Neither of us said anything.

"Well," I said after a long, awkward moment had passed, "I'm going to go now——"

"People could find you, too," he told me. "If the power went out. Because your cheeks are so red. Like, they're flaming. I can actually feel the heat radiating off of you. People would just have to follow the heat."

"That's because between the beet salad without the beets, and the fact that I called your teeth a flashlight, I might actually die of embarrassment in the next four and half seconds."

"That would be a shame."

"At this moment I'm not agreeing with you."

"It would be a shame. If you died in the next four and a half seconds, I wouldn't get to see you again."

I blinked. I didn't say anything.

"I'd like to… see you again," he said when I didn't reply.

I still didn't say anything.

"Would you… not like that?" He asked.

"I…" Pulled my maroon cardigan even tighter around me, locking my hands beneath my armpits. "I… don't understand."

"What don't you understand?"

"I don't understand what you want."

He coughed. "I think it would be cool to hang out with you."

"That's all?"

He nodded. "That's all. We could watch a movie, or get a coffee, or ice cream, or something. Whatever you wanted."

"A movie." After my encounter with Cade, I could only assume what two people did while watching movies.

"You don't like movies?"

"No, I do," I said nonchalantly.

"Okay," he smiled again. "I'll give you my number then." He set the stack of dirty dishes down beside him and took out his tiny waiter pad, scribbling on it. "Here you go," he passed it to me.

I unlatched my crossed arms and accepted it. "Thank you."

"Well…" he piled the dishes back into his hands. "Call me, or whatever. We can hang out. I have a car. I'll come pick you up."

"All right."

"It was good to meet you, Maeve. I should probably get these back to the kitchen."

"Yeah, probably."

"Okay," he nodded. "I'll see you soon, then."

"Right."

Luca smiled as he turned to head towards the kitchen, and I stared at the small paper that had grown hot and damp in my hands. I stared at his name and the numbers until they began to look strange. I turned to go back to Francine, and on the way to the table, threw the paper into the trash. He had been nice, Luca, and his act was a good one, I had to give it to him. He almost seemed genuine. But if Cade Samson had taught me anything, it was that boys, nice boys or otherwise, didn't care about movies or coffee or ice cream. And they certainly didn't care about me.

ELEVEN

MAURICE MORRIS WAS A LARGE black man. He wasn't overweight or fat; he was just large. And he was crusty like Francine had said.

When I walked into his office on the first day, I felt sure I was going to puke right there on the floor in the middle of all that shiny tile. I gathered the notebooks I carried, filled with my poetry as well as a few short stories like Ms. Meyers had suggested, clutching them closer to my chest. Only Levi, Ky, and Ms. Meyers had read them, and then, only a mere few.

I was simultaneously petrified and elated at the thought of someone else reading my work. Francine had told me not to be nervous, but to also be prepared that Maurice was nothing if not honest. That did not settle my aching stomach.

I took a deep breath, lingering where I was on the steps for a few moments, then pushed open the two big wooden doors. I expected to be greeted with an extraordinary bustle of commotion, but all I saw was a receptionist looking bored at her desk.

"Hello." I greeted her.

She looked up at me. "Appointment?"

"Oh. Yes." I stammered and shuffled around my papers and notebook, trying to find the sheet I had written the time and address down. As if that was assured proof that I was significant enough to be there. I showed her the slip.

"Head on back. Last door to the right," she ordered, tossing her head to the side.

"Thank you."

It was at that point in time when I thought I was literally going to be sick. I went through another set of double doors, and there, at last, was where the action was taking place. There were dozens and dozens of desks and cubicles. People talking on the phone or pounding away at their computers. You could hardly hear your own thoughts.

They didn't pay attention to me, and I stood there, gaping, trying to take it all in. It was a new world, and I tried to guess what sort of stories they would be telling that day.

"Hello? Excuse me? Who are you?"

I turned around, realizing that the girl was talking to me. She had dark black hair. I couldn't tell if it was dyed or natural.

She looked at me pointedly. "Can you talk?"

I nodded.

Eyebrow sky high, she asked, "Then who are you?"

"Maeve Parker?" It came out as a question and my cheeks burned. I cleared my throat and tried again. "Maeve Parker. I have an appointment with Mr. Morris…"

"Then I suggest you get over there and stop gawking."

I nodded again. "Right. Thank you."

I found my way to his door. Turned out it was the second to last door on the right, not the last. That receptionist lady should get her doors straight. It was a large door, wooden with a window in it. *Maurice Morris, Editor* was etched into the glass.

I rapped on the door gently.

"You're going to have to knock louder than that for him to

hear you." The same black-haired girl from before said to me, breezing past, a pile of papers high in her hands. She was starting to get on my nerves. I gritted my teeth and knocked again. This time, louder—maybe a little too loud.

The door swung wide and Maurice Morris stood there. "What, do you think I'm deaf or something? No need to take the whole door down with you."

"Sorry."

"Don't just stand there. Come inside." His voice was deep and heavy, and I desperately wanted him to like me.

I pushed the door closed and sat on the chair adjacent to his desk. He had papers everywhere. They were strewn haphazardly across every surface of the room and I wondered how he could ever find anything.

"Francine Sinclair tells me you're a good writer."

I smiled but didn't say anything.

"Well?"

I looked at him, unsure of what he wanted me to say.

"Are you?"

I swallowed. "Am I…"

He sighed and looked tired, pushing his hand deep into the sockets of his eyes. "Are you a good writer?"

I knew I was failing his test, whatever it might be that he was testing me on. I felt sick and embarrassed and I wanted to run out the door with the window on it, push past that pretentious girl and bored receptionist and run, run, run all the way home.

Instead, I planted myself firmer into the chair. "Yes," I told him, begging confidence—or maybe God—to come find me. "I am. But I want to be better."

"Do you believe you could do a good job here?"

"I do. I'm a hard worker. I'll do whatever you ask of me."

He motioned me to hand over the notebook. He leafed through the pages quickly, his hand stroking his chin.

"She mentioned that you're still in high school."

I nodded.

"What grade?"

"Eleventh."

"Young."

"Um… yes."

"Will you be pursuing a career in writing, Miss Parker?" He stroked his chin again.

"I haven't really decided yet."

"Oh?"

If I hadn't failed the test before, I was sure I had failed it now.

I debated lying to him, but even in all his superiority, his ebony eyes seemed almost kind. And also like they'd know exactly when you were lying.

"My English teacher thinks I would be able to."

"Then what's the issue?"

"I don't know if I'll be able to afford school." I swallowed. I was thirsty and my throat felt like sandpaper. "I would like to go to college but… it's very expensive."

Maurice Morris rocked back in his chair and looked at me for a long time. He weaved his fingers in and out of his hands, in and out, in and out, rhythmic, steady. Surely this was the part where he would inform me that I was small and inferior and worthless and wouldn't be needed at this time—which was an acute translation for not being needed ever.

"You know," he told me, his deep voice less crusty and in a way nearly soothing, "If you want something—if you really, truly want something—you must create a way to get hold of it."

I nodded.

"Let me ask you a question."

"All right."

"Do you want to go to school for writing?"

"Yes, sir. I do."

The chair squeaked beneath him as he rocked back and forth, flipping the pages of my notebook, scouring my thoughts and poems and vulnerability. I stared at a floorboard.

"I'm an honest man, Miss Parker. You should know that."

I looked up.

"So I'll be honest with you. Your writing is not great."

I thought I was going to be sick again.

He held up a hand. "Hear me out. It's okay, but it's not great. If you want to write—if you want to be a writer—it has to be great. Don't write because you want to get published. Write because you need to write."

I nodded, but my hands and stomach felt shaky. I stood. "Thank you very much for your time, Mr. Morris—"

"Did I say you could leave?" He asked.

I blinked. "No, sir."

"Sit yourself back down."

I sat.

"I consider myself a fair man. Let me make you a deal."

"Okay."

"I'll hire you, two days a week to write, two days a week to clean. You'll come here directly after school until seven."

I listened quietly. Tried to decide if his offer was degrading or merciful. I had told him I'd do whatever he'd ask of me.

"You'll have three days off. Do whatever you want on your weekend. The other day off I expect you to write from home." He handed me back the notebook. "If you don't continue writing, you won't get better."

I took the notebook from him. "Thank you."

"Miss Parker, anyone would think my proposition generous. In order to work here, you're generally expected to have completed college with a degree in either Journalism or English."

I nodded. "This is kind of you. Thank you."

"It's not kind; it's business. You will get paid the internship wage, which is less than what the other employees make. Monday and Tuesday afternoons you will clean my office, the bathrooms, etcetera. On Wednesday and Thursday afternoons you will write. Clarke can take on the role as your mentor of sorts. Don't be offended if she's offended." He rolled his eyes at that.

"Mr. Morris... I appreciate this."

"Don't disappoint me, Miss Parker."

I got up, gathered my notebook and papers and went towards the wooden door with the window. I could see *Maurice Morris, Editor* through the glass, this time backward. I wondered briefly if someone had once been merciful to him.

I turned to him then, my fingers idling on the brass doorknob.

"I won't."

CLARKE, MY "MENTOR OF SORTS", ended up being the pretentious black-haired girl who caught me staring on the day of my interview. I wasn't all that surprised it was her. Life often seems to work out that way. Maurice Morris showed me to her desk, told her to be nice to me, and walked away, muttering something inaudible beneath his breath.

"Hi again," I said.

I swear she actually grimaced. "I was worried it was going to be you."

"Thanks."

"I'm a writer. Not a babysitter."

"Got it."

"You have to keep up or I'll tell him to fire you."

"Okay."

"Any questions?"

"Just one."

"Spit it out. We don't have all day."

"Do you dye your hair or is it natural?"

AT FIVE P.M. THE FOLLOWING afternoon I decided I was going

to quit.

Then I reasoned with myself that it was most likely the best job I'd be able to find as a sixteen-year-old, and decided against quitting. But if Clarke had any particular talent, it had to be making people want to run as far away as soon as possible. She seemed to be exceptionally good at that.

Maurice had told her—if it was good enough—he would publish some of my poetry in the Art and Creativity section of the paper. And apparently, Clarke, as my mentor and the head of the Arts section, was the one to approve the state of my poetry.

As I was finishing my peanut butter sandwich, I handed her the piece I had written that morning in English class.

His eyes were soft
Blue like a breeze
Wafting over a heart
Gentle
A kind breeze.
His laugh was music
Music from an autumn day
Colorful and bright
And beautiful.
And his hands bore his soul
A mysterious soul
Innocent
Breathtaking.
His voice was a dove
Flying free, flying far
A white dove
A pure dove.
And his lips were compassion
Sunshine
A cold cup of lemonade
Refreshing, bursting with light.
His eyes smiled

His hands laughed
And his lips sang a song of compassion,
A song of songs.

She glanced over it, her black hair falling in front of her face. She didn't bother to swipe the wisps away.

Clarke looked up at me. "It's all right, I guess. But it feels like you're attempting to be deep, or metaphoric, or something. Quit trying so hard. Let it flow out from inside of you."

I sighed.

"There's no need to sigh or be melodramatic. Do you want to be known as 'Maeve Parker the Mediocre Writer'? Or how about not being known at all? Although I have to say, there are very few things worse than mediocrity."

"No. I want to be good."

Clarke sat back in her chair, tipping the two rear legs so the front two were airborne. "Let me give you a free piece of advice."

I sat down. Although she certainly didn't top my list of favorite people, she had her job for a reason.

"I know you're young. How old are you?"

"Almost seventeen."

She nodded, and a small smile came across her lips. "Don't get me wrong. You're not bad for an almost-seventeen-year-old." She snorted. "If I had this job when I was your age I can't imagine where I might be right now. Maybe New York City or something."

"You want to go to New York City?"

Clarke nodded and for some reason struck me as shy. "Not just go to New York City, Maeve. Thrive there."

"There's a difference," I said.

"An astronomical difference. Anyone can go there. I could book a flight right now if I wanted. But in two days' time, I'd be booking one right back home. I want to work at *The New York*

Times, in their Arts and Entertainment section. Can you imagine what you could write about there?"

I couldn't. It all seemed so big. Astronomical, like she'd said. "Would it be hard to get a job there?"

She scoffed. "Hard to get a job at *The New York Times*? How about impossible."

"Really?"

She rolled her eyes. "Do you know anything?"

"Apparently not."

"No one would hire a twenty-nine-year-old girl from *The Dish* in Rutherford to work at *The New York Times* in New York City. No one in their right mind, anyway. I'd have to be a prodigy."

"You're obviously good at something. You work here."

"Yeah, well, Maurice trusts me. He's good at giving chances. Take you, for example."

I smiled.

"We have a budget here in the Arts," Clarke said suddenly as if we'd never spoken about New York. "A small budget, but we have one nonetheless. I'm going to take the liberty to sign you up for an online six-week poetry course. It will help hone your skill. You have a computer, I presume?"

I nodded. I didn't, but Sol did. I would force him to let me use it. "Thanks, Clarke."

"I'm not doing this to be nice, Parker. I get by fine in life without inauthentic compliments."

"Well, thanks anyway. Nice or not."

"You can be done for the day. Make sure to practice this weekend. On Monday, after you're done cleaning, I'll give you the passcode for your course."

I collected my things from her desk. We were sharing one since I wasn't allowed my own (mere intern and all that), although to my complete surprise I was allowed my personal key. *The Dish* had a strange way of doing things.

"Hey, Clarke?" I asked before I left her cubicle.

She looked up from her computer.

"I swear this isn't one of those inauthentic compliments that are given by most of the world." I paused for a moment. "I hope you make it to New York City. I hope you really make it—the thriving kind of make it. I hope someday I walk into *The New York Times* and you're there, running their entire A&E section, being the bossiest and most pretentious you've ever been."

Clarke stared at me for a long minute. Her lips turned out in a half smile. "You can't walk into *The Times*, Parker. You'll need an appointment first."

I laughed. "I'll remember that."

"Parker," She called to me as I was opening the two wooden doors to leave.

"Yeah?"

She paused for a second. "My hair. It's not dyed. All *au naturel* for me."

Grinning, I pulled those doors shut behind me.

TWELVE

TWO WEEKS AFTER JARED THE Boyfriend showed up on Alice's doorstep covered in flowers, Jared the Boyfriend proposed to Alice.

Ky cried. I'd never seen her cry before.

"You need to tell Alice," I told her.

"How am I supposed to do that?" Tears were streaming down her cheeks as we walked from school through the forest to my house.

"I'll come with you. We'll tell her exactly what you've seen."

"She'll think I'm trying to ruin her happiness. She already told me that the other day. She wanted me to go out and see a movie with them; she was calling it Fun Family Time. I told her I didn't want to go anywhere with him, then she said I was trying to ruin the only happiness she'd found." She sniffed hard. "It doesn't matter. I don't care anyway."

"Clearly you care. You wouldn't be crying if you didn't care."

She sat down. I sat beside her.

It was the middle of November and the sky was soft amber, the color of nostalgia. Ky crunched a leaf between her fingers. "How do I bring this up?"

I took a breath. I released it. I looked at her.

"Tonight, you take her out for dinner. She can't make a scene if you're in a public place, right?"

Ky gave me a pointed look.

"Okay, maybe she still can, but it would be less drastic than if you were at home."

"And what do I say?"

"The truth."

"That I followed her boyfriend?"

"Fiancé."

Ky grimaced. "I'll sound like a stalker."

"Tell her how much you love her, and that you want her to be happy—but he has literally been cheating on her for their entire relationship! I'm sure deep down she knows something's not right."

"But we believe what we want to believe, don't we?"

We were quiet for a moment, sitting amidst the orange fallen leaves. I wondered if it hurt when they fell. The season of change seemed to be a constant source of pain for people—I wondered if it hurt the trees too.

"I'm going to go tell her," Ky whispered quietly.

"Want me to come with you?"

"No. This is something I need to do by myself. But thanks, Maeve. You're a good friend. I'll call you after."

I leaned forward and hugged her. I held her for a long time.

When we got up and turned to go our separate ways, I watched her as she walked away. Her shoulders shook as she walked through the dying trees, and I noticed she was crying once again.

WHEN I GOT HOME, GRAY was over.

I could tell he and Sol were drunk even before I closed the door, but that was seemingly the Friday night ritual so it didn't come as a great surprise to me.

Gray saw me come in and yelled, "Beautiful Maeve! Come join us!"

I started walking toward the stairs. "I'm too tired tonight. Sorry. It's been a long day."

"Oh, come on, Maeve," Sol coaxed.

"I'm not lying. I'm exhausted, Sol."

"You never do anything fun," said Gray.

"That's not true. I have fun."

Gray came over to me and placed his hand on my cheek. "But you never have fun with me." He was already slurring.

"Shouldn't you hit on someone your own age?"

Both of them erupted into laughter. I rolled my eyes and muttered, "That wasn't a joke."

Gray took my hand and pulled me toward the couch.

"You've had a long day," he whispered. "That's what you said, isn't it? Come and relax a little. You're hard on yourself, Maeve." He leaned in closer. "You take life too seriously. You shouldn't be so hard on yourself."

"Am I?"

"Yes," his eyes were large and looking at me. "You are. Too hard, Maeve. Too hard."

I sank onto the couch next to him and I was exhausted.

Gray handed me a cup of something he had mixed up. It was heavy and smelled both sweet and sickly, and it burned my throat and lungs as I sipped. After awhile it began to quiver my insides, my mind, my chest. A searing sensation ran through my body and I blinked, sipping it again.

I wanted to be numb.

Gray was talking to Sol and I realized he was still holding my hand, but his hand was sweaty and I didn't want him touching me anymore. I removed my hand from his and held my cup with both of my own hands, and he smiled at me and placed his hand high on my thigh. I didn't want it there. But I blinked and sipped my drink again.

At some point, I realized my cup was empty and Gray filled it up again and I continued to sip, and he continued to put his hand on my thigh, and Sol continued to laugh until there was a knock on the door and three women came in giggling. Sol went and got them drinks. Gray leaned over toward my ear and whispered, "They came for Sol. I came for you."

And then he kissed me.

My drink sloshed down my shirt soaking me, and his clammy hands touched my face and hair.

"I don't want this," I whispered to him. My voice didn't sound like me. It sounded lily-livered and pathetic, like a girl who didn't have the strength to stand up for herself.

He kissed me.

"Get off of me," I said louder, shrugging out of his grasp. I got off the couch, but his hand snaked on my forearm and he pulled me down onto him and he kissed me again.

I pushed him. I pushed him with a strength I desperately wanted to have, and I ran out of the door. I didn't look back. I didn't think I was in my own body anymore.

I WOKE UP BENEATH A blue comforter.

I blinked. The room was light gray and a Beatles poster was tacked on the wall across from me. It hung slightly crooked. The comforter was tucked tightly against my skin, soft and warm on my flesh. I blinked again, trying to remember who had kidnapped me.

My head was pounding and there was a damp cloth on my brow. I groaned. My whole body hurt. The door opened and I turned my head too sharply, causing my body to reverberate.

"Hey," my kidnapper whispered. "You're awake."

"Levi?" I looked around and saw a picture of a beach above his desk. The water was the same color as his eyes. "Am I in your room?" I moaned. "What time is it?"

"Shhh," he whispered again. "It's just after eight in the morning."

"What happened last night?"

He laughed quietly. "You were pretty drunk. I heard someone knocking on my door at three in the morning, and it was you screaming—er, singing, *I Wanna Dance With Somebody*."

"The Whitney Houston song?"

He nodded.

"I love that song. There's nothing like it."

"Then you tried to dance with me."

I slowly closed my eyes. "Maybe don't tell me anymore…"

"It's okay, you passed out after that. And we didn't dance because you fell onto the couch."

I was horrified. "I am so sorry."

"We have to be really quiet. My parents don't know and they're not about to find out. They're awake now but they're dead to the world when they fall asleep—which is nice when things like this happen."

"Things like this?" I raised my eyebrow. "Do these things happen to you often, Levi Fisher?"

Bright pink flushed across Levi's cheeks. "No, not really."

I laughed softly. "I didn't think so. Levi, I'm so embarrassed. How did I get up here from the couch?"

He blushed again. "I… um… I carried you."

"Right," I said after a few minutes. "Thank you. I'm sorry I put you in that position. I swear I don't get drunk often. It was a series of bad decisions, and I feel terrible that I came here of all places…"

"It's okay. No one saw. Are you hungry?"

I shook my head. "I feel awful."

"Apparently you're supposed to eat burnt toast."

I stared at him. He shrugged. "I read somewhere that burnt toast cures a hangover."

"I don't have a hangover. You shouldn't believe everything

you read."

"That's probably true." He disappeared through the door and came back a few minutes later with a sleeve of saltine crackers. "At least try to eat a few of these."

I sat up, slowly, in his bed. "Thank you."

He sat on the edge of the bed. "Were you with Ky?"

"No. With my stepdad, and his friend... Grayson. You don't know him." I sighed and nibbled a cracker. "He's an idiot, and I wanted to get away from him."

"Why'd you want to get away from him?"

I shrugged and bit more of the cracker.

"Has he... has he hurt you, Maeve? You can tell me."

"No," I scowled. "He hasn't hurt me." I swallowed hard, and told him as firmly as I could, "he's harmless."

"You shouldn't be in that house. Not with them."

"Gray doesn't live at our house. Sol's getting better. He's fine when he's sober."

Levi shook his head, "Maeve, this is serious—"

"Levi!" Nora called. "Are you awake?"

I froze.

Levi put his fingers to his lips and pointed to the closet. I nodded and went inside, sitting next to his overflowing laundry hamper. He shut the doors.

"Yeah, Mom!" Levi called back. "I'm up!"

I could hear the crinkling of him covering up the saltine crackers and the bedroom door opening.

Nora's voice. "Morning, honey. Your dad and I are going to Grandpas for the day. I left some money on the counter for pizza." She laughed. "Or you and Simon could actually make yourself food. That would be a wonder, wouldn't it?"

"Thanks, Mom." I heard Levi say.

"Simon's football practice finishes at eleven, so you're home alone until then."

"Okay."

"You sure you don't want to come to Grandpas?"

"Yeah, I'm sure."

Nora sighed. "All right. Love you, honey. Have a good day."

"You too, Mom. Bye."

I heard Nora close the door and pad down the hallway. Levi's voice was close to the closet. "Wait a few minutes, okay?" he whispered. "They'll be gone soon and then it will be safe."

"Okay," I whispered back. I heard the door open and close again, and I sat with my knees tucked against my chest in the closet. I laughed silently, in spite of the situation, shaking my head at what I had dragged Levi into.

Some minutes later, the closet door opened.

"They're gone," Levi said.

"Phew."

He helped me up and went back down and sat on his bed. I sat beside him.

"I think you should go to the police," Levi said.

"What?"

"Your stepdad has hurt you, and you're scared of this Grayson guy. How old is he anyway?"

"I'm not scared of him! I just wanted him to leave me alone last night. And I am not going to the police, Levi. Don't be ridiculous." I shook my head. "I'll be fine. I don't mind Sol. Some days I genuinely like him. In less than two years, I'll be eighteen. I'm saving money. I'll be able to get out of here soon."

"Two years? You can't be in that house for two more years."

"Technically less than two years now."

"Not any better."

"I promise you, Levi, it's not that bad. I've probably been dramatic. I don't see how I have another choice."

"There's always another choice!" he argued.

I ran my hands through my hair. "It's okay," I smiled. "I'm fine."

"That's what they told me in those anger management

classes. They said there's always another choice."

"This isn't your anger management class. Sol has been there for me when my mother hasn't. He's all I've got, Levi."

"That's not true. You've got me."

I bit my lip. He was so tender. "You say that now. You're sixteen, Levi. You've got your whole life ahead of you."

"And so do you!"

"Maybe," I told him. "And maybe you really do believe that now, but in a couple of years you'll be off somewhere new, doing big things. You'll be at your ocean. With a pretty little wife you'll meet in college and like ten babies in a cute beach house."

Levi raised his eyebrows. "Ten babies?"

I shrugged my shoulders. "I feel like you'd be a good dad."

"Are they different ages, or is it like ten-tuplets?"

I laughed. "Is that what that's called? Ten-tuplets?"

"I have no idea... but that seems horrible. Maybe I can have ten kids all different ages?"

I giggled and shook my head. "Nope. Sorry. You are destined for ten-tuplets."

He groaned and leaned back. "Maybe I'll skip the whole marriage and baby thing and hang out with you forever."

I looked at him with a sad smile. "I don't think you'd be able to handle hanging out with me forever. I'm not really the kind of girl you'd want to be with."

"You'd be surprised."

Sighing, I touched his hand for a short second. "Thanks. For helping me."

"Anytime. I mean that."

My phone rang. It was on Levi's desk, which I assumed he put there after he tucked me into his bed. I tried not to think about that. He grabbed the phone and handed it to me.

The caller ID said it was Ky. I had forgotten all about her mission with Alice.

"Ky," I said when I answered it. "How did it go? How'd Alice take it?"

"Maeve?" The voice was crying.

"Ky, what's wrong? Are you okay?"

Levi looked at me.

"Maeve? Is that you?"

"Yeah, it's Maeve. Who is this? Are you all right?"

The voice heaved a sob. "It's Alice."

Levi's eyes were searching mine and I shrugged my shoulders. *It's Alice*, I mouthed to him. I listened closer to her crying.

"Alice, what's wrong?"

"Something's happened, Maeve."

"What happened? Where's Ky?"

Alice didn't speak for a long time but when she did I wished she hadn't.

"Maeve," her voice sounded far away and hollow. "Ky killed herself last night."

THIRTEEN

DURING THE BRIEF TIME AFTER my father died and before Sol entered our lives, Sage took me to the carnival. It was something I believed could only live in the scope of one's mind. But she took me there, and as we walked through the popcorn-littered streets there it was, like an iridescent map unfurling before me. It wasn't the dream I'd assumed it could only be, but rather a real and entrancing place I could feel with tangibility.

"Maeve girl," Sage said. "Come on."

She took my hand with my yellow-painted fingernails, and she brought me down the street, closer to the music and the ice cream trucks and the balloons that waved wild and happy in the breeze.

She bought us each a stick of cotton candy and asked the man nicely if he would swirl in both the pink and the blue. He obliged, and I watched him while he did it, fascinated with the pure magic of it all. That's what it was—magic, really—a place of magical limbo where reality was pushed aside and forgotten; where sugar sitting in your teeth became the only staple. Magic, indeed.

We walked down the streets, our hands and mouths sticky and sweet, and when nighttime fell and the stars sprinkled bright against the sky, it was time to watch the fire woman.

"Watch carefully, Maeve," Sage whispered to me as we stood on the curb of the street, people spilling beside us, encircling the audacious lady.

I watched her, mesmerized by the woman's sequined top and bottoms that had bells sewed in which rang when she danced; like the breeze against a wind chime. The music began slowly, softly. People gathered around the woman as she lit twelve candles, one by one, and the flames flickered and swayed, similar to the motion of the woman's hips and belly.

"Have you ever eaten fire?" the woman called out and her voice thundered against the night sky.

The crowd responded with a low murmur and the fire woman called it out again.

"I asked have you ever eaten fire?"

"No!" Sage cried along with the rest of the crowd, louder that time. The drums in the music began to build with an intensifying rhythm and I could feel that same beat begin to pulse within my very blood.

"My mother always told me fire was dangerous." The woman held the candelabra with the twelve candles in the palm of her hand, while she danced in a circle around us. She looked at me, coming right in close and whispered, "But I didn't listen."

She stayed there for a moment—her eyes boring into mine, black and mystical, the kind of eyes that held deep, ambiguous promises.

"Fire is dangerous," she told me. "But I'll tell you a secret. You want to hear a secret, child?"

Her hair was the longest I'd seen, her eyes flashing as she spoke to me. My heart beat hard and I clutched the safe hand of Sage who stood beside me. I nodded.

"There's nothing more dangerous than people. They'll do

more harm to you than any fire ever could."

She whisked herself away from me and dangled the flame of the candle in between her lips. Suddenly the flames disappeared down her throat. The crowd gasped and she smiled, her lips stretching into a long satisfied grin across her cheeks.

"Ta-da," she sang as she took a bow.

We saw other performances that day, other magical people who presented strange and exotic acts, all of them fascinating to me. But as our tired feet walked back to the car, our stomachs filled with caramel corn and hand squeezed lemonade, I couldn't help but recall what the fire woman had revealed to me: *There's nothing more dangerous than people. They'll do more harm to you than any fire ever could.*

FOURTEEN

ALICE SPOKE AT THE FUNERAL.

Everyone from school came, even Amanda Wright, Brett Meyers, and Cade Samson. Had we been in different circumstances, I might have laughed. I think Ky would have laughed as well, or at least rolled her eyes. I could picture her elbowing me, saying, "Look, Maeve. Look how they flock when someone dies. Look at how the circumstances can change overnight."

Because these people were flaky, that much I knew. I knew they could change in an instant, their opinions holding no weight in the world because they never stuck to what they truly thought. They simply did whatever was popular; whatever gave them the attention they so desperately and repulsively craved.

But Ky was never like that.

She was authentic and real and stuck to what she felt; even when no one agreed with her, even when it was hard, even when it hurt. She was tenacious and gritty and bold—the strongest and bravest person I knew.

But she was dead.

Alice was at the front of the church giving her eulogy, and she was crying. She was crying so hard you could barely understand what she was saying. She kept looking at Jared who sat in the front row as if the measure of looking at him might make her feel more able to continue.

I could see Ky's older sister in the front row beside Jared. There was a man on the other side of her, which I assumed was her father. His new wife sat next to him and beside her were three little boys. I shot daggers at the backs of their heads with my eyes. I hated their family, and most especially, Ky's father. All of these people had ruined her.

You could hear people sniffling and blowing their noses, wailing to one another about how sad they were, how sad it was that such a young girl died. *She killed herself!* I wanted to scream. *She chose to die! And none of us had the decency to stop her.*

The whole thing sickened me if we're being frank. I didn't cry and neither did Levi, because why would either of us waste any emotion on a group of people that didn't actually care? No, we would save our tears for when it mattered.

They didn't know Ky. They didn't know her at all.

"Ky would have loved this," Alice was saying through tears and I could feel my body tighten because I knew that wasn't true. "I know she's looking down, smiling, so grateful that you all came—" she paused and wiped her face. "—that all the people she loved came."

More people were crying.

I wanted to throw up—shove a finger down my throat and get sick, and maybe that would make me feel something else besides the gnawing ache in my stomach.

Levi glanced at me, then down at my hand that was pressing white-knuckle hard against the pew bench. He took it and unfolded my fingers into his own, slowly easing the tension away, like a roll tide washing in and out, smoothing the grains of the shore.

I understand, he mouthed to me.

I nodded. I knew he did. Or at least that he was trying. He was trying to understand and it felt like he was the only one left who could.

Alice didn't want Levi or me or anyone else saying something at the service. Ky's dad refused that, and he spoke before Alice. So did Ky's sister, Hannah. They said nice things, I suppose. Generic, nice things.

Levi thought I might be upset that Alice didn't want me to speak, but the truth is I didn't have any idea of what I would say had she asked me. There would never be a large enough or right enough or poetic enough accumulation of words to describe the mark Ky left on the world. The mark she left on me.

The problem was, the mark she left on the world seemed already to be quickly dissipating. The funeral caused all of these people to remember her, but what would happen when the funeral was done and Ky was buried and everyone went back to living their own pitiful lives? Her mark was shriveling by the moment, and when Alice took her seat and the preacher went back up to say a few more words, I wondered if Ky knew how small her mark really was.

I wondered if anyone knows that.

When you're living, you don't realize how few people really know you. But then someone dies and the living realizes how quickly the dead are forgotten. I wouldn't allow Ky to be disregarded. I would remember her, and so would Levi and Alice. We could carry her on.

Nora and Jonas sat beside Levi, and I watched as Nora wiped tears away.

Music began to play and a swarm of bodies dressed in black stood and started to exit the room. A lowly funeral procession. I'd missed what the pastor had said about Ky. For a brief moment, I regretted not listening. The feeling vanished. He didn't know her. His words were probably the same he'd said about a hundred other dead girls.

"Maeve," Nora said to me. I tried to focus on her, but the air had grown stale and the people were pushing in on me, and there wasn't any more room in the church. I couldn't breathe. Someone was clamping a thousand pounds onto my lungs and I was desperate for just a single breath.

"I need to go to the bathroom," I told her and plowed my way through the throngs of people, not caring about one of them. I pushed open the bathroom stall and collapsed, my lungs heaving. They heaved with great relief and insurmountable grief.

I wept.

I sat on the floor of the stall and wept. Huge, heaving sobs wracked my body.

"Maeve?" A voice called out, quiet.

"I'm okay," I sobbed. "I just need a minute."

"Maeve, honey. Open the door. Please."

I stared at the lock for a long time then curled my fingers around it, finally releasing.

Nora looked at me, her eyes filled with tears. She slipped her feet out of her high heels, crawling onto the bathroom floor next to me. She put her face close to mine and said, "You are a wonderful friend. Don't think you were even slightly at fault for this. This was not your fault. Do you hear me? It's not your fault."

Nora took me in her arms and hugged me so tightly I thought I could break. But I didn't. And I realized she wasn't trying to shatter me, but instead hold me in a way where I might somehow be put back together.

"THERE'S SOMETHING I NEED TO give you," Alice told me once people had withdrawn from the burial site. I wanted to leave too, but Alice had told me she wanted to talk.

Levi touched my elbow. "We'll wait for you by the car. Take your time."

I nodded. "I won't be long."

He walked away toward the car, toward Nora and Jonas, and Alice looked at me.

"Was this my fault, Maeve?"

"I don't think you can ask me that."

She started to cry again, begging, "Please tell me it wasn't because of me. Please. I know I wasn't a good mother, and I know she was depressed, but I never did anything to make her do this. I promise, Maeve."

"I didn't think any of her jokes were serious."

"I thought she was getting better. I thought—well, I thought the worst was over. How ignorant of me."

"She was going to tell you she didn't want you to marry Jared."

"She never liked him."

I shook my head. "No, she didn't."

"She told me that night."

"That she didn't want you to marry him?"

Alice nodded and wiped away her tears. "She told me she hated him, and that he was awful. She said she would run away if I went through with it."

"What did you say?"

Alice cried harder and let her head drop into her hands, the shame of an unforgiven woman written all over her. After a few moments, she lifted her head up. "I told her I didn't care. I told her I loved him and I wanted to be happy." She fumbled for a Kleenex and blew her nose. "Don't look at me that way, Maeve."

"What way?"

"Like you're judging me. Like you're so much better than I am."

"I don't think that."

"I wanted to be happy. Don't you understand?"

"Ky wanted to be happy, too. We all want that. But you're

the mom and Ky's the kid, and moms are supposed to be there for the kid. Don't you get it? Moms aren't supposed to be selfish."

I was crying then and Alice was sobbing. She took a wisp of my hair and twirled it gently around her fingertips; her tears dripping freely down her face. "Oh, Maeve. I would do anything to get one more chance."

She let my hair down and reached into her purse. "I should've given this to you a while ago." She sniffed and brought out a small envelope. "I almost read it. But I wouldn't have been able to live with myself if I had. Will you promise me something?" Alice didn't let me answer. "Will you let me read it after you? She didn't leave me anything, and I just want to know why she…" Her tears didn't let her finish the sentence and she handed the envelope out to me, like a peace offering of some sort. A truce.

I looked down and saw my name scrawled in Ky's loopy cursive.

I watched my fingers reach out and take it, saw my hands peel away the back and lift out a few pieces of paper. I felt my eyes read the words, perhaps the last ones Ky wrote. I heard myself screaming at Alice.

"Did you know about this?" I shrieked at her.

Alice looked bewildered. "Know what?"

I shook the letter in front of her, my body pulsing with rage. "How could you let this happen to her?" I cried. "How could you stand by and let this go on?"

"Let me read it!" Alice ripped it from my hands and I watched as her face turned to horror. She looked up at me. "This can't be right."

"Shut up, Alice!" I yelled. "It is right! And it's all your fault. Ky's dead because of you!"

I took the letter from her and walked away as fast as my legs would take me. I strode past Levi and Nora and Jonas, and Levi

128

called out, "Maeve? Are you okay?"

"I'm walking home," I told him, not stopping or slowing down.

I could hear him running behind me. "What's wrong, Maeve? Tell me what's wrong! Please—I can't help you if you don't talk to me!"

I turned to him and snapped, "I don't need your help, Levi! I don't need anyone."

He looked hurt and helpless. "That's not true."

The tears were coming faster than I could stop them.

"Please let me help you. Tell me what's wrong."

I almost told him. I almost let him read the letter, but it hurt too much. Everything hurt—a fire devouring all of my limbs and bones and muscles and soon I would be ash. "Leave me alone!" I screamed and started to run. I didn't look behind me, but I pictured him standing there hoping I might return. I didn't.

I found my way to the forest, to the spot where I last sat with Ky. I was in a thousand places all at once. A thousand places and nowhere, seemingly all at the same time—the forest, her house, the school, my living room, that stupid dance.

I was furious. I suddenly hated Ky, and an impassioned rage was steeping and boiling deep within me. I could feel it churning. I hated her because she was selfish and didn't tell me or include me or even try and take me with her. I hated her because she had left me alone in this stupid, freaking world. I hated her because she was the very best person I knew—and what are you supposed to do when the best person in the universe irrevocably disappears?

That's the problem with death, you see. It has ugly, intolerable permanence that only the people left in the wake of its destruction might possibly comprehend. And even then, as I, spit out along the side of the road where she blew up, I did not comprehend it for a millisecond.

What I did comprehend: I was a failure of a best friend

because I didn't see the signs.

What I did comprehend: I was a failure of a human being because I didn't stop her.

What I did comprehend: I would do anything to get her back. I would trade anything and everything that I had. And if someone would take all of my measly, now utterly meaningless possessions and events and take me back in time, I would save her. Levi and I were so busy trying to save ourselves that we couldn't see the one person who needed saving more than anyone.

That's the essence of it, really. I should've saved her.

I would go to her home that evening, instead of going to get drunk with Sol and Gray. I would go to her and I would ask her straight up, upfront and confident and totally sure of myself, and I would say, "Ky, are you sad? Are you hurt? Are you going to kill yourself?"

I would know, instinctually, that she was feeling that way. I would see it in her eyes because they would be cloudy and leaden. I would feel suicide permeating from her pores, and I would stop her.

Maybe she would emit a small yes—that yes, she was planning on ending her life that evening—and maybe she would emit it so small I would lean in close, right to her lips in order to hear her. Or maybe she wouldn't emit anything at all and instead she would simply wrap her arms around me similar to the last day I saw her. But I would be there for her, so close our flesh would be touching, and I wouldn't let her do it. And if she told me the only way she would be okay was if she disappeared forever, then I would tell her I would come too, because I would never be able to survive the world without her.

My hands shaky, I brought the letter close to my face and began to read it all over again. I willed the words to change into something else, silently pleading them to turn to something different. They stayed the same.

Maeve,

You will always be my truest friend.

I hope you're not mad at me when you read this. I wanted to tell you so many times, but then I knew you would try and stop me, and I didn't want to hurt you even more. My mind was made up.

I don't want you to be mad at Alice either. She never had a clue.

As you know, I tried to kill myself last summer and was unsuccessful. The truth is, I can't live broken anymore. I don't think I will ever be able to heal.

Jared has been hurting me for such a long time, Maeve. I didn't know how to tell you and I'm crying now as I write this because I know how sad you're going to be. Please try not to be too sad, Maeve. Or at least try not to stay that way. It would be a hard life.

He began long ago, the first time he slept over at the house, which is why I attempted suicide in May. He stripped me of all that I was and all that I felt I could be. After I got home from the hospital, he hurt me more often. I didn't know how to stop him.

Jared told me he would kill Alice if I told anyone. I believed him. I think he would have really hurt her. He's mean, Maeve. Maybe he has been hurting her all along. I wouldn't be surprised.

I know I'm jaded and confused, and maybe I'm actually sick, but I can't live this way anymore. It hurts too much. I want to believe there is hope for me, but I don't have that option right now. I don't know if I ever will.

Jared is going to marry Alice. Alice told me so, and we both know how stubborn she is. She won't change her mind for me. Love is blind, and all that crap. She's so infatuated with him that even if I told her what I'm telling you now, she would accuse me of lying and making the whole thing up. When they marry it will only get worse for both of us. I hope Alice leaves him, but I don't know if she will.

I need you to tell her, okay, Maeve? I need you to tell her to leave him. (Can you also tell her I love her? Because I do, so much. It hurts.) I am sad to think of what he might do to her. I am sad to think I will never see you again. I am sad to think I will not go to Iceland.

Thank you for loving me, Maeve. You're the best friend I could've asked for. I'm sorry I'm hurting you. That's what hurts me most of all. I'm sorry I'm not brave enough to stay alive. I never was brave.

I'm going to have the audacity to ask you to do something for me, even after I have left you this way. I'm asking you to go find Sage. You can't live your life not knowing what happened. Maybe that makes me a hypocrite since I am dying not knowing a lot of things. But I wish so much more for you.

You have to go find her. If you do anything for me, go find Sage.

All my love forever,

Ky xx

PS. I'm serious about not blaming Alice. Make sure Levi doesn't blame her, either. And tell him I think he's one of the best people out there.

FIFTEEN

I WALKED HOME SLOWLY.

When I got back to the house, Sol was sitting at the table, as if he were waiting for me. He stood when I closed the front door.

"What's wrong with you?" I barked.

"Levi came by. He was wondering where you were."

"I'm right here."

"He wanted you to call him when you got in."

"Fine."

I moved to go up the stairs but Sol said, "Wait, Maeve…"

"What?"

"I'm sorry about Ky."

I kicked off my high heels. "I don't want to talk about it."

"Levi told me."

"I'm sure he did."

"Why didn't you tell me? I would have gone with you to the funeral."

I gathered my shoes into my arms and glared at him. "Let me think for a minute. Maybe because I didn't want you at the funeral? Maybe because you mean nothing to me?"

"You don't think that."

"Think what?"

"That I mean nothing to you."

"Of course I do."

Sol started to cry. He was actually crying.

"Don't cry," I ordered. "I can't handle anymore crying today."

"You're all the family I've got, Maeve. Don't you realize that? And I'm all the family you've got."

"No, that's not true. I have a mother. A real mother. A woman with the same blood as mine running through her veins."

"Where is she? Because when I look around all I see is the two of us."

I hugged the shoes closer to my chest. "Why did you keep me? When she left, why did you keep me?"

"Because I—I love you!" It spurted from his lips.

I stared at him, tears threatening behind my own eyes. I blinked them back. I had cried for far too long already.

"Maeve," he came closer to me. "I'm sorry about Ky. And about Sage. I'm sorry I haven't been good enough for you. You're like a daughter to me. My only family." He reached out and gingerly touched my shoulder. "I hate seeing you hurt."

"Where's Sage?" I whispered.

"I don't know."

"So she's never contacted you?"

He let his hand drop from my shoulder, and I watched as his head dropped too. I took a step back. "She has contacted you, hasn't she?"

Sol didn't answer.

"Hasn't she?" I yelled.

He seemed startled at my sudden rage, but the rage wasn't sudden to me. "Yeah, Maeve. She's called a few times."

"And you never thought to tell me? Her only child?"

Sol turned and sat on a chair at the kitchen table. Defeated or deflated or maybe just dejected. I didn't care.

"She didn't want you to know."

"What?"

"She told me not to tell you when she called."

"Why would she say that? I want to talk to her!"

"She thought it would make you upset because she was never ready to come home. She thought you'd beg her to come back."

"Of course I would have. She's missed ten years of my freaking life. Of course I would have begged her!"

"I don't know where she is, Maeve."

"How often does she call?"

"Two, maybe three times a year. She hasn't called in a while."

I found myself collapsing on a chair, letting the words soak in. "She's called every year and she's never wanted to speak to me?"

"I'm sure she's wanted to—"

"But she hasn't."

Sol simply looked at me.

"What does she say?" I asked quietly.

He ran a hand through his hair. "She asks how you're doing, the kind of stuff you're interested in, that sort of thing."

"What have you told her?"

"I've talked about your writing and school and your friends. She's proud of you."

"She's not allowed to be," I told him.

He didn't say anything.

"Does she talk about herself?"

"Not very often. She always says she's still figuring stuff out."

"Unbelievable. Doesn't that make you angry?"

Sol sighed. "It used to. But I love her, Maeve. After all of this, I still love her. She asked me to take care of you, and I know I haven't done a good job at that…"

I raised both my eyebrows.

"I was angry at her and I took it out on you."

"How can you love someone who doesn't love you back? Who literally could not care less about you?"

Tears filled Sol's eyes again. "I have to believe that someday she'll come home and it will all be okay again."

"You think that's going to happen?"

"I don't know, Maeve. But I hope it does."

"Don't you want to go find her?"

Sol traced his fingers against an indent in the wooden table. "It's hard to find someone who doesn't want to be found."

"I don't care if she doesn't want to be found!" I banged my fist against the table and stood up. "I've had enough of her crap about trying to figure out who she is. I'm going to find her. Whether you choose to help me or not."

"How are you going to do that?"

"I'll find a way."

"What happens if you never find her?"

"I'll keep looking."

"What happens if you find her and she doesn't want to come back?"

I blinked.

"I'll figure it out if it comes to that. But it won't. She'll come home with me. You'll see."

LEVI DROPPED BY LATER THAT afternoon. I had a feeling he would. I hadn't bothered calling him.

"You can't shut me out," he said as he walked into my bedroom. "You can try, but it won't work. We're sticking together—I don't care what you say."

I still had my funeral clothes on and I was tucked beneath my comforter and sheets, my head on the pillow.

"I hated that funeral," I told him. "Ky would have hated it."

Levi nodded.

"She didn't like most of those people." I lifted my body out from under my covers and sat up. I patted the section beside me. Levi came next to me and sat down. "Why did Amanda and Brett and Cade and everybody else bother to show up? They weren't friends with Ky."

"But they knew her. I think death does weird things to people. Plus it was a suicide. It's been like a wake-up call or something. I don't think any of us ever thought someone our own age would kill themselves. Not someone we grew up with." His shoulders lifted and heaved down, tiredly. "My dad says grieving brings people together."

"I don't give a crap about their grief," I snapped.

"Don't be angry at them, Maeve. It wasn't their fault."

"Don't you dare talk to me about anger. Just because you went to those stupid anger management classes doesn't mean you actually know anything."

Levi's eyes flashed and I thought he might say something back. Instead, he got off the bed and went toward the door and as he placed his hand on the knob I spewed, "You were wrong. I guess I can shut you out, can't I?"

He didn't look back at me. Just twisted the knob and I watched the door widen.

"Yeah. I guess you can. You win, Maeve. I give up."

Levi closed the door behind him. I lay down on my bed, yanking the covers up against me once more. I wanted to feel satisfied. I could take care of myself. I could handle this pain on my own.

Instead, I simply felt worse.

I didn't want to win.

I wanted Ky back.

I DREAMED OF PARADISE AGAIN.

This time paradise was only me and Ky.

We stood in the water together, her laugh rippling against the waves. She was laughing so hard, her head tipped right back, her hair blowing tangles together in the wind. I dove into the ocean, the water caressing my back, and Ky's laugh went silent as I swam beneath the surface. The whole world goes utterly silent underwater.

I rose from the ocean and Ky was watching me. She wasn't laughing anymore.

I started to walk toward her, but the sand under my feet pulled me away, further and further, and I was on sinking, shifting sand.

"Ky!" I screamed, my lungs burning. "Help me!"

The ocean started swirling me, pushing me out to sea, adrift, alone, untethered to her or anything.

"Ky!"

"Goodbye, Maeve," she whispered, but her whisper was loud and I could hear it echo across the beach.

"No! Don't go!" My voice was hoarse and inaudible and I watched as Ky dipped her hand into the water, resurfacing with a gleaming silver gun, freshly washed and beautiful, the metallic glistening against the shimmering sun.

"Don't do it, Ky!" I tried to scream again. "You can't leave me! Help, please, I need your help! I'm drowning!"

The current was getting stronger. I dug my toes into the sand to try and hold on. I started to sing to her, a sea lullaby Sage had sung to me when I was young:

If I were like the ocean
And you were like the sand
I'd crash down as a tsunami
Would no longer be dry land
But you would mingle with me
Sand and water, rock and sea
As the waves crash high around us
There's no place I'd rather be

She listened to the song and I wondered if she'd stay. If she'd stay for me.

As the last note rang out I watched Ky lift the precious metal to her head, watched her small fingers pull, and watched her crumble into the ocean until I saw her no longer. I let my toes go then. I lifted my arms away and let the current take me. The sea surrounded me, turning red with all that Ky was and all that she left behind.

I woke up crying.

SIXTEEN

AFTER STAYING IN BED FOR four more miserable days, I got up.

I took a shower.

I got dressed.

I put on shoes.

I went outside.

The world looked exactly the same, and yet everything was different.

Sol had been sliding food into my room every so often, knocking on the door and peeking in, I'm sure to see if I was still alive.

My heart is pumping blood, I repeatedly thought, *but it does not feel like I am living.*

"How are you?" Sol asked me when I came down the stairs the morning I finally emerged from my bed.

"I'm going to go see Ky."

He silently offered me a cup of coffee, but I shook my head. I half-wondered where that side of Sol had been the past thirteen years.

"Do you want company?"

"No. I want to go alone."

"It's cold out."

"I'll be fine."

I was wearing my yellow dress from the Sadie Hawkins Dance. I buttoned a heavy cardigan over top and put tights on underneath. I laced up my thrift store army boots Ky and I had purchased together.

I got onto my bike and pedaled to the cemetery far across town. It was cold out. It was nearing the end of November so I shouldn't have been stunned at the chill, but it wasn't usually that bitter kind of cold. The wind stung my face as I rode; my fingers felt stiff; my nose began to run. I pedaled harder. I watched the trees dance as I flew across the city. They waved goodbye to me, their branches swaying and shifting quickly against the next, fast and furious; I was fast and furious, too. I passed the school, and a few minutes later pedaled by *The Dish*. I wondered if I had lost my job. Clarke had been calling me for three days. On the fourth day, she didn't call. I guess she gave up on me. That shouldn't have been a surprise.

When I got to the cemetery, I dropped my bike in the empty parking lot. The wind was strong as I walked toward Ky; I debated letting the weight drop out from under my feet and allowing the wind to carry me to her.

I stopped in front of the plot of land she now belonged to. There were fresh flowers on top of her. I paused for a moment and thought of who might be responsible for them. Surely someone kinder than me.

I had nothing to offer her except what I was wearing. I took off my boots, unlacing them slowly because my fingers were frigid. I pulled them off my feet one at a time. My feet were instantly freezing and my thin tights grew damp from the grass. But I laced them back up and knotted a lopsided bow, placing them side by side a little ways away from the flowers. There was no headstone yet, so I took a piece of paper from my cardigan pocket and laid it down upon the freshly mown grass, tucking it slightly beneath the heel of one of the boots so it wouldn't blow away.

Ky McNeil,
One of the best people in the world
Gone November 15th

(As long as I live, I will never forget you. I hope these keep you warm.)

I shivered and stretched my body out on the grass. I lay beside her.

"I miss you," I said. "The world isn't the same anymore—not without you in it.

"I'm trying not to be angry or sad but no matter what I do, I *am* angry and I *am* sad. I'm mad at you. I wish you would have told me, just said something, anything, so I could have known what you were going to do. Or at least you could have told me about Jared. I would have hurt him so badly, Ky. I think I maybe could kill him. I've never felt this before. It's like a boiling, tangible anger that I can feel simmering within me. I think it's like Levi's pressure cooker. I don't know what to do." I started shivering harder, and I curled myself into the fetal position to try and stay warm.

"We're sixteen," I whispered. I didn't bother correcting my incorrect tense. "So impossibly young and yet jaded by the world we thought only had intentions to hurt us." I began to cry. "Isn't that true, Ky? Didn't we always think the world was out there to get us? Jared and Sage. Sol and Alice. So much pain that felt directed right at us." I took a deep breath, and I could see it in the air.

"But that's not true, you know. The world doesn't intend to hurt us. It's just filled with hurt and broken people who are trying to somehow fix themselves. And when they can't figure it out, they try and hurt others to make themselves feel better. It's a poisonous cycle. We were both caught up in that cycle, weren't we, Ky? We were both terribly broken, so seemingly unfixable, and yet the only thing we desperately sought after was hope." A tear slipped down my cheek into my lips. I tasted the salt between my teeth.

"I don't think I realized that until now. I want to believe hope is out there… somewhere. It doesn't feel real, though. It feels far away and useless. I mean, you were living a nightmare. Where was hope for you?"

I cried quietly then sat up because I couldn't breathe. "I wish there was still hope for you," I whispered.

My teeth were chattering viciously and my fingers had begun turning blue. I wondered what would happen if I froze there, a crystallized icicle on the grave of Ky Aspen McNeil, my very best friend. What a horrifically beautiful way to go.

"Maeve?"

I hadn't heard the car pull into the parking lot nor heard his steps creep up behind me. My head was hurting, making it hard to hear anything. It was cold—everything was so cold. I didn't know how long I had been sitting there.

"Maeve?" Levi asked again, but my body couldn't move very well so I wasn't able to answer him. I thought my fingers might break off. I pictured them snapping away like twigs. Snap. Snap. Snap. Off they go. And then my toes would snap off too. A fingerless, toeless, pathetic girl. I wanted to laugh but couldn't muster the energy.

"You're blue." He took off his hat, scarf, and coat, wrapping them around me. He started to put my boots back on my feet but I managed to scream.

"No!"

Levi's eyes widened, but he put the boots back where they belonged. Gave my offering back to Ky. The wind had picked up again, causing my hair to fly barbarically around my face.

"It's too cold out here, okay Maeve? I'm going to go take you somewhere you can get warm." He was soothing me. I nodded, but my head hardly moved. He looked at me for a moment, and like the ragged, limp girl I was, pulled me up against him and wrapped his arm around my shoulder, leading me to his parent's gray car he must have been allowed to borrow. The wind was loud and strong but I think I heard him whisper, "I'm not going to lose you, too."

I closed my eyes and leaned my head limply against his chest, faintly feeling his heart beat. We're alive, I told myself. We're alive.

I whispered to him softly, so softly he may never have heard, but I had to tell him.

"No, you're not going to lose me, too."

AFTER NEARLY FORTY MINUTES OF the heat blasting and an extra large, extra hot chocolate drink in my hands, I decided it was time to tell Levi about Ky's letter.

"I have to tell you something—something I don't want to tell you."

"What's that?" Levi adjusted the heat on his side of the car. I was still thawing out. He wanted to take me to the hospital because of how cold I was, saying something melodramatic about how he thought I might be suffering from a mild case of hypothermia, but I refused, telling him that the last time I had checked, he was a high school student and not a doctor. We went through the coffee shop drive-through instead. Christmas music played on the car radio, and I leaned over to turn it down.

Levi looked at me, eyebrows raised.

I shrugged. "It's too early."

"It's almost December."

"It's too merry."

He smiled. "Can't argue with that." But he still turned the dial back a little, and blue-eyed Bing crooned softly in the background.

"What were you going to tell me?"

I sighed.

"Is it bad?"

"Yeah."

"Is that why you don't want to tell me?"

"Yeah." I took a sip of the hot chocolate, licking the whipped cream off my lips. "I don't want to hurt you."

"It's not your job to protect me."

"But it's yours to protect me?"

Levi exhaled loudly. "You were going to freeze to death, Maeve. Is that what you wanted?" He raised a hand. "Actually, don't answer that. I don't want to know."

I laughed. "I shouldn't be such a brat. I just... wanted to talk to her again."

"Me too."

"Is that why you were there? To talk to her?"

"Yeah. I've gone every day this week."

"So you're the one who leaves the flowers."

"No," he said. "It's Jared who leaves them. Surprisingly."

"Pull over," I said immediately.

"What's wrong? Are you okay—"

"I said pull over, Levi!"

The car lurched to the side of the road, and I jerked open my door, collapsing on the gravel. I was sick, throwing up in front of me, my body dry heaving discontentment.

Levi was saying something, opening his door and coming round to me. I shooed him with my hand.

"Give me a second. I'm fine, I promise."

"You're sick, Maeve—"

"I'm fine! Just one second—please!" It came out harsher than I intended. He went back to the driver's side and shut the door.

I took a deep breath.

I wiped my mouth against my cardigan sleeve.

How dare he bring her flowers. How dare he be allowed to see her at all.

The rage was simmering again.

I stood up, my legs shaky, but I got back into the car.

"Will you take me to my house, please?" I asked him in the sweetest voice I could bear as I shut the door beside me. "There's something I need to show you."

I leaned forward and cranked the music so he wouldn't ask me any questions.

To my relief, he didn't. He simply drove.

SOL WAS AT WORK WHEN we got to my house, so Levi went and sat on the couch and I brought down the infamous letter. It felt heavy in my hands.

"Do you… want a drink or something?"

Levi smirked. "What's with the sudden pleasantries?"

"I'm trying to put this off for as long as possible."

I sank onto the other side of the couch, gripping the paper closer to my chest. I debated shredding it right there, discarding the evidence so I could sneak into Jared's home and kill him silently. No one would know the difference. I could singlehandedly get justice for Ky.

But then Levi said, "Tell me what's wrong, Maeve," and it all seemed too much for my weary shoulders. So I crumpled beside him and handed over the letter and watched as his face ripped in half, just like my heart did every time I read it.

He was crying when he handed it back to me.

I put it on the coffee table. I didn't want to touch it anymore.

"She's right, you know," I told him. "You are one of the best people out there."

Levi put his head in his hands, defeated. We accept this defeat, I thought in my mind. This terminal defeat.

"All this time and we didn't have a clue." He lifted his head.

"She never told you anything?"

"No."

"How does someone keep a secret like that?"

"I don't know."

"I'd never be able to keep that to myself."

"If the roles were reversed, I would have told her. There's no doubt about it, I would have said something. It was selfish of her Levi, don't you think? To go? To leave us like this?"

Levi was quiet for a second and I watched his head tilt to the side as he gazed at me. "Was it?"

"Yes—I could have helped her! We could have gotten her out of that home, away from him. We could have saved her if she'd let us."

"Maybe it wasn't selfish, Maeve."

"What do you mean?"

"She didn't want to hurt you. Or me, or anyone. So she didn't say one word. She piled all that hurt onto herself so we wouldn't feel a thing. I don't think she was being selfish." He laughed sadly. "In fact, I think she was the most selfless person of all."

I didn't realize tears were pouring down my face until I tasted the salt on my lips.

"I don't want her to be selfless. I want her to be here."

Levi reached across the couch and held me in a crushing embrace. "We're going to make it," he whispered into my hair. "Somehow, we're going to make it."

I wanted to believe he was telling the truth.

When he released me he asked, "What are you and Sol doing tomorrow?"

"What's tomorrow?"

"Thanksgiving. Did you forget?"

I nodded. "We rarely do anything for Thanksgiving."

"This year you are. My mom wants you both to come over for dinner. Say yes."

"Yes."

Levi smiled. There were days where I would do anything to make him smile.

"I'll tell Sol."

"My mom wants to invite Alice as well."

"Please not Jared," I begged.

"No," he said quietly. "I won't let her invite him."

"That's so like Nora. She'd invite the whole neighborhood over if your house was big enough."

"There's always room around the table," he mimicked in a woman's high voice, and I laughed.

"Is there room for one more?"

He looked at me quizzically. "Who are you thinking?"

"My landlord? I know that's sort of random, but I think she might be alone. Maybe not, but…"

"Invite her! My mom will be happy. She's always going on about how everyone is more than welcome."

"Okay. I think I will."

"The kids at school have been wondering where you are."

I sighed. "Maybe I'll go back next week. How has it been?"

"Lonely without you."

"I don't want to go."

"It's been hard, but my parents haven't given me a choice."

"Sol doesn't care. He has no idea what to do with me. Are we the dead girl's best friends?"

Levi nodded. "For now, anyway. I think that will pass."

"Because people will forget about her."

"I hope not."

"It's inevitable, Levi. People will forget. They always do. They'll start thinking about her less and less until one day when they've moved on entirely."

"I don't think moving on is the same as forgetting."

"What do you mean?"

"We'll have to move on someday, too, Maeve. We'll get

older, maybe go to school, maybe move away, get married, have ten-tuplets." He grinned at me and I couldn't help it, I laughed. "But that doesn't mean we'll forget Ky."

"She wants me to find Sage," I whispered quietly.

"I read that."

"Do you think I should?"

"What do you want to do?"

"Some days I want to find her so bad it hurts. It'll be all I can think about, every freaking second, and I plan and dream our reunion and how she'll come home and we'll be together. Finally a real family. But other days I think about how far I've gotten without her, and I feel as though I'd be fine with never seeing her again." I sniffed. "It's all very confusing."

"Would you regret it if you didn't try to look for her?"

A deep sigh rattled from my chest. "Probably. I wish Ky hadn't asked me to find her. I'd regret it more because of Ky. I feel like I have to find Sage if only to fulfill Ky's final wish. I don't know where to begin to look."

Levi ran his hands through his hair. "I'll help you look for her if you want."

"Really?"

"It might be a nice distraction from the present circumstances."

I let out a small laugh. "That's a good point. What if she's halfway across the world?"

"I guess we'll be going on a long trip, won't we?"

Smiling, I said, "I guess we will."

"We're sticking together, okay, Maeve?"

I nodded. "I'm sorry I've been trying to push you out. Sometimes I think that's easier."

"I don't want to be alone in this. It gets too overwhelming... the sadness, the anger. Sometimes it feels suffocatingly lonesome."

"Okay," I said. "We'll stick together."

"We need each other. Let's just accept that."

"Consider it accepted." I held out my hand and he shook it.

"Accepted," he replied.

SEVENTEEN

FRANCINE WAS THRILLED WHEN I asked her to join us for Thanksgiving dinner at the Fisher's. I phoned her the next day and she let out a loud shriek when I extended the invitation.

"Of course you might be too busy," I said quickly.

"No!" she practically yelled. "I don't have any plans whatsoever."

"It's settled then."

Sol took a little more convincing, but he eventually succumbed to my request.

I wasn't sure what one was supposed to wear to a Thanksgiving dinner, so I put on the yellow dress again. I wanted to bring Ky along with me. Everywhere I went I wanted her to be, too.

We brought a store-bought pecan pie—Sol and I were undecided if it would be considered kind or insulting. We brought it with us anyway. Better store-bought than empty-handed, we both supposed.

Nora flung the door wide open when we got there. Her entire outfit was orange.

"Come in!" she said. "I'm so glad you could make it."

Sol awkwardly thrust out the pecan pie. The smells coming from the kitchen made me wish I had put the pie in a Tupperware container, at least to appear like I had made it.

"How kind of you," Nora gushed and took the pie from Sol's hands. She looked at both of us, appearing unquestionably genuine. "Thank you. I really appreciate it."

On second thought, she probably would have seen through my Tupperware trick.

"Sol, you go into the family room. Jonas and the boys are in there watching football. You come with me, Maeve."

I followed her into the kitchen hearing hoots and hollers from Jonas. I smiled. "Thanks for having us, Nora."

She set the pie down on the counter then came and hugged me. She said into my hair, "This is a safe place for you, okay? I want you to know that." She let me go and I nodded.

Nora passed me an apron and I tied it behind me. With the red gingham clashing against my yellow dress, I knew I looked as eccentric as Nora Fisher. I did not point out that the situation was unequivocally sexist—the boys watching football and the girls cooking in the kitchen. I figured Nora didn't care much about sexism, as long as the outcome was a good Thanksgiving dinner.

Nora let me help her finish up the mashed potatoes. My mouth watered at the sight of the large turkey, stuffing, and green bean casserole.

"You went all out."

Nora laughed. "It's Thanksgiving! It's going to be a good day." I couldn't decide if she was reassuring me or herself. I wondered if she felt pressure to make Levi and me happy.

"Is Alice coming?"

"She is."

I was quiet for a moment. "Is Jared?"

When Nora looked at me, her eyebrows were scrunched together in concern. "No... no, I didn't invite him. Levi was pretty adamant about that." She hesitated for a moment. "Is there something going on, Maeve? Something I don't know?"

I could feel tears forming behind my eyes, and I pictured myself falling into her and telling her everything about Jared. About how he was hurting Ky the whole time, about the letter, about the real reason for the suicide. Nora was strong; she could handle it for me. But instead, I blinked the tears back and looked at her, saying, "Ask Levi about it later. Tell him I said it would be okay if he told you."

Nora sighed. "I will."

I stirred the gravy while she sliced the turkey. She said, "I'm sorry about all of this, honey. It's been a lot for you kids. It's been a lot for anyone."

"It's not your fault, Nora."

"I know. But it's my instinct to want to protect you and Levi, to keep you from feeling all that pain."

I thought of Alice and Sage and wondered if all mothers felt that instinct, or if it was a special quality of Nora. "And Ky?" I asked quietly.

She nodded, her eyes filling with tears. "Oh yes. I wish I could've protected Ky."

"Death is hard, Nora. It feels permanent and heavy but also really empty, all at the same time."

"Like there's a hole inside of you that will never go away?"

I nodded. "But... the strange thing is, I'm not sure if I want the hole to go away. If it gets filled up, maybe that means I'll be forgetting her."

Nora put down the knife she was using to carve the turkey. "You won't forget her."

"How do you know?"

She pressed her fist to my chest, tapping it gently against my heart. "Because she's a part of who you are. You don't just forget who you are."

After a moment I leaned in and kissed her cheek, my silent

thank you. She went back to cutting the turkey, and I continued stirring the gravy. We talked about her childhood Thanksgiving traditions and Nora Fisher made me laugh. I hadn't laughed in what felt like a very long time. Nora, I decided, was delight personified.

Francine came a few minutes later. I knew it was her as soon as I heard the fourteen knocks rapping on the door.

I wiped my hands on my gingham apron. "I'll get it, Nora. I'm almost positive it's my landlord." I opened the door and saw Francine's red hair piled on top of her head. Upon closer inspection, I realized she was wearing pumpkin earrings. Only Francine.

"Happy Thanksgiving, Maeve!" Francine beamed at me. She wrapped me in a hug.

"Hi, Francine."

"Help me take this in, will you?" She nodded to the three containers that sat on the ground beside her.

I lifted two of them into my arms. "What are they?"

"Homemade butter tarts! Sixty-five of them." She laughed. "I may have gone a tad overboard, but once I got started I couldn't stop!"

I thought of my store-bought pecan pie.

"You like butter tarts, don't you?"

"Of course I do. Everyone will love them. Don't you worry."

We took them to the kitchen where I introduced Francine and Nora, and Nora gushed over the sixty-five homemade butter tarts, the same way she'd gushed over my very store-bought single pecan pie. I decided I wanted to be like Nora when I got older.

"This looks downright delectable!" Francine raved as she took in the food that sat on all surfaces of the kitchen. "My oh my, I never imagined a feast like this! Can I help with anything?"

Nora smiled and I think she realized what a... enthusiastic... person Francine was. "Would you help me take all of this to the table? Maeve, tell the boys dinner is ready."

I nodded. "What about Alice?"

"We'll set it out and see if she's here by then. I don't want it to get cold. I told her six o'clock."

"All right. I might… go call her, in case she forgot."

I went to the foyer and dialed Alice's number into my phone. It rang eight times and then went to voicemail. I hit redial. Eight more lonely rings rang out without an answer.

"Is everything okay?"

I jumped halfway across the room. "Levi!" I gasped. "You freaking scared me!"

"I'm sorry!" he said earnestly.

I took a breath and tried to slow down my heartbeat. "Don't sneak up on me like that."

"Sorry, Maeve, I didn't mean to. Dinner is ready. Everyone is heading in there to eat."

I nodded. "I know. I'm going to call Alice one more time."

"She isn't here yet?"

"No."

"Maybe she isn't coming."

"Why wouldn't she come?"

He looked at me.

"You don't think she'd be with Jared, do you?" I felt my eyes widen and thought I might be sick.

"I don't know, Maeve."

"What a stupid, foolish woman," I hissed.

"Don't say that. We don't know where she is."

"She is stupid!" I yelled. "She's stupid for being with him in the first place."

"Shhh," he whispered. I lowered my voice.

"How could she not have known what he was doing to her? They were in the same house."

"I don't know, Maeve," he said again, miserably. A parrot, a broken record, a broken boy.

"You guys coming?" Nora called out.

"Be there in a minute!" Levi yelled back, his voice betraying nothing.

"Why do you do that?"

"Do what?"

I gestured my hand around the room. "Pretend everything is normal. Pretend it's all a-okay!"

"It's Thanksgiving." He was exasperated. "Isn't this a day where we could pretend to be okay?"

"It's just another day, Levi. It's not anything special or unique."

I thought Levi might cry. "We're trying to make new memories, Ky, don't you see that—"

"What did you just call me?"

Levi blinked.

"You called me Ky," I whispered.

He took a step back. "I didn't mean to. I'm sorry."

"You called me Ky."

"I'm sorry—"

"No."

"Maeve, I'm sorry. I am, I didn't mean—"

"No."

He sighed and looked at me.

I began to laugh, slowly, but then it couldn't contain itself, coming from the deepest recesses of my body, laughter seeping from my lips as tears seeped from my eyelids.

Levi stared at me, probably thinking I was certifiable. I wondered that, too.

"It was like she was here for a minute."

He smiled, his eyes glistening. "Yeah. I guess it was."

"What would she do if she was here?"

Levi chuckled. "She'd be eating."

Laughter burst from me. I wiped my tears. "Come on," I said and took his hand. "Let's go eat. For Ky."

"Always for Ky." He grinned.

PART OF ME WANTED TO wait to eat until Alice showed up, but I didn't know if she was going to. I tried not to think of her going back to Jared, but I had a feeling that's exactly what she had done. After all, who else did she have? Francine had once said to me, "We need other people. All of us do." That didn't exclude Alice. I just wish in her need for people she would come to dinner with us instead of going back to him.

Nora's food was incredible and the conversation was good. Even Sol seemed to be enjoying himself and acting like a normal, sober human being. That was quite the feat in itself.

Jonas was telling an exaggerated story and I think Francine was crying she was laughing so hard. I leaned in my chair and watched them. Francine throwing her red hair back, Nora's hand covering her mouth, the sound of happiness escaping from Sol's lips. I watched Jonas' arms, hands, and fingers illustrate and animate the story, Simon looking at his dad in wonder, Levi giggling uncontrollably like a little kid beside me.

I wasn't listening to what Jonas was saying, not because it wasn't interesting, but because I couldn't stop watching them. All of these people, bits and pieces of who I was. I wanted to freeze time for one moment. I wanted to capture the feeling I had, bottle it up so I could reopen it some other day. It was a warm feeling, deep inside the lining of my stomach. As if the sun had escaped its orbit and was living inside of me for a moment.

Glasses were clinking; knives and forks scraped against plates to gather the last of the food, and the laughter continued to ring out like an anthem. Faint music played in the background. I made note of all these things—the way Nora's hand was lightly touching Francine's arm like they'd been friends forever, the way Sol made a joke and Jonas grinned and Sol said something about how we should all do this again sometime, the way Levi and

Simon talked about their futures and Levi actually listened while Simon was talking. I made note of it all: the flickering candle light, the kaleidoscope of delicious smells, the ball of sunshine in my stomach.

You would have loved this, Ky.

"Are you okay?" Levi asked when I started to push my chair out.

"I'm doing good." I patted his hand. "Don't worry about me."

I went to the washroom, but before I slipped back in with the rest of them, I wanted to get a bit of air. It was chilly outside but if I stamped my feet and wrapped my arms around myself, I figured I could keep warm for a few minutes.

The rest of the neighborhood houses were lit up, making the street seem like it was glowing. I smiled when I saw the cars piled at Levi's house, evidence of the gathering that was going on inside. I tried to snapshot that in my mind too. One of the cars parked out on his street was idle, and I squinted my eyes to see who might be sitting there.

Alice.

I bounded down the Fisher's steps and ran to her car. I rapped on the window and she jerked her head up at me, petrified. She didn't yell at me the way I'd yelled at Levi for scaring me. The window rolled down and I saw mascara streaked long down her cheeks.

"Hi, Alice. Sorry for scaring you."

She opened the passenger door and I slid in beside her.

"Do you want to come inside?" I asked. "Nora's made such good food, and dessert hasn't even begun yet! Which, of course, is the best part. Nora was looking forward to seeing you. She'd love for you to come inside." I paused. "I'd like that, too."

Alice sniffed.

I stared at my yellow dress for an exorbitant amount of time until I turned to her. "I'm sorry I screamed at you after the funeral. I was—no, I'm still—furious about this whole thing. Sometimes I lay awake at night going over all the conversations she and I ever had, and I search for something, for anything really, that might clue me in on what was happening. She was obviously good at keeping secrets. You and I both know that. I can't find even a small hint that would have led me to know what was going on."

Alice was staring down at her lap. I reached my hand to touch her wrist gently. She flinched but let me keep it there.

"It's not your fault, Alice. It was never your fault. I shouldn't have said that to you. I was searching for someone to blame and you—"

"I am to blame," Alice uttered softly.

"No," I told her in the firmest voice I could muster. "This is not your fault. You're not to blame." I turned to her. "I admit I've been blaming you. But I'm wrong. It was Ky's choice, not yours."

Alice started to cry. She looked up at me, eyes widened and wet, the picture of desperation, "I was her mother, Maeve. Her *mother*. I should have known."

One or two or maybe more minutes passed, I can't remember, before I whispered, "You still are her mother. You still are."

She grappled my wrist with her fingers. "Do you hate him?"

"I'm not sure if that's a strong enough word."

Alice took a breath. "I know you don't think of me as a particularly brave person... but I'm going to try and press charges."

"You are? Against Jared?"

She nodded. "I may need your letter for evidence."

"That's fine. Do you think I'll get it back?"

"I think so. I don't know much about this."

"No, neither do I."

We sat silent for a few minutes. "Ky would be proud of you,

Alice. Her strong, brave mother... fighting for her. You're doing now what mothers are supposed to do."

Alice was crying again.

"Let's go inside, okay? We don't want to miss dessert. I hope you've come hungry because my landlord made sixty-five butter tarts."

I think Alice smiled. Or maybe she didn't. But at least she was coming inside.

LEVI IMMEDIATELY PULLED ANOTHER CHAIR around the table when he saw the two of us come through the front door.

"Are you hungry?" Nora asked Alice.

Alice sort of nodded but her grip tightened on my wrist. I felt like I was leading a frightened baby bird to her slaughter.

"It's okay," I murmured. She sat down beside me, still clutching my arm with a heavy grasp.

Nora placed a plate of steaming food in front of her and Alice's eyes widened. She turned her head to me and I shrugged. "I told you. Nora's a good cook."

Nora blushed but smiled. No one else said anything.

Jonas cleared his throat. "So, Alice is it... cold out there?"

I knew he was trying to make conversation, but I couldn't help but glare at him. Really? The weather?

"Yes, it's cold," I said flippantly, "because it's the end of November."

"Maeve," Sol warned.

I felt Alice take a breath beside me. In a wavering voice, she said, "Thank you for having me here today. It was kind of you."

"Of course!" Nora breezed. "It's our absolute pleasure. Isn't it, Jonas?"

"That's right," he affirmed.

The once comfortable rhythm of the evening had disappeared in an awkward spurt.

Francine said, "I'm sorry I didn't introduce myself. I'm Francine Sinclair."

"Alice McNeil."

"It's very nice to meet you, Alice."

I tossed Francine a smile. "This is my stepfather, Sol," I told Alice, and Sol gave her a nod, "and that's Simon, Levi's brother." Simon smiled. "And Nora and Jonas."

Francine clapped her hands together. "I think I'll bring in those butter tarts now!"

"I'll come with you and bring in the pies," Nora offered.

Jonas started saying something about football to Sol, and they got lost in their own meaningless conversation.

Levi turned to Alice. "I'm glad you came."

The corner of her mouth turned up slightly.

"I've been to see Ky almost every day," he continued. Tears brimmed over Alice's eyes. "I talk to her about all sorts of things. I like to think she wants me to fill her in."

"I'd like to think she wants that too," Alice told him.

"I want to tell you something, but I don't want it to upset you."

She sighed. "Go ahead."

Levi lowered his voice. "I'm angry at Jared. I've never been this angry before. And—I get angry a lot—but this feels different."

Alice's eyes drooped, and I noticed layers of bags had sunk into her skin. Her face looked weary and she seemed older than she had before. Grief ages you, I supposed. It squeezes out every drop of life you felt you had and wrings you till you're old and gray and wasted. A fragment, a shell of what you once were.

"Is that what you wanted to tell me?" Alice finally asked.

Levi nodded. "I wanted to ask you something, too."

Alice didn't say yes, but Levi asked anyway. "Will you leave him, Alice? Will you stay away from him now?"

I watched her lower lip quiver, tears cascading down her

cheeks. "I love him," she whispered. "Even after all of this, I still love him."

A shiver prickled my spine, and the hair on my neck stood straight. "How?" I burst out. I didn't mean to speak, but the cry escaped from my mouth before I could take it back.

"Haven't you loved someone before? They get inside of you, beneath your skin, into who you are. They become a part of you. You can't erase that or simply stop loving them. When you truly love someone, you have to look past their mistakes, past their faults—"

"It wasn't a simple *mistake*, Alice!" I didn't mean to shriek, but the syllables seeped out and I felt the eyes of everyone upon me. Nora and Francine rushed into the room. Everyone was staring.

Alice was crying harder. "Don't you think I understand that, Maeve? He killed my little girl," she cried. "He killed my baby."

"And yet you love him still." Levi was staring at her, disgusted. I felt wrenched, simultaneously feeling pity and unadulterated repulsion.

"Yes, I love him!" Alice wailed, and I wondered if she might be on the brink of hysteria. I also wondered if it was me who drove her there.

Nora flew to her side, rubbing her back, soothing her with words I didn't care to listen to.

"Stop it, Mom," Levi ordered.

"Levi and Maeve, go to the other room," Jonas commanded. "Leave Mrs. McNeil alone." Neither of us moved.

"I thought you were going to press charges," I offered weakly.

"I was," Alice said. "I am. I—"

"She was your daughter," Levi spit. "And you're going back to him? After what he did to her? After what he might've done to you?"

"Levi!" Jonas.

"*I didn't know*! Please," Alice begged. "I swear I didn't know what he was doing."

"Ky said she didn't know," I told Levi. "In the letter, she said Alice didn't have a clue."

"How is that possible? How could her own mother not know?" I thought he might cry, but he was too angry. It was a palpable anger, one you could see like a vapor around him.

"I didn't know," Alice whispered.

"We know," I told her.

"I don't believe it," Levi said.

The three of us stared at one another. Nora continued to rub Alice's back as if it would rub away the tension in the room. As if one's anger could dissipate that quickly.

"Pie, anyone?" Francine asked suddenly, breaking the silence. We all looked at her then back at each other.

"We'll help you press charges," I told Alice. I gave Levi a pointed look.

"For Ky," he said. "But you need to stay away from him."

Alice looked down at her lap. Her makeup had long since worn off, and her cheeks were sticky with half-dried tears.

"Remember," I urged her softly. "Remember how brave you're going to be? A strong, brave mother?"

"For Ky," she whispered.

"Yes. You're going to be a strong, brave mother for Ky. You're going to fight for her. You're going to leave him and never go back, even if you love him still, even if it hurts you, even if the pain is unbearable at times, because you're fighting for her. For Ky."

Alice's eyes were shiny as she hugged me and I thought about how she must not hold grudges for very long because I had just screamed at her in front of everyone. Yet there she was, hugging me. She hugged Levi too, and he held her for a while. I contemplated how small she must feel in such a gaping, cavernous world.

Nora lingered around us, and I could feel her watching, most likely wondering what had happened in the middle of her once perfect Thanksgiving dinner. She and Francine sliced the pies and dished out plates with pieces of pie, ice-cream and butter tarts. The conversation grew quietly and not one person screamed at another again.

As we finished our dessert, Levi dinged a fork against his glass and stood.

"I want to make a toast," he announced. He looked down at Alice, his arm outstretched holding his drink. "A toast to Ky. I wish her the happiest Thanksgiving... and I hope she knows how much we all miss her."

Alice stood, and the rest of us followed suit.

"For Ky," she said.

"For Ky," we echoed.

For you, Ky.

EIGHTEEN

I WAS BACK AT THE newspaper gathering the remainder of my things. It was the day after Thanksgiving but with everyone still off work, I was alone. I was fine with that.

I looked at Clarke's things, photos of her and her boyfriend tacked on a corkboard in the cubicle. In one of them, her head was tipped low against his chest, her black hair blowing in the wind, her smile extended long across her face. She looked radiant, as if sunbeams were caught deep within her lungs. Alice had talked about what love meant to her, how love was when you chose to forget the mistakes the person had made, to look beyond their faults and shortcomings. I wondered what love meant to Clarke. I wondered if it meant something different to everyone.

"Did you quit, Miss Parker?"

My heart almost lurched out of my chest. I spun around to see Maurice Morris.

"Oh…" I sputtered. "Mr. Morris, hello. You scared me. I thought I was by myself."

He ignored me. "Did you quit, Miss Parker?"

"No sir, I didn't."

"Are you planning on quitting, Miss Parker?"

"Um… no sir…"

"Then may I ask why you're packing up your belongings as if you were planning on leaving my newspaper?"

Every word I knew jumbled together in my mind. Taking a deep breath, I tried to speak coherently. "I've been gone for quite a few days, sir." That was an understatement. "I assumed I had been fired."

"Do you feel you deserve to be fired?"

"Well, I wasn't very reliable during the time I was gone. I didn't give much of an explanation or anything, and I never returned Clarke's phone calls. I don't suppose any of that is good work ethic."

"No, I don't suppose it is." He stroked his chin.

I stood there and watched.

"Where did you go, Miss Parker? You said you were gone."

I hesitated. "My best friend killed herself." The words hung in the air—a thick and intolerable smog.

"November fifteenth. She was sixteen years old. A gun—just shot herself, I guess. They said it only took one bullet to do the trick. I was with her the day before and then suddenly she was gone. Here one minute, and the next… permanently disappeared. Things keep happening, like little unimportant things, and I keep thinking: I have to tell her. And then I realize all over I'll never be able to tell her those things again. She was smart, too. I don't know if she thought she was, but I did. I wish I had told her, you know? I mean, I wish I had said a lot of things, but I wonder if she would have stayed longer if I'd told her…"

I looked up to find his brows creased together, his ebony eyes reaching deep into mine.

"Dear Maeve," he said after a long moment. "My sincerest apologies. I had no idea she was your friend."

I nodded.

"Then you'll be the one to write the article."

"What do you mean?"

Maurice Morris went into his office, and when he returned he was carrying a newspaper. He chuckled as he handed it to me. "I suppose I should have made it mandatory to read our paper. I'm going to take an educated guess and assume you don't."

I blushed.

"That's all right, Miss Parker. Not many people do."

I looked at the article and felt my breath catch in my throat.

LOCAL GIRL FOUND DEAD
By Bernard Peterson

A local Rutherford girl was found dead in her bedroom early yesterday morning.

Police have confirmed it to be a suicide at gunpoint. Ky McNeil was sixteen-years-old.

Her mother, who found the girl, refuses to comment at this time. Police say the reasoning for the suicide is yet to be determined. Information on the funeral proceedings will be released later this week.

It showed a photo of Ky from the Sadie Hawkins Dance that Alice must've taken. Ky's arms were crossed against her purple dress, her red lips pursed, her eyes gazing straight at the camera in a way that made you feel as if she knew your deepest secret. Just as I remembered her. "We wrote this?"

Maurice nodded. "Bernard Peterson did." He pointed to a cubicle.

"Please tell him not to hound Alice. It's not fair to her. She's grieving."

"This is the only one we've written about it. It's not us who are hounding her, it's the larger papers. They'll stop soon. They always move on to something more interesting. A suicide becomes boring after a while."

My head snapped. "My best friend killed herself and you

think that's boring?"

Maurice leaned against a desk. "It's not a homicide. They're not searching for a killer. She killed herself. It's over. That's the end of the story. Unless it's not…"

I thought I was going to be sick. "You want me to write something that keeps this story going longer."

"I would love for you to write a story on why she did it, but I somehow doubt that's going to happen."

"And you would be right."

"I want you to write an article: something less informative, but much more personal. Perhaps a letter to her or—"

"No."

His eyebrows rose.

"I'm not using my best friend's death as a way to advance this newspaper."

"I didn't mean it that way," he said.

"Oh? And which way did you mean it?" I snarled. I took a deep breath. "I'm sorry. I didn't mean to get upset. It seems that's all I am these days."

"I don't doubt how hard this is for you. I thought maybe the article would be good for you, as well as for the community. I thought you could use it as a tribute to your friend, a way of honoring her."

"I'm a horrible person," I confessed.

Maurice laughed out loud. "Miss Parker, why would you say that?"

"I naturally think people are trying to get something for themselves. But… that's kind of you, Mr. Morris. I think I would like to do that."

"I look forward to reading it."

I thanked him, then took my coat and bag. "Sir…" I said before I left. "Can I ask you something?"

"Of course, Miss Parker."

"Does this mean I'm not fired?"

Maurice Morris smiled. "No. You're not fired. Next time, don't make an assumption. You know what they say about that."

A grin grew across my face.

"But," he warned firmly, "call Clarke and apologize. And please, for the love, start coming back to work."

"Thank you, sir. I'll see you Monday."

I REMEMBER HOW MUCH SAGE loved Christmas.

She refused to put up an artificial tree, even though the real ones were much more expensive, plus you had to actually keep them alive, and neither of us had anything remotely close to a green thumb. She often forgot to water it and the pine needles would fall off covering the floor. The tree always ended up looking barren and slightly desperate. But Sage loved imperfection. She sought out the most crooked tree in the lot and when she found it she'd point like she'd won the greatest prize, hollering, "Maeve, baby, look here! Isn't this the grandest tree you ever saw?" It never was—not by a long shot—but I'd nod my head at her anyway.

"I love it," Sage would sigh, taking a saw, unfailingly hacking off pieces that in all likelihood shouldn't have been hacked away. Then we'd tip the tree over and claim it as our own.

We'd somehow stuff it onto the roof of our car, hoping it would still be intact by the time we made it home. Sage had a rule that we'd adorn the tree with handmade ornaments only—none of that store-bought junk that only encouraged consumerism—and the evening we bought the tree we would have a craft night. Compare it to even the ugliest Christmas tree and it would have most definitely been uglier, but you'd have never known that by the look on Sage's face.

Once the lights and the handmade ornaments and the angel were up (always an angel, never a star, because she liked to think the angel was watching over us) Sage would basically set up camp beside the tree. She would sleep on the couch, eat beneath the twinkly lights that she pretended were stars, and draw or play music or write—depending upon what her fascination was at the time.

Not too much changed when Sol moved in. Sage would still blast the Christmas music, constantly playing it throughout the house, and Sol would sigh and go into the silence of their room. Sage would roll her eyes at me and whisper, "Scrooge."

I would giggle and she'd let me ice the sugar cookies she would be making. We'd eat them piping hot and they'd burn going down our throats. We'd have a funny sensation on our tongues for the rest of the day, but it was always worth it.

Looking back, I wondered what people thought when they glanced at us. A quirky pair we must have made. At least in the winter, Sage didn't wear a sunhat. Instead, she donned fur earmuffs she'd scored from a thrift store. They made her feel rich, she told me. Some days she would even let me wear them, and it was quite the honor when that happened.

I wondered if I would be embarrassed by her now. I never was back then, but I was a little girl living in a state of blissful oblivion, completely unaware of the blindside that was soon coming for me. Not even in my wildest dreams would I have thought she'd leave. And if you sat me down and told me that was just what was going to happen, I'd have told you that you were flat out wrong. And if you'd somehow convinced me you were right, I'd have told you not to worry, because she would come back for me.

Sage was going to come for me. Of that, I was sure. Or at least I used to be. But years passed and lines blurred and I slowly became not so sure anymore.

IT WAS LATE. MAYBE ONE. Maybe two. Late for a school night, anyway.

Levi was knocking hard on the door.

I answered it. He was crying.

"Are you okay?" Even as I said it I knew it was a stupid thing to ask. He obviously was not okay. No one had been for awhile.

"Do you wanna go to the forest with me?"

I nodded but disappeared into the house to grab a coat and a flashlight. It had snowed a little bit the day before and the air was nippy. We crunched our way to the forest.

We didn't talk for a long time. We found our stumps and sat. We hadn't been to the forest together since Ky had left. Nothing was ever more prominent than that third stump which stayed empty.

Levi stared out into the blackness. Then he told me.

"I hurt him, Maeve."

"Hurt who?"

"I hurt him real bad."

He turned to me, and I didn't think I had ever seen someone look sadder. He grabbed my hands and brought them towards his chest, brought me towards his chest, and I went willingly.

"Jared."

I was crying then, too.

"You hurt him?"

Levi nodded, tears cascading onto our entwined fingers. Tears entwining together. Tears beget tears beget tears.

"I was so angry." He let out a sob. "I've never been that angry before. I saw him in the 24-hour grocery store down by the bar. I've been trying to push the anger down, think different thoughts—happy, stupid, positive thoughts," he laughed bitterly. "I've been trying to write about it, talk about it, not talk about it, but nothing is working. And when I saw him go into the store... the anger rushed up so fast I couldn't stop it. I didn't want to stop it. So I waited for him to come out."

"Did anyone see you?"

"No. No one was there, and his car was parked near the

Dumpster. I just… I hurt him so bad. And the weird thing was, he didn't try and fight back. He just let me hurt him."

"Is he dead, Levi?"

Levi shook his head.

"I wish he was," I whispered. "I wish you'd killed him."

Levi got up, off that stump and went to a tree, a large one. He punched that tree. He punched that tree so many times I thought his knuckles might fall off. He cried while he did it, making these low guttural sounds I'd never heard before. I cried while I watched him.

Can you fix someone? I desperately wanted to. I wanted to fix him, and I wanted him to fix me, and we both wanted to fix Ky, and all I could think was that if I could—if I could—I would plunge in headfirst, fill and occupy all of his vacant spaces and make it so he'd never know this empty sort of pain again.

Then I'd ask him to do the same for me.

When he finished punching and kicking that tree he fell onto his knees on the ground, in the middle of the lonely forest.

I went to him. I wrapped my arms tight around his shoulders and burrowed my face into his neck. He shook my whole body as he sobbed.

"I'm sorry," I whispered.

"I couldn't save her," Levi said after a long time.

You can't save anyone.

He turned around, pressed his bloody palm against my cheek, my tears spilling down his arm.

"Maeve girl. How did this happen?"

I pushed my cheek further into his hand, willing the pressure to ease the pain. "How did we not know?" I asked him. "I keep replaying everything, over and over in my head. I should have known. All the signs were there." I paused. "She was such a sad girl."

"I just thought she was cynical."

I laughed a sob. "She was."

"Do you remember when we were here a few months ago? When we were playing my game?"

"I do."

"You asked us what we were afraid of. You remember what Ky said?"

I nodded. "She said death."

"Tell me, Maeve, why would someone kill themselves if their greatest fear was dying?"

I paused for a long moment and then said to him softly, "There must have been a greater fear."

"What do you mean?"

I gave him a sad smile. "I think she was afraid of dying, yes. But I think she was even more afraid to live."

That was the saddest truth of all.

Levi's knuckles were bleeding, terrible amounts of blood, the most desolate kind. So I kissed them, though the blood bled to my lips, though I tasted our briny tears and wretched, unforgivable lives. I kissed them.

After all, that's what Ky would have done.

NINETEEN

CHRISTMAS THREW UP ON THE world. In one swift motion, everything was transformed to tinsel and lights as if Sage had orchestrated the entire thing.

We rarely decorated for Christmas; most years we didn't even celebrate. Sol had always said we were skipping it that year. I think it reminded him too much of Sage. But you can't really skip Christmas. You more miss out, as opposed to disregarding it. You sit there by the window and watch the snow fall and pretend it's another day while seemingly the rest of the universe celebrates, partaking in what you only wish you could partake in. Each year after Sage left, I sat by the window watching the snowfall, wishing I belonged to a real family that didn't try and skip Christmas. I wanted to be a participant, not a skipper.

We did celebrate one year. It was in the peach house in Sycamore, the year I was fourteen. Sol's mom came over. She was a nice old lady. So nice in fact, she let me call her Grandma. I cooked her ham and scalloped potatoes because she had told me they were her favorite. It was the best Christmas—I think in history. She made Sol buy me a tree and she helped me decorate it with real ornaments, not homemade ones. She took me to midnight Mass on Christmas Eve and it was beautiful. A choir sang *Silent Night* a cappella and I remember thinking my feet must have been on holy ground. Sol spent the days she was here drunk, so she and I kept one another company while he wasted himself away the next room over.

She died the end of that February from a massive heart attack. Sol and I attended her funeral, and he didn't cry but I did. She was a kind woman and made me feel like I had mattered. Her hair was so white it was almost light blue, and she was small and frail and the only grandparent I had. I didn't know where Sage or my father's parents were. I didn't know if they knew I existed, and I supposed that was mutual since I didn't know if they existed either.

Sol came in from work and hung up his coat, stripping off his winter boots. "It's snowing again," he told me.

"Think it will be a white Christmas?" I asked.

"Don't know, don't care."

"I want to decorate this year. I want us to buy each other presents. I want us to, like, do Christmas."

"Why?" He grabbed a glass of water and sat on the chair adjacent to where I was on the couch. I lowered the volume on the show I was watching, the one that highlighted people's strange addictions.

"Because that's what normal people do."

Sol laughed, "Who said we were normal?"

"Very funny. But I'm serious."

"What would I get you?"

I thought for a moment. "We could make lists. People do that."

He sighed, running a hand through his hair. "I don't know, Maeve. That was more Sage's thing than mine. I don't mind skipping it."

"Look, Sol, I'm not going to let Sage ruin Christmas for us. We've let her ruin far too many already. We can make our own traditions together."

His eyes narrowed into slits. "Like what?"

"Like… we could get an artificial tree. Totally fake. Store-bought ornaments. We'll figure the rest of it out along the way."

"Do you think if we 'do' Christmas this year, Sage will come home? Because I wouldn't get your hopes up, Maeve. She hasn't come home any other year and I doubt this time will be any different—"

"No, that's not why I want to do this. I know she won't come home. I don't care anyway. I'll find her when I want to find her. I just want to do something like a real family for once."

"We did that when my mom was here."

"She and I did. You were drunk the entire time."

"Not the entire time…"

I rolled my eyes. "Right."

"It's my coping mechanism, all right? Everyone has 'em."

"Why would you need to cope while your mom was here?"

"Trust me," he said and took a sip of his water, "you'll need to cope when you find yours."

I bit the inside of my cheek to keep from smiling. "Okay, grab your keys. We're going to the store to get ourselves the fakest tree anyone's ever seen."

Sol groaned but got up. We came home with an artificial tree, a box of assorted colored Christmas balls, and a shiny gold star for the top.

This is what you get, Sage, I thought. Not two moments later I chided myself. *Shut up, Maeve. It's not like she's going to find out you openly defied her Christmas traditions. She's not coming back.*

And yet, like a child on Christmas morning, I held onto the tiniest sliver of a measly thing called hope, that maybe—just maybe—this would be the year she would.

DEAR KY,

I stared down at the paper, twisting the pen in between my

fingertips. Maurice wanted me to write Ky a letter—an easy task if it were just her reading it, but what could I write that the whole town might see? At least only a handful of people read *The Dish*. That was a comforting thought.

Oh Ky, I thought. *If you were here, what would I tell you?*

My phone rang, interrupting my scattered thoughts.

"Hello?"

"So I hear you're not fired," the female voice said.

"Uh… you heard correctly. Who is this?"

She laughed. "Who do you think?"

My mind was blank. "I have no idea."

"It's Clarke, you idiot. Who else would know you're not fired after ditching work for a dozen consecutive days? I'm calling you because you're supposed to apologize."

"You're calling me because I need to apologize? Shouldn't I be the one calling you?"

I could hear her scowl through the phone. "Obviously. But you weren't going to, were you? Naturally, I took matters into my own hands."

"I'm sorry, Clarke. I should have answered your calls or phoned you back or something. I shouldn't have left you hanging."

"No, you shouldn't have. I seriously covered your butt. You owe me for… oh, the rest of your life should do it."

I smiled. "But then you'd have to *see* me for the rest of my life."

She grimaced. "Good point. We'll lower it to owing me for the rest of the year."

"The year is done in like twenty days." I pointed out.

I think she growled. "Fine, Einstein, you owe me for the rest of this year and the rest of next. Happy?"

"Sure," I laughed. "I am sorry."

"Me too. I didn't realize she was your friend."

"Yeah, my best friend."

"Maurice told me you're writing an article."

"I'm trying to do it right now, actually."

"How's that going?"

"Harder than I thought. It's different than if I were writing to only her, but it's like I'm writing to our whole town."

"You are writing to her," Clarke said. "But a few other people might read it."

"That's the problem," I muttered.

"Look, Parker, it has to be decently good. It's a pretty big deal to get an article in the paper, especially at your age. I know it's only *The Dish*, but still. Think of this as your test to get into the big leagues. If it's not good, you won't get asked to write seriously for awhile, or possibly ever again. If it's decent, you may get a few more opportunities."

"Is it your goal in life to make people feel worse about themselves?"

Clarke laughed. "It's called realism, cupcake."

"This isn't easy."

"I have a motto for you—one I vow to remind you of every day."

"Great."

She cleared her throat as if something profound were about to be spoken. "'Quit whining and start writing.'"

"That's the motto?"

She ignored me. "Quit whining and start writing, Parker!"

"I'm trying."

"Clearly not hard enough."

I sighed. "I hate the motto. It's stupid."

"You think I care? Remember the motto; breathe the motto; live the motto! *Carpe diem!* Don't even think whiney thoughts— stop that, I can hear them from here."

"You cannot!"

"Yes, I can. I can hear you thinking how you can't do it, how it's too hard, etcetera, etcetera, etcetera. Would you like some cheese with your whine?"

I almost growled at her.

"Repeat after me, Parker, 'Quit whining and start writing.'"

I sighed again.

"Repeat it," she demanded.

"Quit whining and start writing," I muttered.

"That's right," she sounded pleased, her voice syrupy. "Now go forth and finish that article." The phone clicked off and she was gone, without a goodbye or see-you-later.

I looked down at the paper.

Dear Ky,

I picked up my pen.

The days have stretched like infinity since the day you left. They're never ending, not marked by dawn or eve, simply sinking into the next without realization. My world has spun out of control. I'm trying to grab hold of anything that might keep me from teetering off the edge of this planet, but the stars have shifted and what once anchored me has been wrenched away. The day you left, the Earth collapsed beneath my feet, and its imbalance has remained and I am still grappling.

I wonder if you realize the damage you have created. I wonder if that is a menacing thing for me to wonder.

I scratched out those last two sentences.

I wonder if you realize…

How much havoc you have wreaked. How much pain you have caused. How much I wish I could have saved you… How much I wish I could have been you…

I wonder if you realize how much we miss you.

Yes, that was safer, less vulnerable, for me and the general public.

All of us. The universe really. It's a tangible loss, one I can smell and taste, stagnant and bitter on the back of my tongue. The air feels different, and in the morning the birds sing a new kind of song, a mourning song. In the morning the birds gather to sing their mourning song. Perhaps someday I'll put lyrics to their tune; maybe when the world slows down enough for me to swallow this new reality, or at least enough to dig my heels in and gain a smidgen of traction in this sand.

We read somewhere once, I think in your sister's magazines she had left behind, something about how 'you change the world simply by living in it.' I remember how we laughed about that, both agreeing it was a stupid and pathetic quote, one therapists must tell their clients to cheer them up. But now I wonder if we were wrong because the world does feel changed now. You did change the world by living in it, but more than that, you changed the world by leaving it.

I wrote the next part for Alice. Sometimes you have to write half-truths in order to honor the people who are still living. They're the ones reading it, after all.

On behalf of your town, your friends, your family… on behalf of all the people who loved you the most, I promise you we won't forget. We couldn't forget, even if we tried, because the truth of it is: you're unforgettable, Ky. Truly, unequivocally unforgettable, always to be remembered, forever to be deeply missed.

All my love, your best friend,
Maeve Parker

THE DAYS LEADING UP TO Christmas break seemed to pass quickly, with loads of assignments to finish and a few more articles (much smaller than the letter to Ky, which Maurice had been quite pleased with, bringing me a mixture of nausea, relief, and excitement) to write for *The Dish*. Sol and I had written a few things we wanted on lists, tacking them up on a kitchen cupboard so we wouldn't miss them. The tree looked nice, albeit very fake, and I sort of missed the evergreen smell that filled the room when Sol's mom had been over years earlier.

But at least we were partaking.

The last day of school was a half day, so we watched *A Christmas Carol* in Herman's class, but no one was really watching, and I'm pretty sure Herman had fallen asleep at his desk. I whispered to the girl who sat across from me, Molly, that I was going to the bathroom. She shrugged and kept drawing in her notebook. Occasionally, I would sneak glances at what she would draw in her notebook—she was drawing, always—and most of the time her drawings were cartoons of people blowing up, fires surrounding them. Frightening.

I went to the bathroom and saw Levi sitting in the hall.

I kicked his shoe softly. "Hey."

He grinned as he looked up at me. "I was hoping you'd come."

I sat down beside him. "How could I not? Herman's asleep, and you can't hear the movie because everyone's talking so loud. Also, I'm pretty sure some people were hooking up in the back of the room." I crinkled my nose as if I'd smelled something particularly foul.

Levi laughed. "Yeah, Miller put on a movie, too. He wanted to grade our final projects today so he didn't have to do it over the break."

"How'd yours go?"

He shrugged. "I made a birdhouse. I'll give it to my mom someday. She cries whenever we give her something homemade."

"Did you get her something for Christmas?"

"Gift certificate to the nail salon."

"She'll love that."

"She told us she wanted one, so she won't be very surprised. What'd you get Sol?"

"He wanted warmer socks, new gloves, and a twelve pack of beer."

"I'm shocked by that last one. How are you gonna get the beer?"

I wiggled my eyebrows. "Oh, you know me. I have my sources."

"Right. Gray." The disdain was evident in his voice.

"You say that as if you don't like him."

"I don't."

"Why? You can't have a good reason, because you hardly know him. Besides, he's gotten better. Sol's gotten much better too, since... well, things are turning around. The two of them don't get drunk nearly as often and when they do I make sure to be more careful—"

"You shouldn't have to be careful—"

"Look," I said, frustrated. "I don't want to talk about this! It's almost Christmas. It's going to be good this year, okay, Levi? Don't make this bad for me."

"I'm not trying to make Christmas bad for you, Maeve. But I don't think you should be around Gray."

I scoffed. "Are you jealous, Levi Fisher?"

"No!" He practically barked. "You shouldn't surround yourself with people like him."

"Oh, yay," I rolled my eyes, regret brimming over but I did not stop it. "Bring on the lecture. Let's hear it."

Levi slammed his fist on the ground. "Stop making it all about you, Maeve! Honestly! I'm trying to help you!"

"And for the hundredth time, I don't need your help!"

We sat silent for a moment, breathing. Our chests sinking in, seconds later pushing out. Spoken and unspoken words; things we wished we'd said, things we'd wished we hadn't.

"We have different lives," I said quietly. "You have to accept that."

"I know our lives are different," he looked over at me. "But we don't have to accept when people treat us poorly."

"We all have stories, don't we, Levi? And our stories predict the future. Sol's getting better, but I've stopped blaming him if he gives me a smack every once in a while when he's drunk. Sometimes that's how you deal with things. We all have our ways of dealing with things."

"You can't think like that."

I cast him a sardonic grin. "I can think whichever way I like."

"You're wrong, anyway. Our stories don't predict the future."

"I think they do."

"No. What a hopeless idea to believe in. If our stories—if our past—determined what our future would look like, I doubt anyone would want to live past tomorrow. I know I wouldn't."

An image of Ky flashed through my mind. Her delicate fingers holding the heavy weight of a gun, lifting it slowly to her temple, blowing her brains out until they permanently decorated her bedroom floor.

I looked at Levi. "Agree to disagree?"

He shook his head. "No. But I'll agree to let it rest until after Christmas break."

I let myself laugh. "If you're so concerned about Gray—"

"—which I am—"

"—which you are," I laughed again. "I'm going to his house after school today to pick up the beer for Sol. Why don't you tag along?"

"Fine," Levi said.

"Please. Your excitement is overwhelming."

He smiled. "Meet you here at twelve once the bell rings."

We both went back to class and *A Christmas Carol* was finishing. At the same time, Herman was waking up from his nap.

"Sorry Mr. Herman," I went to his desk, apologetic. "I needed to use the restroom and didn't want to, um, wake you."

The tips of his ears turned pink. "It's all right, Maeve," he said, stifling a yawn. "Class dismissed. Merry Christmas, or happy holidays, or whatever the politically correct saying is these days."

My next class with Miss Meyers went by more slowly. I had English with Ky, so the desk beside mine sat empty. Miss Meyers was a better teacher than most, at least in my opinion, and she didn't fall asleep or plug in a movie for us to watch. She sat on her desk, ankles crossed, palms splayed casually on the surface.

"So, in fifty minutes Christmas break will officially begin."

A few cheers and hollers floated through the classroom. Miss Meyers laughed. "All right, all right, calm down. I know you're all excited. Trust me, so am I. Don't tell anyone, but I have a hunch my boyfriend is going to propose this Christmas."

The class let out some *oohs* and *aahs*, and Miss Meyers blushed.

"Like I said, don't tell anyone."

I liked Miss Meyers, but she was a little strange. What—did she think our whole class was going to stalk her boyfriend and find out when he was planning to propose? I went to roll my eyes with Ky, but the empty seat was all that greeted me. I had forgotten, for that brief moment, that Ky was gone. I didn't have anyone left in the class to roll my eyes with.

Miss Meyers wanted us to go around and say what our favorite memory of the class was, but after three students not being able to come up with a response, (because it's English class! Who has a favorite memory of English class? The answer is no one.) Miss Meyers called it quits and let us chat until the bell rang.

The students clustered into groups and Amanda Wright said something that caused her little squad of girls to erupt into laughter, and they all turned and looked at me. I looked back at them, right in the eye, because I sure wasn't about to let them think they could scare me. They did, of course—girls are exceptionally horrifying—but they weren't about to know that. I felt Miss Meyers plop her tiny body into the desk beside mine. Ky's desk.

"Have you had an enjoyable time in English class this semester, Maeve?"

I nodded.

"You're a good writer. You've done well," she said kindly. "Even after... what happened." She took a small breath. "Are you... happy here?"

I blinked. "In your class?"

"Well, yes, but also in general. At school. At home."

"Happy... probably isn't the word I'd use. I'm trying to figure things out, I guess."

Miss Meyers bobbed her head. "Of course." She hesitated. "Some of the teachers... We're worried for you."

"Worried?"

"Well, you didn't come to school for awhile after it happened, which we fully understood! Had it been me at your age I probably wouldn't have come back at all. We wondered if you'd had any counseling or anything?"

"No, but it's not—"

"Mrs. Greene offered to talk with you maybe once a week or so. So you'd feel like you had someone you could talk to besides your mom and dad."

I sighed. As if I wanted to spill my guts to the guidance counselor. "That won't be necessary."

"Mrs. Greene is lovely, really. Maybe you could try it one time, Maeve? After the Christmas break?"

"I'm doing okay, I promise."

She patted my arm. "I know. But sometimes we push down our emotions, and then our insides become so cluttered and heavy, well, then we just explode."

"If you're suggesting I'm playing with the thought of suicide, I can assure you I'm not."

Her cheeks reddened. "That wasn't what I was suggesting. We care for you, Maeve. We want to see you succeed. You're very intelligent." Tears filled her eyes. "It breaks my heart what you must be going through… what she must have been going through."

"You can say her name."

"All right." She pursed her lips together thoughtfully. "I didn't know. Sometimes that's… a trigger."

"No. Not for me. I like when people talk about Ky. It's like she's still alive."

Miss Meyers nodded sympathetically. I didn't have the heart to tell her that the last thing I wanted was her sympathy.

"How about—for Ky—you could try it with Mrs. Greene? She won't pressure you in any way. It's a pressure-free zone. You can say anything you want."

"I'll think about it," I told her, adding quickly, "but probably not."

She patted my arm again and said reassuringly, "Yes, please think about it! It would do you good. Talking about our pain is healthy."

To my relief, the bell rang signaling Christmas break had begun. Miss Meyers looked disappointed that our conversation was cut short, but she smiled and wished me a Merry Christmas, and I wished her the same.

And then I met up with Levi.

LEVI'S PARENTS HAD BEEN LETTING him borrow one of their cars to go to school because it had gotten quite cold out, so Levi strapped my bike on the back, and I jumped into the passenger side. I loved riding in his car. It was warm and smelled like worn leather and fast food.

I pointed the way to Gray's. He lived on the town's edge in a very small, not very well-kept house.

"It would have taken you ages to bike here," Levi said.

I shrugged. "I'd have managed."

"Like you always do."

"That's right."

He put the car into park on the gravelly driveway, and I hopped out to go knock on Grayson's door. Levi followed behind me.

"Hi Gray," I said when he opened the door.

"Maevie Parker."

"Don't call me that."

Gray laughed. "I see you brought company."

"This is Levi Fisher. Levi, meet Gray Henderson."

"Hello, Gray," Levi said curtly.

"Hey there, Levi Fisher," Gray practically drawled. "Keeping Maevie company, or coming along as her bodyguard?"

"All right, that's enough," I said and pushed past Gray. "Where's the beer, Gray?"

He laughed again, going to the pantry and pulling out the twelve pack.

"How much?" I asked.

"For you? Free."

I rolled my eyes. "No seriously, just tell me what it cost you."

"Twenty bucks, but I can cover you this time."

"No thanks." I fished the money out from my backpack. "I don't like owing people."

"It'd be a gift."

"I'm okay."

"You don't like gifts?"

"She said she's fine," Levi cut in.

Gray put his hand to his heart, mocking. "Are you her boyfriend? How cute."

"No," Levi said. "A friend."

"Quit that! The both of you." I glared at them. "Get over yourselves. Honestly."

Gray smiled, but Levi still looked annoyed. I sighed. "Thanks for getting this for me, Gray. I appreciate it."

"Anytime," he said.

We walked toward the door, and Gray said, "I have an idea. I'm throwing a small party on New Year's Eve, just a couple of friends. It'd be fun to have a few younger people there to liven it up a bit. Why don't you two come? You can bring some friends if you'd like."

I looked at Levi. He was frowning.

"Probably not a good idea," he said. "What if the police come?"

"The police don't bother coming this far," Gray assured us.

"It could be fun, Levi," I said. "I never do anything on New Year's Eve."

"I think you'd like my friends," Gray said.

"I still don't think it's wise," Levi cautioned.

Gray looked at me. "Is he always this boring?"

I stifled a laugh. Levi grabbed my hand. "C'mon, Maeve, we should go."

"We'll think about the party, Gray," I promised as Levi pulled me out the door and into the car. I pulled the car door shut and braced myself for another lecture, but Levi was silent.

"You can go if you want," Levi said after a few minutes. "But I'm not going."

"Wow," I said, sarcasm dripping. "It's so kind of you to allow me this opportunity."

"What do you like about him?"

"What do you mean?"

He repeated his question, slower. "What do you like about Gray?"

I shrugged. "I don't know. I didn't use to like him. But people change, you know? Maybe I was judging him too harshly before.

He's... different. Sort of mysterious. Nobody treats me the way he does."

"Doesn't he, like work or anything? What does he do all day?"

I shrugged. Again. "Never asked him. Not really my business."

"Don't you find it odd he wants two sixteen-year-olds to come to his party?"

"It's not that weird. He probably wants a variety of friends."

"How old is he, anyway?"

"Twenty-one, maybe?" I knew that was a lie. He must've been older than that, twenty-five at least.

"Right," Levi said, casting a sideways glance at me.

"Maybe twenty-two?"

"Yeah, maybe."

We drove quietly for awhile. I asked him, "Why wouldn't you want to go to his party? Do you have other plans?"

Levi shook his head.

"Would your mom and dad not want you to go?"

"Unlikely, but that's not why."

"Then why not? It might be fun, Levi. I haven't had fun in such a long time."

"They'll just want you to get drunk."

I shrugged my one shoulder nonchalantly. "So?"

"I thought you don't like drinking because of Sol."

"I think I can control myself a little better than Sol can. I'm also old enough to make my own decisions, thank you very much. If you go, you don't have to drink."

Levi sighed, running a hand through his hair. Some of it fell across his forehead and I suppressed the urge to take my fingers and brush it away.

"I don't know, Maeve."

"I think you're afraid."

"Of what?"

"Letting loose? Being sixteen? Ky would have come. You know that."

"That doesn't mean I would have."

"Yeah, it does. If she was here, you would come. I know it. There was nothing for you to be worried about back then. Not really. But now you never have fun. You just worry about me."

"I worried about you before."

"But why, Levi?" I asked, exasperated. "I'm fine. I'm doing fine now, the same way I was doing fine before. I'm not some little girl in need of looking after. If anything, you should have been worrying about Ky. She's the one who ended up dead. Not me." I regretted the words as soon as I said them.

"You're right." He pulled the car to the side of the road ending in a stop and leaned his forehead gently against the steering wheel.

"I'm not right. I shouldn't have said that. I'm sorry. It's not your fault she's gone. It's not."

I looked out the window. The day was gray, what all the bleak midwinter days seemed to look like, overcast and sad and dreary. Even the snow looked gray. It had long since lost its purity.

I unzipped my backpack, pulling out a small box.

"Here," I said. "Merry Christmas."

Levi looked up, then over at me. He accepted the box. "What is it?"

"Guess you'll have to open it to find out."

He gingerly lifted the top off and peered inside. He took out a piece of paper. "Ingredients for Levi Fisher's ocean," he read. He smiled at me.

I smiled back.

He placed the ingredients one by one on the dashboard. A container of water. A small bag of sand. A message in a bottle. A satchel of salt.

"I wanted to bring you the sea," I told him.

"You did good, Maeve, you did so good. Almost like the real thing. Thank you."

I leaned in and held him. I whispered *imsorryimsorryimsorry* in his ear. I kissed his cheek. I straightened up. We wiped our eyes.

"Now, your turn," he said. He reached into the back seat and handed me a package.

"For *moi*?" I feigned surprise.

"Yeah, yeah, just open it."

I ripped the wrapping, tore it right off, hoping Levi didn't want me to try and save it or something.

"Levi!" I gasped wistfully. "This is beautiful!"

It was a leather notebook. It was brown, but a warm brown, the kind of brown that was a mix of burnt embers and spicy chocolate. The notebook opened up with leather flaps and closed by wrapping a long leather band around it. I unwound the band and opened it onto my lap. The paper was cream onionskin, thin and brittle and old. I smelled it. It was lovely.

Levi was watching me. "I've never seen someone try to eat a journal before."

I laughed. "Did you smell it?" I shoved it in his face before he had the opportunity to reply. "Smell it!" I demanded.

He sniffed.

"No, I mean smell it. Take a good whiff!"

He inhaled sharply, then looked at me.

"Doesn't it smell incredible?" I asked.

"Smells like leather to me," he admitted.

I sighed, shaking my head. "Not just leather, Levi. Vintage leather."

"Right."

"There is a difference, you know. It smells like a story."

Levi laughed. "I'm sure it does."

"It's wonderful," I told him. "Thank you."

"You're a writer," he said to me. "You needed a good notebook."

I held it to my chest, and he started the car. When we got to my house, I thanked him again. "Think about the party, all right?"

"I'll think about it," he said.

"It could be fun," I offered, tantalizing him. "It's something different."

"Maybe."

He unloaded my bicycle for me.

"Thank you for the journal."

"Thank you for the sea."

"Merry Christmas, Levi."

"Merry Christmas, Maeve girl."

TWENTY

"WOULD YOU LIKE TO GO to church?" I asked Sol on Christmas Eve.

He was nursing a beer on the couch under the glimmer of light from our artificial Christmas tree. He hadn't said as much, but I think he'd fallen in love with that tree.

"When did you become religious?"

"I didn't. Your mom took me a few years ago. I thought it might be nice to go back—for tradition's sake."

"Yeah," he took a sip. "That was always more her thing than mine. Gray might come over later, so I think I'll stay here."

"Doesn't he have family to spend Christmas Eve with?"

Sol shrugged. "Don't think so."

I changed into a black dress—what was one supposed to wear to a Christmas Eve service?—even putting on some red lipstick and combing my ashy blonde hair back. I looked in the mirror and the red lipstick reminded me too much of Ky. I wiped it off.

I went downstairs and saw Gray.

"Maeve." He was staring at me. "You look beautiful."

"Oh." His words surprised me. I felt my whole body flush. "Thank you."

"Where are you going?"

"To… church. Midnight Mass."

"Church?" He raised his one eyebrow. "I never knew."

"I… don't go very often." As in, have been once.

Sol came over, handing Gray a beer.

"Could you give me a ride to church? I would take my bike but it's freezing out." I asked Sol.

"I'll take you," Gray offered.

"That's a good idea," Sol said, taking Gray's beer and going back to the couch.

Gray smiled at me. Kindly.

"Thank you," I said again. I grabbed my coat and shoes, quickly putting them on. Gray opened the front door. "Bye, Sol," I called out, but couldn't hear his reply. I felt Gray's hand on the small of my back; felt him guiding me toward his truck.

"Careful," he warned, "it's slippery." His breath was cold, close to my ear.

"Thanks." I looked up at him smiling, and at the same moment felt my foot slip out from underneath me. I shrieked, sliding on the ice. I was envisioning my fall which would surely be fatal, when suddenly his hands swooped beneath me, his large hands, pulling me up, pulling me to safety. I was close to him— safe—his arms wrapped around mine, my heart pumping adrenaline and blood and wonder throughout my entire body. Every nerve was alive and tingling. I shifted my face up to see him. He seemed different, somehow. Still strong, seemingly unbreakable, and yet soft, as if he wanted to protect me. His dark eyes peered into mine, and I realized if either of us moved less than an inch closer our lips would be touching. Not in the drunken, rushed way he'd kissed me before, but slow and golden and Christmassy.

"Careful," I whispered. "It's slippery."

A laugh gurgled from his throat, and the flirt of a smile played on my lips. Then, as I instinctively knew he would, he kissed me. He stroked my cheek, my body shivering beneath him.

"Let's get you warm," he said, and we got into his truck.

He held my hand on the way to the church, rubbing his thumb in circles on my palm. Despite the heat blasting, my insides trembled. I looked at his profile as we drove. His long hair was wavy and wild, his cheeks rough, his nose strong. His hands enveloped mine—and I was small within him. Like I hardly took up any space at all.

"Your boyfriend wouldn't have liked that," Gray said.

"He's not my boyfriend."

"No?"

I shook my head. "We're good friends."

"I bet he likes you."

"He doesn't. He's a bit protective, but he doesn't like me... like that."

"I do." Gray smiled at me.

"I realized that," I said in a soft voice. I had wondered for a while, but it still felt nice to hear him say it.

"I'm glad."

We drove quietly for a little while. Gray asked, "Why is he protective?"

I sighed. "Our best friend killed herself a month and a half ago. Did you hear about that? Maybe Sol told you. Anyway, we all found it hard, obviously, but Levi... he's been taking it harder than anyone, it seems. I think he believes it's his fault."

"Is it?"

"His fault? No. Of course not."

Gray said nothing.

"It was her choice," I countered. As the words fell from my lips I became aware of how true they were. "That's what it was. Her choice. Not mine or Levi's. I wish Ky hadn't chosen what she did because I miss her—I can't even find words for how much I miss her—but it doesn't change that it was her choice."

We were at the church, a large Catholic cathedral with a steeple reaching high into the night sky as if it were peeling past stars and searching for Heaven. Perhaps it was. Maybe we're all desperate to find anything larger than us. To envelope our hands and make us feel like we don't take up any space at all.

"I'll come pick you up when you're finished?"

I shrugged. "That depends on how much you've had to drink with Sol."

Gray laughed. "I can handle it."

I smiled, regardless of knowing how wrong he was. "I'll let you know." I loitered for a moment, not ready to brace the cold. Finally, I shoved the door open and slid out.

"Hey," he leaned across the seats, warmth exuding from the truck. "Merry Christmas, Maevie."

I wrinkled my nose. "I hate that nickname."

"Yeah, I know," he grinned, his teeth showing. I was stunned by how frightened and safe I could feel around a person, all at the same time.

"No one calls me that but you." I arched my eyebrow. "I suppose we can keep it that way." I leaned in but didn't kiss him. I was quite sure I would be frozen if I lingered much longer. "Merry Christmas, Grayson."

He gently tugged a few strands of my hair. "You're the best person I've ever met."

"I'm the coldest person you've ever met."

"No," he said, leaning in closer, "the warmest." He tried to kiss me, but I pushed him away.

"I'm going to die of hypothermia and you'll be to blame."

"Fine," he said reluctantly, "but I'll miss you."

I rolled my eyes and shut the door. I saw him grinning through the window, and when I turned to make my way into the church, I felt myself grinning, too. Maybe people aren't always what they seem. Maybe there's more to them than we realize.

"MAEVE PARKER?"

I turned at the sound of my name.

"It is you! I thought that was you! And then I thought, 'No, I'm almost positive Maeve Parker isn't Catholic,' but then you turned around and it really is you!" Francine was enveloping me into her tiny arms. We were in the lobby of the church, about to walk in and find a seat. "Hi, sweetheart," she said.

"Hi, Francine," I smiled. "It's good to see you."

"Are you Catholic?" she asked, almost suspiciously.

I held back a grin. "No. I decided I wanted to visit. It's Christmas... you know?"

"Ah," she nodded her head knowingly, "I feel the same way. It feels like a sacred place here in general, but most especially at Christmas. My mother used to say, everything feels more divine at Christmas time."

"She was right. It does."

I could hear music swelling in the sanctuary. "Well, come on now," Francine said, grabbing my arm. "I don't want to be late for Jesus!"

There were a lot of people there—more than I expected—and we could only manage to find seats near the back.

Francine leaned over and whispered in my ear, "Most of these folks don't usually attend. Like you said, it's Christmas. And I should warn you, the service can get a little confusing what with the reciting and standing up and kneeling and all that, but you follow along the best you can. Nobody's judging."

I nodded and whispered back, "Thanks, Francine."

She smiled, probably excited at the prospect of Maeve Parker getting converted—and in her very own church, too!

I wondered if that was why Francine had always been kind to me. Church people automatically had to be kind, didn't they? But then again, I guess no one had to be anything they didn't want to be.

Francine was right—there was a lot of standing up, and sitting down, and saying random phrases back to a girl who stood at the front. The girl at the front sang some songs, and the church recited words in between her singing. She had a nice voice. It was high and light and airy. I liked to listen to her.

The priest came out and gave a sermon. Was I supposed to do confession? I'd heard of that before. I wondered what I would confess. I pictured myself getting into the little confession booth I'd seen in movies, waiting for the slate to shift open beside me, and saying to the person on the other side, *Hello, I'm Maeve Parker. Am I supposed to tell you my name? I don't know. For the past month, I've regularly thought about killing someone. I know it would be committing a crime—and a bad one at that, because I'm thinking murder is on the top of the list of bad things you can do—but lots of people want him dead, so I think I'd actually be doing the world a favor. Now tell me, what are your thoughts on that?* Perhaps the priest would banish me from the church.

Was thinking things a sin? Did I need to confess that? Would I need to admit to the priest who, exactly, I intended to kill?

I turned to Francine and asked quietly, "Do we do confession at this?"

Francine shook her head. "That's during the week. It's totally optional."

I nodded. Thank God—or whomever.

Finally, the priest was finished speaking. He had talked about the Lord coming as an infant, a vulnerable little baby—fully human, and fully God. Born in a barn for the sole purpose of dying for the world. He said God loved all people, despite the mistakes they may have made. I didn't understand. How could God even love Jared?

The choir ushered onto the platform as if they were one entity—their long black robes and white, pristine collars. I wondered if they were nuns. I always liked the idea of nuns— these fascinating creatures who didn't marry or have sex or anything. Did they tire of praying, of dedicating their life to God? How did they wholly love their life—one of ritual, routine, and no relations? I couldn't begin to fathom. They began to sing.

Francine was swaying gently beside me, her fingers clasped, eyes closed. "Handel's Messiah," she whispered, "my favorite."

It was beautiful. A young blonde girl came out, beginning to light candles along the sides of the aisles as the choir sang their hallelujah chorus. The chorus grew and grew in a crescendo that was both holy and sensational, and I felt satisfying shivers settle against my spine.

When they finished, I sat breathless.

People stood and filed out. I clicked my phone; it was officially Christmas. 1:02 a.m. I could see some children yawning, their excitement radiating in lieu of their exhaustion.

"Santa's coming tonight," a little boy said to his sister as their parents whispered a few pews away.

"Not Santa," the girl said. "Jesus."

"No, Jesus comes on Easter. Santa comes on Christmas."

The girl scrunched her nose. "I thought Jesus came on Christmas."

He shrugged. "I can't remember anymore. But I do know Santa brings presents."

"Oh yes!" She clapped her hands. "I can't wait."

Their parents collected them, and they left the church to go home to their stacks of presents and mismatched theology.

"Did you like that?" Francine asked me. We were almost the last ones in the sanctuary. I didn't want to leave. It was safe, warm, cozy.

"Very much so." I watched the girl who lit the candles begin to blow them out. One by one. "That choir... for them to sing like that... well, I would imagine they must be very close to God."

Francine turned in the pew, curious.

"I mean... they sang like they knew him."

"I think they do."

I nodded. I looked up. I wondered what the stained glass

windows looked like in the day with the midmorning sunlight streaming through. No more darkness, only light. I looked out at the altar. A statue, of who I presumed to be Mary, had her hands folded together. The priest had talked about her, the mother of Jesus. Mary's lips were arced in a permanent half-moon smile. She gazed across the wooden pews at me. "I couldn't be a nun."

Francine laughed. "Nor could I!"

"But they're remarkable. And I respect them, you know, living their life for God."

"You don't have to be a nun to do that," Francine answered quietly.

"I guess not."

We sat silent for a long moment.

"Let me take you home," Francine offered.

I let her.

CHRISTMAS LEFT THE SAME WAY it came: quickly. Sol, of course, didn't want to make it last any longer than absolutely necessary.

He was thrilled with the beer. I had also gotten him wool socks, new gloves, and a travel mug that was supposed to keep his coffee extra hot. He gave me a gift card to the mall in the next town over, a few books I was excited to read, and new boots that were a soft gray suede on the exterior and faux fur on the inside.

"I couldn't remember what size feet you have," he had said, embarrassed. "I tried looking at your other shoes but couldn't find the size. The lady at the store said to go with a size eight. They were on sale, so I don't think you can take them back..."

"They're perfect," I had told him, even though I wore a size seven. I figured I could layer on a couple pairs of socks and it would all be just fine.

Christmas had come and gone, and I still hadn't heard back

from Levi regarding Gray's party. I hadn't seen him since Christmas break had started, and was unsure whether to tell him that Gray had kissed me. I wished Ky were around. I would have gone to her house on Christmas Day and explained everything that had happened the night before. I tried to imagine what she would tell me. She'd be intrigued by the thought of an older guy, but she had never been a huge fan of Gray. Neither had I up until a few days ago. But circumstances change. So do people.

What were you supposed to do when a boy—or in my case, a man—liked you? I grew angry again, knowing Sage was missing my life and wondering if she cared at all.

I decided to leave it. If Levi wanted to come to the party, he could come. If not, well then, I was fully capable of taking care of myself. I didn't need a boy to protect me. I didn't need anyone.

Alice knocked on my door on New Years Eve day.

"I went to the police." She sat down on the couch.

I closed the door.

"I told them…" her lip quivered, "…I told them everything."

"Would you like a cup of tea?"

She nodded. As the water boiled, she explained to me what happened.

"I went to the police station. They knew about Ky. They were the officers who had come to the house when I called the day I found her. I went in and told them about him, and about the note. It must count as evidence. It must!" Her voice had grown high and frazzled. I took her hand. "They didn't tell me anything, only that they'll be by your home later today to collect the letter."

"Okay."

"I'm scared, Maeve."

The kettle hissed, screeching loudly, signaling its finish. I went into the kitchen and made Alice's cup of tea. I didn't ask her how she liked it, just stirred in a bit of milk and honey the way I always made mine. I brought it out to her and she wrapped her fingers against the comforting warmth.

"You make a good cup of tea."

"Thank you."

"The world doesn't tend to work in my favor," she admitted. "It didn't work out with Charlie, and Hannah won't speak to me anymore. She refused to look at me at Ky's funeral. She used to live with Ky and me during the summers or Christmas breaks, whenever she wasn't away at school. Now she goes to Charlie's. She never liked him, but now she prefers even him over me. I have no idea what he's been telling her." She let out a rattled sigh and took a small sip of her tea. The steam rose, curling against her eyelashes. "In one day, I lost both my daughters. And Jared... I don't know where he is. I came home a few days ago and he was gone. All his stuff was gone, too. I know you'll be happy to hear that, but I don't have anyone anymore." She peered down at her cup and said softly, "I miss my girl."

I knew I should have been more sensitive and allowed her to dwell on Ky, but I couldn't get past Jared. "He left? He's gone?"

"Well, he hasn't come home."

"Where he is?"

"I don't know."

"We have to find him, Alice. How is he supposed to go to prison if we can't find him?"

She was calm, taking a sip of her tea. "That's the job of the police. They'll find him."

"Oh yeah? And what if he's taken off and gone to Honolulu or something?"

"He's hardly the type to do that."

I huffed. "I can't believe you're not worried."

She stared at her cup. "I'm too tired."

"Did you not sleep well last night?"

Alice let out a small laugh. "Sleep? I don't sleep. I close my eyes and see Ky, dead and bleeding across her bedroom floor. I close my eyes and hear the gunshot ring out, echoing through my brain, the last sound ever associated with my child. So no, Maeve, I don't sleep." She drained her tea and went to the door.

"I don't know what time they're coming," she said, her hand draped loosely on the knob. "Just be ready with that letter."

I shut the door behind her.

EVEN THOUGH I HADN'T DONE anything wrong, terror welled within me when the police knocked on the door.

"Hi there." The lady was smiling next to the man who wasn't. "Are you Maeve Parker?"

"Yeah, that's me. Come on in."

"I'm Detective Haddon," the lady said as she took a seat on the couch, "and this is Officer Gervais." She smiled again. The man—Gervais—sat down beside her but still didn't smile. I felt like I was on the set of a movie.

I remained standing. "Can I... get you a drink?"

Detective Haddon shook her head, and the man remained mute. "That won't be necessary, Maeve. Why don't you take a seat? You're not in any trouble. We only want to talk to you."

I sat on the chair adjacent from them. I fiddled with my fingertips. My whole body felt jittery and nervous like I had drunk too much caffeine. The letter was on the coffee table in between us. I looked at it, and so did they. None of us made a move to pick it up.

Detective Haddon cleared her throat. She was pretty, I thought. Pretty, in that sort of unsuspecting way. Her eyes crinkled when she smiled and she seemed to smile often. "So Maeve, can you tell us about your relationship with Ky McNeil?"

"What do you mean?"

She crossed her legs comfortably. "Let's start with when you became friends."

"In September. We had moved here, and I met her on my

first day at the school."

"Oh? That recently?"

I nodded, slowly. "We became good friends right away. We hung out all the time."

"So you were only friends for about two and a half months before the suicide."

"I guess so. It felt like longer, though. We were best friends."

The man spoke. "After two months, you couldn't have known her that well."

"That's not true! We knew each other really well. We told one another everything."

"Did she talk to you about Jared Smit?" Detective Haddon asked.

"No," I said quietly. "I didn't know anything about him doing that to her."

"I guess she didn't tell you everything," Gervais said. I didn't like him.

"Why are you here?" I felt brazen. "I don't care what you say, I know my friendship with her was real and true. I miss her. But I appreciate you suggesting we didn't have a friendship at all."

Haddon smiled again. "We're not saying that. Simply trying to get to the bottom of this."

"Jared Smit was raping Ky." I pointed to the letter on the coffee table. "It says so—in her very own handwriting—right in that letter. *That's* the bottom of this. Arrest him. Charge him. Do whatever it is you do with criminals, but he was sexually abusing her since last May and that's why she killed herself."

"Did you see Ky at any point on November 15?"

"Yeah, all day at school and then we hung out in the forest when school was finished."

"The forest?"

I nodded. "We go there a lot... I mean went."

"Did you notice anything different about her that day? Did

she seem upset or angry? Anything to suggest why that night would be the breaking point?"

"She was going to talk to Alice about cutting it off with Jared. He had proposed and Ky was incredibly upset. Now I obviously know why. But back then I thought it was because Jared had cheated on Alice so much."

"Had he been cheating?"

"Oh yeah. Ky had followed him a couple of times after he had left her house. She wanted to see where he went, and he always went to be with another woman. It was always someone different than the last. Ky didn't want Alice to marry him because he was cheating on her like crazy."

"What was Ky planning on saying to Alice?"

"She told me she was gonna tell her about the other women. Alice told me Ky did tell her that night, but Alice had said she didn't care and was going to marry him anyway. It must have been too much for Ky. She was depressed," I explained. "She had been for a while. But she seemed to be doing better on certain days… I don't think she had planned the suicide. I was shocked when Alice called me."

Detective Haddon put tight blue gloves on, the kind a dentist used and opened the letter. "Who's Levi?" She asked after she had read it. She passed the letter to Gervais who had also put gloves on, and he read it too, then deposited it into a little plastic bag.

"Levi Fisher, our friend from school. The three of us hung out a lot. I'll get that letter back, right?"

"Maybe," Gervais answered.

"Yes," Haddon confirmed.

"It's all I have left of her."

Haddon smiled again, a sadder smile, nodding her head. "We know. We'll give it back. We'll need to talk to Levi Fisher."

"He doesn't know anything about it. Less than me."

"We'll still pay him a visit. We like as much information as possible."

I gave them Levi's address, then stood, indicating their cue to leave. "It would be a mistake to not find Jared. A girl killed herself because of what he did to her. Please don't let him get away with that."

"We care as much as you do, Maeve," Haddon said, placing her hand delicately on my shoulder. I somehow doubted that they did, but didn't say anything. "Thank you for answering our questions. We'll let you know if we have any more."

They went to the door and as they were walking down the pathway to their car I called out, "Wait. Can I ask you something?"

Haddon turned to me. "Of course."

"How did Ky get a gun? Nobody told me, and I couldn't find anything in the papers."

"No, we haven't said much to the media. It's been nothing short of miraculous how we've kept it under wraps." She looked past me, out at the forest that sat across my street. After a long moment, she said, "The gun belonged to Alice. She told us she had always been a little afraid of Jared herself."

She blinked at me and didn't smile, then went to the car and climbed in beside Gervais.

I tried to remember how to breathe.

TWENTY-ONE

THERE WAS A PIECE OF paper taped carelessly on Gray's front
door.

JUST COME IN, it read in messy writing. I could hear music
pounding through the walls, even as I stood outside. I turned to
wave at Sol who had driven me, but he had already left. He was
going to his own party, apparently. And I wasn't supposed to
worry if he wasn't home until tomorrow. I didn't want to think
about what that might mean. I also didn't want to think about
the absurdity of our lives. For a brief moment, I wished Sage was
back home, still together with Sol, and at least then I could
pretend to have two semi-functioning parents. I blinked. This
was not the time to think about it.

I opened the door and stepped into Gray's house, the music
suddenly growing louder. It had a thumping bass that matched
the thump of my beating heart. I cringed. There was a pile of
shoes in the entryway, so I carefully slipped off my boots and
placed them among the rest. I shrugged off my winter jacket and
laid it on top of the accumulation of coats, which were piled
haphazardly on the stairs.

Gray's house was not large by any means, but I did not know
if I should walk further into the house or wait where I was until

someone happened to find me. Without meaning to, it ended up being the latter.

A girl carrying a paper cup rounded the corner. She wore circular glasses and was small—at least a head smaller than me. I felt large standing next to her. The girl had short brown hair that cut jagged beneath her chin and earlobes. Her eyes were dark. I kept thinking that if she wasn't so mean looking, she might be pretty. Maybe mean wasn't the right adjective to describe her— more like scary. Intimidating and terrifying. Her shoulders sat squared and I immediately knew she was confident.

"You must be Maeve."

Her voice was lower than I thought it would be; her tone almost accusatory. I could feel my spine lock up.

"We've heard a lot about you."

I didn't know who the *we* she was referring to might be.

"Good things, I hope," I joked lightly.

The girl shrugged. "Honest things, anyway."

I blinked. "Sorry—what's your name?"

"Missy. I'm one of Gray's oldest friends."

"Right. Of course. I've heard a lot of… honest things about you, too," I lied. She laughed as if she knew I wasn't telling the truth. The bones began to simmer beneath my skin.

"What do you do?" she asked me. She was chewing a piece of gum, punishing it loud between her teeth.

"I write."

"Like books?"

"Yes, well… someday. Poetry for now, and some articles. They get published in newspapers, and other places." My, how grand I was at stretching the truth, especially when it came to someone I wanted to thoroughly impress. *Be jealous of me!* My brain cells were screaming.

Missy nodded. "That's cool, I guess."

"What about you?"

"I'm a part-time bartender, and I'm in my final year of

college for urban planning."

I didn't know what urban planning was, but I wasn't about to ask. It sounded useless, dumb, and quite pretentious to me. I was relieved when Gray came into the room. A grin flew across his face when he saw me. "Maeve! You came!"

"That's right."

He reached for my hand and I gave it to him, happily. "Did you offer to get her a drink, Missy?"

"No." Missy snapped her gum again. "She has two perfectly good legs and so do you." She spun on her heel and stalked down the hallway.

"I see you've met Missy." He took his other hand and traced my jawline, cocooning me.

I giggled. "Yes, I did. She's..."

"Crazy?"

"I was going to say terrifying."

"That, too."

"She said you've been friends for a long time."

Gray nodded. "We grew up together. Our moms were practically sisters. Missy's not known for her sparkling personality."

I laughed. "That's surprising."

He squeezed my fingers. "Let's get you a drink." He took me down the hall to the kitchen and I could hear people laughing in the next room. Groups of people were in the kitchen, all drinking, some from bottles, some from the same paper cups Missy had.

Gray lifted our joined hands when we entered. "Maeve Parker, everybody!" I blushed but smiled, and a few people hooted, and a few others waved. There were more people present than I thought. Missy must have been in the next room. Not that I cared.

"No Levi?" Grayson asked as he poured me a drink.

"No Levi," I replied. "Not his sort of thing, I guess."

"I won't complain."

"Sure you won't. Probably makes you happy."

Gray smiled.

"You hide it so well," I teased.

"How's he ringing in this exciting New Year?"

I shrugged. "I don't know—I never asked. I haven't talked to him in a little while. It's been a rough couple of days."

"What do you mean?"

"The police came by my house today. They were asking me about Ky."

"Ky?"

"My best friend. Remember? The one who killed herself?"

"Right. Sorry. Are you in trouble?"

I shook my head and took a sip of my drink. It was gross. "No. They just had a few questions. They're launching an investigation, I think. Finally," I sighed. "I should probably talk to Levi. The police were going to go visit him after they left my house. I should call him and find out what they wanted."

"Right now?"

"Yeah." I felt a sudden unquenchable need to talk to him and find out what Haddon and Gervais had to say. "Keep my drink safe for me?"

Gray nodded and I passed my cup. "Try not to be too long… I wanted to spend tonight with you."

Heat deepened within my cheeks. "Of course. I'll be back in less than a minute."

I piled my boots and coat back on and stepped out to Gray's sagging front porch. I dialed Levi's number. "Please pick up," I whispered beneath my chilled breath.

"The cops were here," he answered in lieu of hello.

"For how long?"

"Like a half hour."

"Me too."

"What did you tell them?"

"Nothing they didn't already know. I gave them the letter."

"What did they say?"

"Nothing. What did they ask you?"

"Just where I was on the 15, if I had a hunch Ky was going to do it... stuff like that."

I sighed. "Yeah, me too. They better get Jared, Levi. They better freaking get him. They don't even know where he is!"

"I know they don't," he breathed.

"They better find him."

"They will."

"How do you know that?"

"I don't, but... maybe if we say it, it'll be more likely to happen."

"Jared's stupid," I reasoned. "They have to be smarter than him."

"I'm sure they are."

"Although I did not like that officer man. The lady was nice. The man was rude."

"He was nice to me."

"He's probably a misogynist."

"Yes," Levi said dryly, "I'm sure that's the answer."

"Everyone's nice to you."

"Not Gray."

"It's not like he was *mean* to you. And you definitely weren't all peachy to him."

"Are you with him now?"

"I'm at his house. I'm not standing next to him if that's what you're asking."

"I figured you'd go."

"I told you I was going. What are you doing tonight?"

"I'm about to head out to Carl's. Most of our class is going to his place."

"Why would you go there?"

"Because I was invited."

"You were invited here. Won't Amanda Wright and her crew be there?"

"Probably," he said, "but so will lots of other people. I could come pick you up if you wanted."

"No. You could not pay me enough to spend the last day of the year with Amanda Wright. Or any day of the year, actually."

Levi laughed. "You wouldn't have to, like, *sit* beside her. There will be other people there, too. You might be able to get by the entire night without seeing one another."

"Thanks but no thanks. I hope you have an absolute ball."

"The sincerity in your tone is touching."

I smirked. "You'll have to call me tomorrow and tell me all about it."

"Yeah, yeah, you too. I want to hear all the gory details."

"There will be gore," I said, laughing.

"I'm sure." His voice quieted some. "Happy New Year, Maeve."

"You're not supposed to say that until tomorrow."

"Whatever."

"There you go, being all rebellious again. You're a bad influence on me, Levi Fisher."

"My goal in life!"

"You've succeeded."

"Thank you."

"Happy New Year, Levi."

I THINK IT WAS GRAY'S friend Pete who began the countdown when it was ten seconds away from midnight. "Ten! Nine! Eight!" he began, and more voices filled in, chanting along with him. "Seven!"

Gray's hand wrapped closer around my waist, pulling me tight against him. I looked up and smiled.

Six!

I felt dazzling.

Five!

As if my lips were rubies and I was a pearl: sparkling, shimmering, like a diamond cut against the sun.

Four!

I watched him watching me, the way his eyes didn't look at anything else in the room, just me, just his gleaming eyes watching my dazzling face.

Three!

He cupped his hand around my chin, and I pressed my own hands against his chest.

Two!

He kissed me.

One!

I kissed him back.

Welcome to the New Year, I thought when one of us finally peeled away. I wasn't sure who.

There was a flurry around us, soft and blurry with action— people kissing, people clinking, laughter ringing throughout the house, echoing along the rafters like a memory. Like what last year had suddenly become: a flitting memory.

"Come with me," I told him.

He tried to kiss me again but I shook my head and repeated myself. "Come with me." I rolled off his lap and yanked his hand to try and get him to follow.

We wove our way through the people refilling drinks and telling tales and cheers'ing *Happy New Year*. I put on my coat and boots. He looked at me for a moment, then put his on too. I opened the door and he trailed behind me.

"Do you have your keys?" I asked.

He nodded.

"Good. Give them to me."

He did, and I got into the driver's seat of his truck. He was too drunk to drive, or at least I thought so, and I wasn't, or at least I thought so. I had driven Sol's car a few times to know what to do, so I felt semi-confident. Gray didn't ask me where we were going; instead watched me with a wiry, glittering smile, his hand never leaving the spot above my knee.

I pulled in front of my house.

"Sol's not home," I said as I shut off the ignition and turned to him, my sweaty fingers clutching the keys. I stared at the form of his body, his broad frame filling the side of the truck. He kept me safe, didn't he? I touched his hand still resting on my knee, and took a deep breath. "Sol won't be home till morning."

I hopped out of the car, not waiting for him to follow behind me.

But he did. I knew he would.

I WOKE EARLY THE NEXT morning.

January, I thought.

The sheets were crumpled around us, and a light breeze blew through the open window. It made me cold and I wrapped the quilt tight around my body. I wanted to feel content, but instead, I only felt empty. I looked at Gray lying beside me; watched his bare chest move up and down, slowly, steadily, the beat of a drum, the rhythm of a metronome. He looked serene lying there. He seemed young and naive as if the world had yet to engrave its scars upon him.

How different a person seems when they're asleep.

Gray had been kind to me, and yet I couldn't help but think of Levi. I wondered if he was still sleeping. I daydreamed that it was him asleep beside me, instead of Gray.

I would tenderly push back the hair that had swept across his forehead during the night. I would quietly slip away and bring back two hot mugs of coffee: black for him, cream and sugar for me. I would sit with him in bed, talking, and we would stay there for the entire day, refusing to leave until dusk broke out across the city when we would go and pick up Ky, the three of us driving into the night with only the stars as our companions. I pictured us driving down the endless roads, leaving the town, the country, the world. We could keep driving, away from the Jared's and the Grayson's and the Sage's, and we could go to Iceland and to the ocean, hundreds of different oceans, no turning back... no turning back.

I smiled.

Gray stirred and I stopped smiling.

Because it wasn't Levi beside me.

Because we wouldn't go out that night and pick up Ky.

Because we'd never pick up Ky again.

Gray's eyes slowly opened and he blinked. He reached for me, pulling me close to him. He grazed his lips hard against mine.

"Morning," he said.

"Hi."

"How are you?"

I looked at him. How can a single night alter the course of one's entire existence?

"I'm fine. I'm good."

"Me too," he said. "The best."

We were quiet for a long time. It was awkward. I kept reminding myself at least he stayed the night, at least I could make him breakfast, at least he wasn't like Jared. I realized I didn't want to make him breakfast and I tugged the quilt tighter around me.

Gray pulled me toward him after a while. He kissed my forehead. My nose. My lips. I waited to see if the emptiness would fill. It didn't.

"You're a good girl, Maeve. A nice girl."

"Are you saying that because I slept with you?"

He laughed, but I hadn't intended it as a joke. "No, that's not why I'm saying it."

"You should go," I heard myself telling him.

He blinked. "Why?"

I got out of the bed and wrapped some clothes on my body. "I think you should go. You need to check on the state of your house or something. Who knows if it's still standing."

Gray climbed out, too. He came to me and kissed my cheek. "We should do this again sometime."

I choked back a scream. "Yeah, maybe."

He got changed, and after what felt like years, left me.

I went to the bathroom mirror to stare at my reflection. An old woman appeared in front of me. I was reminded of Alice: sunken skin, eyes rimmed in a bluish tint, brittle bones, innocence forgotten.

That's when I started to cry.

I missed Ky. I missed her so deep I could hardly breathe. I needed to fill myself up to remove the sadness, but nothing was working. My insides were suffocating me. I went to the shower. I didn't take off my clothes. I simply got in and allowed the water to pound down through the layers onto my skin. To try and erase the memory of what happened the night before, of what happened my entire life.

TWENTY-TWO

"So HOW WAS YOUR NEW Year's?" asked Levi. True to his word, he had called me.

"Good," I nodded. "Yeah, really good. You missed out."

"I'm glad Gray was as entertaining as you'd hoped."

"Definitely." I swallowed. "How about you? What was yours like?"

"Great!" he breezed. "Pretty much everyone in our grade went. A few people asked me where you were."

"What'd you say?"

"That you were at another friend's."

"I don't know why they'd ask you that—it's not like they care if I'm there or not."

"Not true. A bunch of people said they wished you had come."

I laughed sharply. "Right."

"It was really cool," Levi continued, ignoring my tone. "At one point someone—I can't remember who—brought up Ky and we all talked about her and shared memories and stuff. I wish you had been there for that. It was sweet. It felt like we were really honoring her, you know?"

"Why would they do that?"

"What do you mean? They wanted to talk about her."

"They hardly knew her!"

"The school's not that big, Maeve. They knew her."

"But hardly."

"Maybe we make a bigger mark in this world than we realize."

"Thank you for that, O Philosophical One. I'm not in the mood for this."

"Are you all right?"

"Fine."

"Did something happen?"

"No," I heaved. "Aren't I allowed to be grumpy?"

"On the first day of January? Seems like a crappy way to start the year off."

"Well, maybe this will be a crappy year."

"I hope not," he said seriously. "Last year was bad enough."

I sighed. "I know. This year will be better. Even a crappy year would be better than what last year was."

"That's true."

"I wonder what this year will feel like. At least... at least last year was a year she was with us, standing beside us. This year we won't have that. We'll never be with her again."

Levi was quiet for a moment. "Maybe this could be the year we look for Sage."

I sighed. "Part of me wants to find her, like, today. The larger part of me never wants to see her again."

"Maybe we won't have to look for her. Maybe she'll come and find you."

"I doubt that will happen."

"Me too," Levi agreed. "But you never know. Hey, it's still pretty cold out. I'll pick you up for school tomorrow so you don't have to walk."

GRAY CAME OVER LATER THAT NIGHT. Sol and I were watching television together when he knocked on the door.

"Come on in!" Sol hollered, both of us too lazy and relaxed to get up.

"Gray," I said when I saw it was him opening the door. "Hi. Are you okay?"

"Of course I am." He came over and kissed me—with Sol sitting right there. I looked at Sol. He stared back at me. He excused himself to his room.

Once Sol was gone, Gray started laughing.

"That was awkward," I said.

"He needed to know."

"Know what?"

"How I feel about you."

Right. That.

I turned the volume on the television up and we watched a show for awhile. Sol appeared from his room around an hour later and announced he was going out.

"Where are you going?" I asked. "You look nice."

He scratched the back of his neck, his face blooming with color. "Out to dinner." A moment later, "I have... a date."

"With who?" I shrieked.

"Her name is Lucy. I met her a few nights ago at my work party. She's a nice lady. Kind of short, but nice."

"Wow." I was impressed. "Not holding out for Sage any longer?"

"I don't know." He looked sad. "I'll try this out with Lucy tonight and see, I guess."

I nodded. "That's great, Sol. I'm happy for you. Really, I am."

Sol came over and kissed my head gently, softer than the whisper of a breeze, and more tentative, too. "Thanks, Maeve," he said into my hair. "I don't know what time I'll be home. You both... uh, have fun."

"You too! Open the door for her—and make her laugh but don't be too corny." I turned to Gray. "What else should he do?"

Gray shrugged. "Seems like you know more than me."

I laughed and looked back at Sol. "Just be your charming self. And pay for dinner. Or at least offer to pay."

"Okay." He pulled the collar of his shirt out from his neck.

"Are you nervous?"

He nodded and I laughed again.

"She's a person, not a monster. You'll be fine." I reassured.

"I haven't been on a date in a long time."

"You'll do great."

"Okay," he put his coat on. "I'll see you later."

"Good luck, Sol!"

"Thanks…" he muttered as he went out the front.

Gray turned to me when the door shut. "So. We have the house all to ourselves tonight."

"Sure seems that way, doesn't it?"

"It seems so." He smiled and began leaning in close to me.

I interrupted. "Does Missy hate me?"

Gray sat back. "Why would you ask that? She doesn't know you."

"It feels like she hates me."

"Don't take it personally. Like I said before, she's moody."

"Is that how you would describe me?"

"What?"

"To other people. Is that how you describe me? As moody?"

He frowned at me. "Maybe at this moment, yes. But no, I've never said that about you before."

"Tell me, then. If you were to tell someone what you thought of me, what would you say?"

"I would say…" He stared at me for what felt like a long time then brought me closer to him, his fingers draped loosely around my waist. "I would say…" He began to undo my shirt, slowly, one button at a time. "I would say…" He kissed my collarbone.

"You're beautiful," he whispered.

I wanted to be beautiful, but I wanted to be smart, too. And creative and witty and driven. I wanted to be so many impossible things.

"Am I?"

Gray delicately slid his hands through my hair, as if I might break had he pressed his fingers in harder.

"Yes," he traced my eyes with his index finger. "I would say this is beautiful," he traced my nose, "and this is beautiful," he traced my lips, "and this is beautiful…" He ran his finger down my flesh whispering *and I would say this is beautiful* and *this is beautiful* and *this is beautiful* and…

He grabbed my hand to take me up the stairs to my bedroom. I didn't know if I wanted to go with him, but he did, he desperately wanted me to—I could tell by the way he looked at me, and no one had looked at me that way before.

He saw my hesitation and pulled me in closer. "It's okay," he whispered. "You're safe with me."

I nodded and climbed the stairs beside him.

"You deserve everything, Maeve, and—I want to be that everything for you." His voice was soft, soothing.

As he kissed me I wondered: can someone be everything for you? Can one singular person really be enough to fill you up and make you whole?

He didn't want me to be empty anymore. I knew that. I didn't want to be empty, either.

I knew that as we laid there, the red numbers on the clock on my bedside table shifting from 11:59 to 12:00, beginning the start of a fresh, new day. I knew that—after he was finished kissing me, after he had whispered goodnight, after he had rolled over and drifted away. I knew that he wanted to fill me, and when I turned my body to watch him sleep, I knew that he never could.

A FEW WEEKS LATER, IN the middle of the school day, I was

called to go visit the office.

My psychology teacher let me go. It was the second semester, so I didn't have Herman or Miss Meyers anymore. I grabbed my stuff and walked down the stairs. Mrs. Greene, I presumed, was waiting for me.

"Hi!" she said enthusiastically. "I'm Merry Greene, one of the school's counselors. Are you Maeve Parker?"

"Yeah. Am I in trouble?"

She laughed breezily. "No, honey, not at all! Here, come into my office. I want to chat with you." She motioned to some plush red chairs so I set my backpack down and sank into one of them. She shut the door and sat down on the other.

"So," she folded her hands casually in her lap. "I wondered if you wanted to talk about Ky McNeil."

"Not particularly."

"I can't begin to understand how hard this is for you. I wish we could've talked sooner, but Miss Meyers felt you needed more time." Mrs. Greene was wearing a lot of makeup. Deep blue eyeliner had been drawn out against her stretched eyelids. I kept watching her blink and wondered how sticky her eyelashes would feel if she gave someone a butterfly kiss.

"Are you going to call down Levi Fisher?"

She blinked again. Definitely sticky. "Levi Fisher?"

"Yeah. He was good friends with Ky, too. If I have to go through therapy, I think he should have to as well. It's only fair."

"Oh honey, this isn't a punishment. This is so you can heal."

"I've healed."

Her immaculately penciled eyebrow arched high on her forehead.

"If I have to do this, I think he should too." I slouched deeper in my chair.

"Okay," she pursed her lips. "I'll keep that in mind. I'll at least write down his name." She scrawled it on a pad of paper. "But his would be separate, and most likely with a male counselor."

"Fine."

Mrs. Greene hesitated. "You know, I can't force you to talk to me. I can only strongly advise and encourage it. Do you want to be here, Maeve?"

"In therapy? No."

"Do you feel like you need to be here?"

I thought of my imaginary confession from Christmas Eve. "I don't know," I muttered.

She must've taken that as an affirmative because she said, "Talking about our grief is nothing to be ashamed of. Why don't we start with something simple? How do you feel about the absence of Ky?"

"That's starting with something simple?"

She said quietly, "I don't know if any of this would be classified as simple."

"No... probably not." I looked down at my lap. "Some days I'm jealous of her. She doesn't have to feel anything. No pain, no confusion. She doesn't have to make any hard decisions. I picture her blissful, and that makes me jealous. I want that sort of bliss. I don't want to have to feel anymore. I'm tired of feeling. It's exhausting."

Her eyebrows were knit together. "Have you been having thoughts of suicide, Maeve?"

"No. It's not like that. I wish I didn't feel things; I don't wish I were dead."

"There's a difference." A statement, not a question.

"I think so. Don't you?"

She nodded. Not in agreement, but as if she were processing the information I had flung at her.

"Have you been having trouble sleeping?"

I shook my head. "Not especially. A few bad dreams here and there, but nothing too awful."

"What were the nightmares of? Can you remember?"

"Um… the one was of Ky and I. We were at the beach, at an ocean. I don't know which one—I've never been to the ocean before. We were swimming, or I was. I was swimming underwater and when I resurfaced I was a long way from Ky. She was at the shoreline, and I was fairly far out in the ocean. I watched her take a few steps into the water, and then I saw her pull out a gun. I started singing to her, some song my mom taught me. I guess I thought it might make her stop. I could see her watching me. It was really vivid like it was actually happening. It seemed like she wasn't going to do it, but she did. She shot herself. I looked down and realized I was swimming in her blood. Then I woke up."

"Horrifying," Mrs. Greene murmured.

"Yeah."

"Are you angry with Ky?"

I sighed. "I think I used to be. I don't know if I am anymore. I think I understand why she did it, which helps. Now I just feel… sad."

"What does the sadness feel like?"

"I think it's emptying me."

She tilted her head.

"Like… whatever fills you up, whatever makes you feel full… I don't have that anymore. The sadness feels like it's eating away at my wholeness. I'll be empty soon."

"Did you begin to feel this way after Ky died?"

"You mean after she took the gun and killed herself? She didn't die, Mrs. Greene. She made a decision."

"Do you think still you might be a little angry?"

"It depends on the day. I have mood swings."

"Don't we all," she said with a light laugh.

"The emptying process didn't start with Ky's death," I realized. "It started long before then. The year I was seven. On March 13."

"What happened that day, Maeve?"

I put my head in my hands and groaned. "Am I going to have to tell you my entire life story?"

She laughed again, and the sound was pretty. "Maybe. But probably not. How about you start from the beginning?"

"Okay." I took a deep breath. "I'll start from there."

TWENTY-THREE

I WAS SURPRISED TO SEE it was Missy who opened the door when I went to Gray's house one day after school, a few weeks later.

"Oh," I said when I saw her. "What are you doing here?"

She smiled sadistically. "Hello to you, too."

"Where's Gray?"

"At the gym or something."

"Why are you at his house?"

She thrust her tiny hip against the doorjamb, crossing her arms. She couldn't possibly have an ounce of fat on her body. "Pete's here, too. We come over all the time."

"Right."

She laughed. "You can come in and wait for him if you want."

The idea of being stuck with Missy for an unprecedented amount of time seemed like another circle of hell if you asked me. But she was already walking back inside, and even though it wasn't freezing it wasn't really warm either, and I had hoped to talk to Gray.

I sighed, then followed behind her and closed the front door.

"Pete," Missy called. "Gray's little girlfriend is here. I invited her inside. Be nice."

Pete was playing video games on the television, and gave a grunt—I was pretty sure in my direction.

"Hi, Pete," I said.

Missy flopped on the couch beside him, and I sat on a sagging—what I believe to have once been yellow—chair.

"Is something wrong, Maeve?" Missy inquired, leaning her elbow on her knee to stretch closer to me. Pete erupted into a shout, cursing the game he was playing. I jumped, startled.

Missy shook her head. "Don't be freaked," she said. "He does this all the time. You'll learn to ignore it. So, is anything wrong? What are you doing here?"

"I wanted to see Gray. To talk to him."

"About what?"

I narrowed my eyes. "Is it necessary for you to know? It's not exactly your business."

She sat there, waiting, her expression bored yet unreadable.

"I know there's something up," she finally said. "I can see it all over your face."

"Right."

She laughed. "If you don't tell me, I'll have to start guessing."

I sighed, annoyed with her, annoyed with the world. "Or you could leave it alone."

"That's not going to happen."

She disappeared for a moment returning with a purple and white box.

"Here."

"What is it?"

"What do you think?" She rolled her eyes. "A pregnancy test. Obviously."

"I'm not pregnant."

She didn't look convinced.

"What?"

"You better tell Gray—"

"There's nothing to tell—"

"—unless," she cocked her head, "it's not his baby."

"You think I'm out sleeping with other guys?"

She smirked. "So you do think you're pregnant."

Disgusted, I looked at her. "Who do you think I am, Missy? You?" I sighed, frustrated. "This is ridiculous. This is none of your business, and I am not pregnant. That's impossible."

"Are you a virgin?"

I flushed. "No."

"Are you unable to bear children?"

I pictured Francine. "No, I don't think so."

She nodded slowly, her eyebrow snaking high on her face. "Then it is possible, isn't it, little girl? It's very possible, in fact."

"But," I lowered my voice, "we've always been very... careful."

Missy cackled. "Oh sweetie, you can be as careful as you want. It doesn't mean he won't knock you up."

I looked at the box in my hands. "You... have one of these? Lying around handy? At Gray's house?"

She shrugged again. "You never know when you might need it."

I felt stupid, but I asked the question anyway. "Have you needed one before?"

She started to apply some lip balm, and she smacked her lips as she nodded.

"Were, um, were any of them positive?"

"Yes."

"What did you do?"

Pete cursed loudly again and I felt myself jump. Missy gestured her arms wide around the room. "Maeve, darling, does it look like I have a child?"

I shook my head. "Did you give it up for adoption?"

"No." She handed me the test and patted my hand. "How young and naive you are. Just a baby yourself." She looked at me, almost nostalgically as if I was reminding her of someone. Maybe of herself. "No, I didn't give them up for adoption, Maeve. I aborted them. Both of them."

"I'm sorry," I said after a while.

She laughed. "It's not your fault. They weren't babies at that point anyway. They were apparently smaller than the size of a blueberry. Hardly a child. Besides, I'm not ready to be a mother."

I nodded.

"Go. Take the test. If it comes out positive, remember: you always, always have options."

"Do you regret it?"

Her eyes looked sharp. "I regret sleeping with them." She laughed, but it was hollow. "It's funny, isn't it? It takes two people to have sex, and yet when the girl gets knocked up and fat, suddenly it's her fault. As if I would purposely plant a kid inside of my uterus."

"Were they mad at you?"

"Mad?" She mulled that over for a second. "More like appalled. Or horrified. One was confused and asked how that could happen. Let me tell you something, Maeve. If you're pregnant and you keep the baby, your life will be ruined. Gray won't stay."

"Maybe he's different than the guys you were with—"

"No," she snapped, "he's not. They're all the same. He will leave, I can promise you. You'll be stuck with a child. You'll be a single mom. And you'll have no more prospects—not for a career, not for anything."

She was quiet for a moment, and I was, too.

"I can't say it's not painful," she said softly, reminiscent. "I mean, I was called a murderer by the group of people standing outside, both times I left that clinic. And I wonder sometimes, you know, what they would have been like. If they would have looked like me. What I would have named them." Her eyes flared up at me. "But if you keep it, you won't have a chance at a future. It's hard enough to picture the future as is, let alone with a baby strapped to your hip."

I looked at the purple and white box. I didn't want it. I wasn't pregnant. I couldn't be. No matter what Missy thought, the mere idea was ludicrous.

"Go," Missy prodded.

I thought of Francine as I carried the box into the bathroom. I thought of Francine as I ripped the contents open and took the test. I thought of Francine as I waited. I thought of Francine as I watched the two pink lines form, the two pink lines that were forever burned into my memory, the two pink lines that signified how life would never be the same. I thought of Francine as I realized she had spent years trying to get pregnant and never could, and how I hadn't tried at all, hadn't wanted it even for a remote second.

And yet, here I was, with the only thing Francine had wanted and with everything I couldn't bear to have.

WHEN I EMERGED FROM THE bathroom, once I'd dried my tears and soaked my face to ward off the oncoming puffiness, Gray had arrived home.

Missy looked at me when I came back into the room. I couldn't meet her eyes.

I plastered on a grin as Gray turned to hug me.

"Maeve! I didn't know you were coming."

"I wanted to surprise you," I said, hoping the tears in my throat were hidden. I couldn't tell if they were. They felt as if they were going to erupt from me at any moment.

"It's a good surprise," he kissed me.

"I actually have to go," I told him.

"This soon? You just got here."

"I wanted to come say hi. I'll see you tomorrow though,

okay?"

He grazed my cheek. "Okay. Are you all right to get home?"

"Yeah, yeah," I said, waving my hand nonchalantly.

"Great. I'm gonna go hit the shower. I was at the gym and I reek."

"I was going to say something about the awful smell…"

He laughed.

"I'll walk you to the door, Maeve," Missy offered.

"Okay. Thanks, Missy."

Gray beamed at me from the stairs, and I was certain he was thinking Missy and I would soon become best friends. Maybe he'd buy us matching friendship bracelets. I tried to smile back.

"It was positive?" Missy asked when were safely outside.

"Yes." Tears filled my eyes and I pinched the bridge of my nose. "What am I supposed to do?"

She patted my arm. "You have options. Go home and think about it. You're early. You have some time. Remember what I said."

"Don't tell Gray. Please."

"I won't. It's your news, not mine."

I stared at her. "I'm glad you changed your mind."

"About what?"

"Hating me."

She laughed. "I don't hate you. You're just young, Maeve… so young."

Her voice drifted like she had no more words to say. I began to walk down the street.

Just young Maeve… so young.

I called Levi before the tears in my chest blew up within me.

"It's Maeve," I said when he answered. "I need you to come pick me up. Now. Please," I added.

He asked me where I was and I told him, and he said he'd be there in ten minutes. I wanted to sit down on the grass because I had grown tired. The snow had melted some, the temperatures crawling a bit warmer, and the grass was flattened from the heavy weight of the snow. It looked dead, void of any color.

I looked down at my coat. I was looking at my stomach. I wanted to touch it, but I was afraid. Would it feel different the way it was suddenly bursting with life? But it wasn't bursting anything yet, nothing except a deep and dreary sadness that felt stronger with every heartbeat. Or, two heartbeats, I supposed.

I heard a car pull up to the side of the road, and Levi looked at me through the window. I opened the passenger door and slid into the seat.

"Thank you," I said.

"Are you okay?" The tears escaped then because no, I wasn't okay, nothing was okay, the world might never be okay again.

"No," I said after a long time, after we'd driven for a while. "Can we go see Ky?"

He nodded.

When we arrived, I immediately went to her grave, the tears streaming freely. I could hear Levi lock the car and follow behind me.

"I'm pregnant," I said without warning. I was explaining it to Ky, but it was Levi who heard me.

"What?" he asked, incredulous.

I ignored him. I stared at Ky's headstone that had been placed there a few weeks prior. I leaned in and traced my fingers against the engraved words, *beloved daughter, sister, and friend.* "That's right," I told her. "You heard me. Bet you didn't see that one coming, huh?"

I could hear Levi saying something but I couldn't decipher what it was, and I didn't care to try.

"I didn't see it coming either." I pretended Ky was laughing. "Go ahead, laugh. But it's not that funny."

"No, it's not funny at all, Maeve—"

I spun around and glared at him. "I was talking to Ky. Not you."

He placed his hands firmly on both sides of my shoulders. "Maeve," he said strongly, his voice slushy and thick, "she's not here."

I tried to shrug out of his grasp, but he was too strong. "I know."

"She can't hear you."

"I know!" I was crying. "But I need her!" I succumbed to his grip, my head falling against his shoulder. "I need her."

Levi held me for a long time. I wiped my tears and looked up at him.

"I'm pregnant."

"How?"

I tilted my head.

"No, I know how. Who? Did someone take advantage of you?"

"No." I drew a small breath. "You're going to be so angry."

He shook his head.

"Gray."

He didn't say anything; just blinked a few times as if he were sorting the news out in his head. "Are you going to keep it?"

"I don't know! I found out about it like ten minutes ago! I haven't told Gray yet. I don't know what to do, Levi."

"We should tell my mom."

"What? No."

"She's a good person to talk to when things like this happen!"

"Really? Things like this? Because they happen every day, don't they, Levi? I'm sure you get a lot of knocked up girls strolling through your front door!"

"Don't talk like that. Please. Don't call yourself that."

I shrugged. "Why not? It's what I am."

His blue eyes were cloudy. *I make him cloudy*, I thought. *I take away his transparency and leave him all murky inside.*

"Missy thinks I should have an abortion," I said after a few minutes.

"Who is Missy?"

"Gray's friend."

"And you trust her?"

"She's more… experienced than I am."

Levi whipped around and kicked the trunk of a tree. He swore under his breath.

"What's your problem?" I yelled.

"I can't believe this is happening!"

"How do you think *I* feel?"

"I know you're sad, Maeve, and I am too, but this," he gestured wildly, "is not the answer!"

"Are you kidding me, Levi? Do you think I was trying to get pregnant?"

"Why were you sleeping with him in the first place?"

"Because he loves me!" I yelled at him. I took a breath and quieted my voice. "I think he actually loves me."

Levi shook his head, disgusted. "He doesn't love you, Maeve."

"You can't say that. You don't know him!"

"I know exactly the type of person he is."

"Stop it!" I was crying again. "Stop being judgmental, and acting like… like you're better than he is. He's a good person. And he loves me! What's so wrong with that? Why don't you want me to be happy?"

"All I want is for you to be happy, Maeve!" Levi yelled.

We were quiet for a few moments.

"Well, what if he's my happiness?" I asked.

"Do you love him?"

I sniffed. "I… I don't know. I think so."

"I guess you should figure that out before you have his baby," Levi said, his voice dripping.

"How dare you. You can't be mad at me."

"Why not?"

"Because I'm feeling very alone right now and I need you."

"Isn't that convenient."

"What are you talking about?"

He sighed. "Most of the time you act like you don't need anyone. You push people away, push me away, but then you'll call me and I'll come. The cycle repeats and you'll push me away again. I don't think I can handle it if you keep doing this. You have to make up your mind. Do you want me or not?"

"I'll stop," I promised. "I won't push you away anymore."

"I've heard that before. Many times."

"I know. I'm sorry, Levi, I am. I'm so sorry."

"Me too." He sighed again—deeper this time. "Me too."

"Sage had me," I said abruptly. "She was seventeen. She didn't have an abortion, and she could have, you know, she could have. But she didn't. Instead, she chose me."

"So you're going to keep it?" he asked me gently.

I looked up at him, tears pooling in my eyes. "I don't know what else to do."

TWENTY-FOUR

GRAY STARED AT ME.

It was a week later. I'd avoided it, somehow, but it finally had come time to confess.

"Say something," I begged. "Please."

He ran his fingers through his hair, starting to pace back and forth across the bedroom. I steadied myself on my bed, watching him.

He checked his phone. "If we leave right away, I bet we can have this done and over with in the next few hours."

"Done and over with?" I repeated. I stood, my overprotective hand finding its way to my belly. According to Levi, who had done thorough research, the baby was the size of a flax seed. Even still, my entire perspective on my body had changed.

"Come on, I'll drive you to a clinic."

"A clinic?" My voice was high and hysterical. My fingers grappled at my stomach.

He froze. "You're not... you're not actually thinking about *keeping* it... are you?" He looked as though he had tasted something vile.

I tried to swallow a breath and sat back down. "I don't know if I want to… if I want to do that." I couldn't say the word.

Gray came and placed his hands gently on both sides of my arms. "Maeve, it's normal. Lots of girls have abortions. You're sixteen—"

"I'm almost seventeen—"

"—and I'm hardly making enough money to support myself. We're not ready for this."

He took my hand, pulling me to my feet. "Let's go. I'll take you to the clinic. You won't have to do this on your own—I'll be with you the entire time. It's going to be okay, Maeve. Everything will turn out fine. You'll see."

My head was swimming and I felt like I was drowning, deep and quick and panicky, as if Gray was the one keeping me held firm beneath the waves. "No. Wait. I can't. I'm not doing that. I don't know if I want to do that."

He dropped my hand and said, "I'm not staying with you if you keep it." It was fast, the threat he made.

I blinked and tried to focus. "What?" So Missy was proven right after all.

"I'm not staying with you if you keep that." He restated, but I hadn't actually wanted to hear it again.

"But—but I've been making a plan!"

"A plan?"

"Your house has two rooms," my voice was shaky. "I don't have a lot of money, but I'm making some at the newspaper and—"

"You want to move in? That's your grand plan?"

I nodded. "I'm not saying we need to get married or anything like that. But we could make this work… the three of us. I can quit school. I can get another job." He didn't say anything so I added quickly, "Did you know Francine can't have babies?"

Gray stared at me. "Who's Francine?"

"My landlord."

"Okay… and you're telling me this because…?"

"You want me to… get rid of this baby, when a woman down the street is unable to have one?"

"Why are you bringing her into this? She has nothing to do with us."

I shook my head. "It's not right, Gray. This doesn't feel right."

He rolled his eyes. "Does goodbye feel right, Maeve? Because that's what you're asking for."

I sat down on the bed again, trying to make my head stop hurting. "Can you give me a week to think about it? I need some time."

"I'll give you three days."

My shoulders fell. "This isn't an easy decision, Gray."

"It didn't take me long to decide."

"This is a baby. A real baby. A human. Our child." I whispered the last two words almost inaudibly.

He simply looked at me.

I splayed my fingers across my stomach, imagining the tiny person being formed at that moment deep inside of me. "We made it. It has pieces of you and pieces of me." A small smile played on my lips. "It's a miracle, in a way."

"It's not a miracle," he snapped. "It's a mistake. If you keep it, our lives will be ruined. You'll drop out of school and won't be able to go to college."

"Am I a mistake?" I asked softly.

"No, Maeve." He sighed, tipping his head back. "You're being selfish. You never asked me what I thought about this."

"I think it's been made fairly clear what you think."

He sat down next to me on the bed. "Maeve. Even if I thought this was a good idea, we couldn't afford it. I could not afford you moving in with me."

"I could help! I'll work!"

"Not enough. Do you love this thing more than you love me?"

It felt like he had hit me. "It's not a thing. It's a baby—our baby."

He whispered his fingers against my cheek, twirling a wisp of hair around his finger. "Do you love me?"

"Yes." I leaned into him. "I do. Of course, I do."

"Because I love you, Maeve. Since the day I first walked into Sol's house, I've loved you. Think about me for a second, will you? This would ruin my life."

I was quiet for a moment. "You know my mom was going to abort me."

He didn't say anything.

"My mom could have easily gotten rid of me. But she didn't."

"Is her abandoning you much better?"

It stung.

"That's different," I managed to say.

"Are you going to abandon this baby?"

The water rushed into my head again and I couldn't think straight and he was pushing me deeper into the sea.

"No. No, Gray, I wouldn't abandon it. Ever."

"Maeve, think about it. You could be more like your mom than you realized. You could hate this baby in four years and wished you had done exactly what I suggested."

"No." I was crying. "I wouldn't hate it. I would never leave it. I would keep it safe. Always."

"But you can't promise that can you?"

"Why are you being cruel?" Tears streamed down my cheeks.

Sighing, Gray pulled me into him and held me tight. "I'm not trying to be mean. I'm sorry. I don't think keeping it is the right decision."

I was quiet. "I'm not saying I want to keep it..."

"What do you want, Maeve?"

I dried the wetness from my face with the cuff of my sleeve. "I don't know."

"Maeve. Compare your life to your mom's. They're not so

different when you think about it, are they?"

He was right and that's what I hated most of all.

Because after all I had done to try and rid myself of anything remotely resembling Sage, my life unequivocally and without realization had suddenly become a very sorry replica of hers.

I DIDN'T TELL SOL BECAUSE I didn't know how. His date with Lucy had gone better than expected and he was happier than I'd ever seen him, except for when he had first moved in with Sage and me. He'd been real happy back then. The good old days, as I remembered them. But maybe there were good days ahead for us as well, or at the very least for Sol. Maybe the good times weren't all behind us. It was a nice thought, anyway.

The three days had passed and I hadn't seen Gray. I knew what he wanted, clearly, but every day—every minute—I felt something new. I wanted it; I didn't want it. I could raise it; I could destroy it. I'd be a good mother; I'd simply be another version of Sage. I knew instinctually what I wanted and yet had no real idea at all.

I obviously was not good at hiding my inner turmoil because Clarke had immediately asked me what was wrong. I told her nothing, but her eyes slanted thin in suspicion, so I told her I was still mourning Ky. Which was true—unbelievably so. Clarke seemed to accept that and didn't press any further.

I asked Sol if he could lend me a ride to Gray's. He obliged but said, "Don't stay at his place too long. Lucy is coming over tonight and I'm cooking us dinner."

I stared at him in disbelief. "You're cooking dinner?"

"Sure am. It's not that shocking, is it?"

"Yes," I said laughing, still stunned. "It is." But I wasn't about to say anything more in case it changed his mind, and I didn't want his mind changed because this Lucy lady seemed, to me, like the best thing that had ever happened to him.

As we got closer to Gray's house, I asked Sol if he would wait for me, as I would hopefully only be a few minutes.

"You could ask Gray to dinner tonight if you wanted."

I nodded. "Yeah, maybe I will."

I hopped out of the car and went up to the front door. His truck wasn't in the driveway, and when the door opened it was Pete, not Gray.

"Hi, Pete. Did I miss Gray? His truck isn't in the drive. I need to talk to him. Do you know where he is? It's urgent. Like, an emergency."

Pete looked like he had rolled out of bed. His hair was tousled and messy. "Hey, uh..."

"Maeve."

"Right. Maeve." He blinked.

"Grayson? Do you know where he is?"

"No, uh, no I don't. Sorry." He scratched the back of his head.

"Any idea at all? Did he say when he'd be back? Is Missy around?" I tried to peer my head inside the house.

"No, uh, Missy isn't here either." He rubbed his eyes. "I don't know how to say this..."

"Say what?"

He looked down at his bare feet.

"Spit it out, Pete, come on. Where is he? I need to see him now."

Pete blinked again. "Missy and Gray left last night."

"Oh. Where did they go?"

"They didn't tell me..."

"Okay, well, when are they coming back?"

His eyes drooped a little. "I don't think they are... coming back..."

"What? What do you mean?"

"They left together and I don't think they're planning on coming back. They packed up most of their stuff and left. Gray gave me the key. Said the house is mine now."

My head was spinning.

"Did you know I'm pregnant?" I could hear myself telling him. "Did you know I'm pregnant with Gray's child? And did you know that he wanted me to have an abortion and I didn't want to? And that he told me I could have three days to think about it—just three days!—so I did, Pete, I thought about it very hard, and I came here today to tell him that okay, all right, I'll have his abortion if that's what he wants me to do, because I believed he loved me, Pete. I was a fool and I believed he actually loved me."

Pete didn't say anything for awhile. "I knew you were pregnant."

"You did."

"Missy thinks I'm stupid, but I was listening when you came over that day. When you talked to her about it. Missy... she's been infatuated with Gray for a long time. She hated anyone he paid attention to."

"She told me she didn't hate me."

Pete gave a half smile. "She was probably lying. I heard her talking to Gray two nights ago about how you were going to keep it."

"She didn't know that!"

He shrugged. "She's manipulative. Trust me. You don't know Missy. Her life is a game and Gray's her favorite pawn. She somehow convinced him to run away with her." He looked at me sadly. "It... didn't take a lot of convincing."

"I'm such a stupid girl," I murmured. "I thought he loved me."

"He might have," Pete offered. "For a time."

"That's not good enough."

He nodded. "It never should be."

I thanked him, albeit weakly, and took a few steps back toward the idling car which held Sol.

"Good luck, Maeve," Pete called out. "I, uh, I hope you find some happiness."

Happiness is limited, I wanted to tell him. Fragmented and loose, never lasting, not for anyone. Particularly, I hoped, for Missy and Gray. Maybe that made me a bad person, my wish of a lifetime of unhappiness for the runaway couple, but I didn't care. I didn't care much about anything.

"Did everything go okay?" Sol asked when I got into the car.

"Can I tell you something?"

"Sure, you can."

"But if I tell you, you have to promise not to completely freak out."

Sol looked nervous. "Okay…"

"Stop giving me that weird look." I sighed and pressed the heels of my hands into my pants. "I… Don't get into an accident, all right? Stay calm."

"Just tell me, Maeve! What's going on? You're freaking me out."

"I'm pregnant," I blurted. "It's Gray's. And Gray has quite conveniently run away." I swallowed something bitter. "With someone. So. Yes. That's what I had to tell you. I hope you're not too disappointed in me."

I looked out the window as we drove, and even though it was only early February you could see a few signs of spring. There was hope that the last snow of the season had already fallen, so maybe spring would come quicker this year. I felt as though I needed spring, almost desperately. I didn't know if I could handle any more gloom.

"Um." Sol coughed. "Are you… are you planning on… uh…"

"Keeping it?"

He nodded.

"Gray wanted me to have an abortion." I sighed. "Sol, maybe you don't want to talk about this, but I can't help but think of

Sage." Sol didn't say anything, so I continued. "I mean, she and my dad had me when they were really young. She was seventeen…"

My voice drifted and Sol said, "And you'll be seventeen next week."

I nodded and choked back a laugh mixed with a sob. "Sage told me that my dad wanted her to have an abortion. But she didn't. I always think of him as a good man, because he still stayed with her after she told him she wanted to keep me. Gray didn't do that."

"Gray's not a good man," Sol muttered. "I should have kept him away from you."

"I know Sage has done things… other things, and I'm not forgiving her for those. She shouldn't have abandoned me. Abandoned us. But she was brave enough to have me, even when everything else was falling apart and life was uncertain. She still had me. I have to respect her for that, don't you think?"

Sol took a deep breath before he answered. "I've not been good to you, Maeve. I know that. I'm so sorry for it. If I could go back and do it over again, I'd look past myself to see you. I was too selfish for that. I guess this is as good a time as ever to tell you that I'm trying to stop drinking."

"You are? Seriously?"

He shrugged. "I've been going to meetings. I want to stop—especially now if you're bringing a baby into the house. I don't want to hurt you anymore. I don't want to hurt your baby."

My eyes welled with tears.

"We make mistakes, Maeve, sure. I can't recall all the ones I've made, there's been so many. But Lucy has been telling me… I'm trying to remember the word she used… she said to me, 'Sol, your mistakes don't… define you'. That's the word: define. And you should know that too, Maeve. Your mistakes don't define you."

"They change your life."

244

"Yeah, maybe they do. Maybe some people would say me loving Sage was a mistake. But I got you because of it. That doesn't seem like a mistake to me."

A smile bloomed out from within me. "I never would have thought that."

"I've not been good at showing it. I didn't realize until recently."

"What made you realize it?"

He pulled into our driveway and shut off the ignition. "Well, Lucy has been helping me realize a lot of things. She says she can't wait to meet you."

"I'm looking forward to it, too." I shifted my body to look at him. "Sol, thank you for not giving up on me. For not walking away or leaving. You could have—I know you could have."

Sol's head tilted against the headrest. "I could say the exact same thing to you."

LUCY WAS SHORT AND COMPLETELY delightful. She had light skin and inky, dark hair. A long, silver scar danced along the right side of her face. She reminded me of a night sky with the smallest smattering of clustered stars. She had been in a bad motorcycle accident a few years earlier, Sol had told me before she came over. I thought she was beautiful. So did he.

"You must be Maeve," she said, her voice calm and low.

"That's me. And you're the legendary Lucy."

I saw a hint of a smile. "I don't know about legendary."

"Well, you are in this house."

"I hope I live up to the name—and the stories."

I laughed. "Likewise."

Her eyes were twinkly. "You already are."

She didn't try to give me a hug or shake my hand, unlike Francine or Nora, and I liked how she liked her space. I liked mine too. I had a feeling we'd get along just fine.

TWENTY-FIVE

FRANCINE WAS AT THE HOUSE when I got home from school a few weeks later. She was at the kitchen table talking to Lucy. Lucy was almost always over. She and Sol cooked dinner together nearly every night. The other day Lucy, waving a spoon dipped in spaghetti sauce, told me I didn't need to cook unless I wanted to. Some nights I did, but most nights I didn't. It was a nice change.

"Maeve!" Francine got up from the table and ran to hug me. "I haven't seen you since Christmas. I've missed you."

"I know, it's been a while! How are you doing?"

"Oh, I've been fine! I just dropped by to see how everything was going and Lucy invited me in for some tea."

I smiled. "That's very nice. Lucy's kind, isn't she?"

Lucy said, "Do you want some tea, Maeve? I can put honey in it."

"Okay." I nodded. "Thanks."

Lucy pulled a seat out from the table and offered it to me. I sat down.

"Nora's on her way over," Francine informed me.

"Nora? Like Levi's mom?"

"That's right. She and I were going to go out for coffee today, but when Lucy invited me to sit down, I thought it would be nice for Nora to come here instead."

"You guys are friends?"

"Oh yes. Ever since Thanksgiving." Francine reached across the table and grasped my hand. She gave it a tight squeeze. "That's because of you, Maeve. Because you invited me."

"It's not a big deal, Francine. I'm glad you came."

Lucy set a steaming cup of tea in front of me. It smelled good. "Thank you," I said to her. Her eyes smiled, and she took a sip from her own mug.

There was a knock at the door and Francine rushed to get it. Lucy and I remained in the kitchen.

I looked at Lucy. "Did Sol tell you? About…"

She nodded.

"Francine doesn't know."

"You don't have to tell her. Not today."

"I'm guessing Levi already told Nora."

"I want to meet him."

I smiled. "You will. Soon."

Nora and Francine came into the kitchen and Francine introduced Nora to Lucy.

"What a pleasure it is to meet you!" Nora said in her enthused sort of way. She hugged Lucy. Lucy wasn't a real hugger, and I noticed she pulled back as soon as she could. I stifled my laughter.

Nora hugged me. She smiled, softer than she had before, and as she released me I knew she knew. It was a knowing smile. I could tell.

"I'm sorry," I whispered, the feeling of shame washing over me afresh.

She shook her head.

"Tea, Nora?" Lucy offered.

"I'd love some. Thank you, Lucy."

We each sat at our respective spots around the table, and as I looked down at my tea I announced, "Well, I'm pregnant." There was no gentle, gradual way of saying it. Or maybe there was, but why put off the inevitable.

I looked at Francine. Tears were already gathering in the corners of her eyes, threatening to spill down her cheeks.

"I'm sorry," I told her.

"No honey," she said, waving her hands away. "This is a weird thing I do. It's a me thing. It's not you. Hormones and all that." She forced a high laugh.

"Francine, I am sorry."

The tears coursed down her cheeks without permission. "Oh sweetheart," she said grasping onto my hand, "I'm happy for you. You're having a baby!"

I looked back down at my tea.

After a moment Francine asked quietly, "You are having it, right?"

"Yes. Yes, I am."

She sighed with ease. "Thank goodness. You would have shattered my heart."

Nora said, "Levi... told me in passing. He didn't tell me much." She hesitated. "Can I ask you something, Maeve? Something personal?"

"Okay."

"Is it... is it, um, the baby... Levi's?"

I stared at her, gaping. "Are you asking me if he's the father?"

She nodded, her eyes laced with concern.

"No, Nora! No! Please tell me you didn't think that."

She sat back in her chair with literal relief. "What was I supposed to think? You two are so close."

"Not like that. He's my very good friend. That's all. My good friend."

"I know he is, honey. I know."

"Do you hate me?" I asked Nora.

"Hate you? Why would you ask me that?"

"Because of who I am. Because of," I spread my hands softly over my still flat belly, "what I've done. I'm not the type of girl you'd want your Levi hanging out with."

Nora slipped off her chair and crouched down beside mine. "Maeve," she said, taking hold of my hands. "I could never hate you. We love you." She nodded toward Lucy, then Francine. "Do you see us all here? We *love* you."

Tears filled my eyes. "Okay."

She hugged me and I burrowed myself into her neck.

I told them—a little—about Gray. The bare minimum, only what I felt they needed to know. They knew I was pregnant; they did not need to know every intimate detail. I told them that, to my surprise, he had left and in all likelihood would not be returning. I omitted Missy. I didn't want to completely smear his name. Not completely, anyway.

"The baby won't have a father," I said. "That's probably a bad thing."

"It will have a good mother," Nora assured me. "And three aunts!" She grinned at Francine and Lucy.

Francine kissed my cheek and said she had to go. "We'll need to have a big baby shower! When's the baby due?"

"Oh," I said. "I don't know."

"I'll take you to the doctor," Lucy offered.

"Yes!" Francine clapped her hands, "and then we'll plan a beautiful shower for you and the baby."

"Okay. Thanks, Francine."

She kissed my cheek again and left. Nora followed soon after. As I shut the door behind them, Lucy came over to me.

"They're nice," she said and sat on the couch. I sat beside her.

"Yes. Though they love to hug."

Lucy wrinkled her nose. "I noticed that."

I laughed. "You'll get used to it."

"I was thinking something," she said, and crossed her one leg lazily over the next, draping them on the coffee table.

"What's that?"

She seemed to want to broach the topic carefully. "Sol has been telling me a lot... about your lives. About Sage."

I didn't say anything.

"He mentioned that you were thinking about looking for her. He said you had talked about this quite awhile ago—after everything that had happened with Ky. Sol told me about her, too. He wasn't sure if you were still planning on trying to find Sage or not."

Lucy was waiting for an answer, but I didn't feel like I had one to give.

"I don't know," I said.

"This is likely none of my business," Lucy told me.

"But..."

She smiled. "But... I keep thinking how much she should know about this." Lucy gestured to my stomach. "That's her grandchild."

"She chose to leave, Lucy. I didn't make her."

"I know," she said gently. "I realize she's missed a lot of your life. But I would hate for her to miss even more."

"She could be dead."

"She could be," reasoned Lucy, "but she's not."

"What do you mean? How do you know that?"

Lucy took a tentative breath. "After Sol told me what had happened, I wanted to find her. All I wanted was to get a good look at her. Just drive by and see her. I wanted to know what kind of person would leave the two of you."

"You found her?"

Lucy nodded. "I think so. I drove by last month. I don't know if she's still there."

"Where was she?"

"Your old house. The one in Sycamore. The one that's painted peach."

I took a breath and let it out slowly, Ky's last words ringing through my head.

You have to go find her. If you do anything for me, go find Sage.

SUDDENLY I WAS SEVENTEEN-YEARS-OLD. It happened quickly, from one minute to the next, and I woke up on my bed finding myself a year older. I looked out the window and felt much older than that. I got changed, half wondering when my pants would begin to feel too tight, and when my shirts might start to stretch against my growing skin.

I went down the stairs to find streamers and balloons draped haphazardly along the railing and kitchen chairs.

The spectacular golden birthday, Ky would've joked. Seventeen on the seventeenth. She and I had talked about what it would be like—if it would feel different than the other birthdays. I thought it would feel the same, but Ky felt certain it would be slightly more magical than normal birthdays. Ky's golden birthday wasn't supposed to happen for a long time. She'd have to wait until she turned twenty-nine on April twenty-ninth, something she felt was particularly disappointing. Normally, Ky had informed me, by the time you're twenty-nine you've forgotten how spectacular and magical a birthday is supposed to be. She said I was lucky having it fall on my seventeenth because seventeen-year-olds were allowed much more leniency when it came to believing in the spectacular.

I twisted my fingers around a yellow streamer, knowing Ky wouldn't see that spectacular golden day, nor the birthday before or after that. Never twenty-nine; forever sixteen.

A birthday card was leaning against a plate with a sprinkled donut on it. I smiled, the work of Lucy written all over.

Dearest Maeve, the card read.

Happy 17th birthday! You're a treasure. Sol and I are grateful for you. I wish you the best year of your life, one filled with love and adventure.
Lucy

The other side read,

You're getting old, kid. Don't grow up too fast. Happy birthday.
From Sol

Two twenty-dollar bills were tucked inside the envelope. I warmed the donut in the microwave for eleven seconds and took a small bite, the flaky pastry melting against my tongue. Lucy had taped a note to the refrigerator that said, *Come home right after work—we have a surprise for you. Happy birthday.*

I wondered what the surprise would be. Sol had never made much fuss about my birthday, and the truth was I'd never made much fuss about his. Lucy was clearly trying to change that, too. I didn't mind.

I walked through the forest to school, slowly, noticing more green than white. Spring was coming—a spring without Ky. I placed my hand against my stomach as I walked, shifting my school bag on my shoulder to try and make it more comfortable.

"Hi baby," I said softly and I wondered if he could hear me. "It's my birthday today. I turned seventeen. Do you know what that means? It means I'm the same age my mom was when she had me. Your grandma, I guess. That's bad, you know, because it's another reminder of who I seem to be becoming. I don't want to be like your grandma—that's the honest truth—and I always want to be honest with you. My mom wasn't honest. She left when I was seven, but she told me she was coming back. She lied, little baby. She didn't come back." I crunched a twig hard beneath my shoe.

"I wouldn't leave you, okay? I won't be like my mom. You'll be safe." I walked a little further, past our three empty tree stumps.

"There's another bad thing about turning seventeen. I'm officially older than Ky. We'll never be the same age again. I wish you could meet her," I said wistfully. "I keep thinking about what she would do if she were here." I laughed. "Ky would be buying you the weirdest clothes, and I bet she'd think of the dumbest names. But I know she would love you. She'd be trying to track down your dad. Ky would be furious with him." I sighed. "I'll be the only one to love you. But that will be enough. I promise."

I KNOCKED HARD ON THE door that was inscribed with *Merry Greene*, then twisted the knob open.

A girl was sitting across from her.

"Hi, Maeve! I'll be with you in just one moment." Mrs. Greene chirped. She turned back to the girl. "Stop skipping class or you're not going to graduate. I mean it. Do you want to be here for another three years?"

The girl mumbled something indiscernible.

"I didn't think so." Mrs. Greene replied. "You may go now."

The girl grabbed her books and backpack and got up. She shut the door with a slam behind her.

I went and sat on the red chair the girl hadn't been sitting on.

"Everything okay, Maeve? We don't have an appointment until tomorrow."

"I wanted to see you now."

"Of course," she said. "You're welcome to come see me at any time."

"Sorry to interrupt."

"You weren't interrupting. Sasha wanted to get out of here anyway." Mrs. Greene laughed, coming around from her desk to sit on the other red chair. A poster hung above her desk that read, *All you need is love! (And maybe some therapy.)* "What did you want to talk about?"

I took a breath. "It's my birthday today."

She smiled. "Is that so? Happy birthday! How old are you?"

"Seventeen. Officially older than Ky."

Mrs. Greene didn't say anything.

"We'll never be the same age again."

"That must be hard."

"Harder than I thought it would be."

"Are you going to do anything to celebrate your big day?"

"Sol and his girlfriend said they have a surprise for me when I get home. I didn't tell anyone at school. I didn't want it to be a big deal, you know? Ky and I would have done something... maybe gone out with Levi. I don't know if Levi knows it's my birthday. I don't think I told him. He's been feeling far away recently. And a lot of the kids here don't like to talk to me because of what happened to Ky. Not that they liked me that much before."

"Why does Levi feel far away from you?"

I shrugged. "It's my fault, not his."

She tilted her head to the side as if she were silently urging me to go on.

"I keep pushing him away. Accidentally. It's... this thing I do. I always think I can do everything on my own. I convince myself that I don't need anyone. I've done that to Levi a lot. But then I realize I do need people and I call him. I was seeing this guy Levi doesn't like, and he told me I should stay away from him but I didn't. And now," I looked down at my limp hands, "I'm pregnant."

I looked up at her when she didn't say anything.

"Maeve, honey," she said kindly, "You have had a hard few months."

"It's my fault. I chose to have sex with him. He didn't force me."

"That's true. You did choose. But it doesn't make this any

easier."

I started to cry. "The guy left, Mrs. Greene. I told him I was pregnant and he left and I don't know where he went. I pushed Levi away and Ky's gone and I don't know what to do."

She leaned in and wrapped her arms around me.

"You have options," she said when we pulled back.

"I know my options. I've already decided."

"You have?"

"I'm going to keep it—the baby."

"You are."

"I know I'm only seventeen, but Sage kept me. That's what I keep thinking. Sage kept me; Sage chose me."

"Have you been thinking a lot about Sage recently?"

I nodded. "I want to find her. Maybe she'd come back if she knew there was a baby."

"Do you think that would happen?"

I shrugged. "I have no idea. I don't know her anymore."

"What does your stepfather think about you keeping the baby?"

"He was very supportive. He's going to A.A. meetings now. Lucy—his girlfriend—she's been good for him. Good for me, too. I think she likes me."

Mrs. Greene smiled. "I have no doubt she likes you."

"I don't know if I'll be able to go to college, anymore. Or even finish next year—"

"Now I want you to stay in school, Maeve."

"I might have to get another job to afford to have—"

"Look at me," she said firmly, putting her hand under my chin and bringing it up toward her face. I looked into her heavily made up eyes. "Look at me. You're going to stay in school. You have a year and a half left until you graduate, and you will graduate. You will graduate with honors, because your marks are good, and because you are smart."

Tears wove their way down my cheeks.

"Do you hear me? You are a smart girl. You have a good future, Maeve. A bright future. You will not let the absence of your mother, or Ky's death, or this baby determine what your future looks like. I believe in you. You understand? I believe you can do great things. So don't you dare quit school. I won't let you." She grabbed my hands. "If you think you're going to quit school you'll have to first get past me, and my husband says nobody gets past me."

"I don't know how I can do it all…"

"Oh honey, you can't. Nobody does it all. That's a lie if I ever heard one. You let people help you, that's the key, and you focus on school because that's important. I have no doubt you can go to college."

"Except there's no way I'll have enough money—"

"We'll figure out the finances when it comes to that. Don't you dare give up on this, Maeve Parker. I believe in you too much to allow you to give up already."

"Mrs. Greene… can I ask you something?"

"Of course. Anything."

"How come you believe in me?"

"Because, honey," she squeezed my hands twice, her eyes never leaving mine. "You're worth believing in."

"SURPRISE!" A CHORUS OF VOICES filled the living room as I opened the front door to my house.

"Happy birthday, Maeve!" I was looking at Lucy and Sol and Levi and Jonas and Nora and Simon and Alice and Francine. I even saw Clarke and, who I presumed to be her boyfriend, standing behind them.

"Wow," was all I could say and Francine raced to wrap her arms tight around me.

"Happy birthday, sweetheart!" she screeched in my ear.

"Thanks, Francine," I laughed, and one by one people were

hugging me.

Lucy went around serving cupcakes, her silver scar glistening as the late afternoon sunlight strewed in through the windows.

"Oh Lucy," I said when she handed me a cupcake with little yellow sprinkles on top, "you didn't have to do this."

"I know. But I did it anyway."

"But why? You didn't have to."

She tipped her head back and laughed, the music flowing out from her lips, filling the room. "Would you quit asking questions and go enjoy your birthday party?"

Levi grabbed my hand, spinning me around. "Happy birthday, Maeve girl."

"Thank you. You're actually talking to me."

"Of course I am. Why wouldn't I be?"

"I wasn't sure if you'd decided to disown me or not."

"You know the truth is, birthday girl, I could never disown you." He leaned in close to me. "It's impossible. Even if I tried I never could."

I leaned in closer still. "Why's that?"

"Because I like you too much."

"Parker, are you seriously going to talk to everybody but me?" Clarke pushed her way past Levi, but I kept my eyes on him, and his eyes were so blue, so tantalizing. I wanted to dive deep into the ocean.

"Hello? Parker?"

"Clarke!" I turned to her. "I was getting to you. Sorry."

"Oh I see," she smirked, "saving the best for last."

I laughed. "Yeah, that's right. This is Levi."

Clarke shook his hand then turned to the boy standing next to her, the boy from her pictures. "This is Alec," Clarke said, "my boyfriend."

"Fiancé." the boy corrected.

"Fiancé?" I gasped. "Since when?" I fumbled for Clarke's hand. "Where's the ring?"

Clarke blushed a deep red. "He wishes. I keep saying no."

"She'll say yes one of these days," Alec grinned.

I pretended to be exasperated. "Alec, how do you put up with her?"

He laughed and wrapped his arm around Clarke's waist. "It's easy. The wonder is how she puts up with me."

Clarke didn't refrain from rolling her eyes. "Happy birthday, Parker. We have to go now... Alec's mom has some supper club meeting she makes us attend. We're already late."

"Thank you for coming. It was really nice to meet you, Alec."

"You too, Maeve," he said kindly, "and you as well, Levi."

"Yeah, good to meet you, Levi," Clarke echoed.

Levi smiled, nodding at both of them.

"He makes her softer," I mused to Levi after they'd left. "Together, she seems almost... nice. Almost human."

Levi laughed. "You were terrified of her your first day. Remember that?"

I nodded. "I'm still scared of her."

He laughed again. "You're not scared of anyone, Maeve."

"That's not true. I'm scared of this baby."

"It's going to be okay."

"I'm glad you think so."

"I do."

"I've been talking to a counselor. From school. Have you been talking to anybody?"

He shook his head.

"I think you should."

"Why? I don't need it. I did the anger management stuff already."

"That's what I thought, too, that I didn't need it. But it helps Levi, I swear it."

"What do you say to her?"

"Anything I feel like. The baby, Ky, Sage... you."

"Me?"

I nodded.

"What do you say about me?"

"That I'm a bad friend to you."

"You're not—"

"We've covered this before. I am. You and I both know it. But I want to get better."

"Me too."

"You're already a good friend."

"I'd like to be better."

"Okay," I said. "If that's how you want it. Then I have a favor to ask you."

"Anything."

I laughed. "I wouldn't say that to me, Levi. You have no idea what you could get yourself into."

"But I mean it, Maeve. Anything."

I looked into his eyes, his dark, long lashes curling over the endless blue. "Take me to find Sage. I think I know where she is."

He watched me and I wished, not for the first time, that I knew what he was thinking inside of his head.

"Like I said," his lips curved up toward his cheekbones. "Anything."

TWENTY-SIX

LATE IN THE NIGHT, DEEP in the middle of the summer, after the stickiness had faded and the earth had slightly cooled, Sage would take me to the backyard and fold my hands around a mason jar.

"Shh," she would say, index finger to her lips. I would trail behind her, watch her long hair spilling down her back in a messy braid. "Quiet, Maeve," she whispered so softly I could hardly hear, "we don't want to scare them away."

I could see them through the screen porch: fireflies, dancing to the sound of their own music, blinking like hesitant Christmas lights. Sage opened the back door silently, and we slipped out to the grass, bare toes pressing into the chilled and hardened dirt.

She wiggled her eyebrows and unscrewed the lid of her jar, reaching up ever so slightly and waiting for the light to dance again. It did, and she capped it quickly, the firefly zipping around the small container.

"Look," she whispered and brought the jar down to my face. "What should we name him?"

I thought for a moment, grabbing the glass with my pudgy, tiny-girl hands, staring at the firefly as he blinked his light on and off, on and off, on and off. "I'll name you Starlight."

"Starlight?" Sage laughed. "Why Starlight, Maeve?"

"He reminds me of a star," I told her as if it weren't obvious already.

"That's true," Sage agreed. She looked down at my jar. "Hello, Starlight," she whispered, "hello."

I held onto him, memorizing the incandescent fragments of light that illumined my face. Sage caught three more in her jar. Her face lit up as she stared into them. I held tight to Starlight.

"They're so pretty, Sage," I told her.

"They are pretty, aren't they, Maeve? Just like you." She nuzzled her nose lightly against mine. It tickled.

"Can I keep them forever?"

"No," she shook her head sadly. "We'll have to let them go tonight."

"But why Sage? Why can't I keep them? I love Starlight. I love him a lot."

"I know you do." She lifted me onto her lap, bringing my head to her chest. She rocked me for a few moments then kissed my head. I felt my eyes grow heavy. "But sometimes we have to let things go, Maeve."

Sage uncapped the jars and we watched the fireflies fly away free. She stood up, still holding me, and carried me inside. She kissed my head again and before I fell asleep, she whispered against my unruly hair, "Sometimes we have to let things go."

I STRIPPED OFF MY PAJAMAS and looked at myself in the mirror. My skin was stretching, I could see it. I placed my fingers against my stomach, cupping the slight roundness that had begun to form. Placing my hands at my sides, I stared at my naked body. Blue lines crisscrossed my breasts and abdomen, full and plumped veins carrying blood for two people who didn't yet know one another.

"Maeve!" Lucy called from down the stairs. "Come on! We're going to be late."

"I'm coming, I'm coming," I yelled back. I got dressed quickly but had to sit down because I felt dizzy. I often felt dizzy.

Finally, we got into Lucy's car—a tiny, blue, two-door sedan.

"Are you nervous?" She asked as she peeled out of the driveway.

"I guess. I don't really know what's going to happen. Do you?"

"I think they'll determine your due date and maybe take your blood. How good are you with needles?"

I shrugged. "I don't hate them. I don't love them either…"

"Did you eat?"

"No."

"Want me to get you a burger or something?"

I shook my head. The thought of fast food made me nauseous. "Does the morning sickness ever end?" I asked weakly as I closed my eyes and leaned my head against the headrest.

"Let's hope so," Lucy murmured. I kept my eyes closed until she pulled into the doctor's office.

We sat in the brightly painted waiting room for awhile. I looked at the other girls who sat there flipping magazines. Most of them were much more pregnant than me. Their bellies bloomed out from within them and they all appeared very relaxed and excited at the prospect of the new life they'd soon be bringing into the world. I wondered if any of them were as scared as me.

"Maeve Parker?"

Lucy and I turned to the sound of my name and a lady in scrubs was looking at us.

"Come with me, please."

We followed her and waited another while longer in a different room. Eventually, the doctor came in.

"Good morning, Maeve," she said, looking down at her

clipboard. "I'm Dr. Carson, your practitioner. How are you feeling?"

"Uh, pretty good. Sort of sick."

Dr. Carson laughed and sat down on a chair across from Lucy and me. "That's not uncommon. The nausea should hopefully go away fairly soon. Aside from that, anything worrying you?"

I shook my head.

"Good, I'm glad to hear it. Today we're going to do some tests and check you over. I'll get you to answer some questions about your medical and sexual history, but other than that, it's all pretty basic today. Just our standard procedure."

Dr. Carson took me to another room to do the tests and Lucy went back to the waiting room. Once the tests were completed, the doctor took me to her office.

"Will I get to see the baby?"

She smiled. "You'll book an ultrasound today and you'll be able to see the baby in about two to three weeks."

"Okay. When's the baby due?"

"We're estimating your due date to be around September 16. You're ten weeks pregnant right now. That means your baby's major organs have fully developed, and we'll soon be able to tell if it's a boy or a girl. Everything looks great to me, Maeve. There's no need to worry."

I thanked her then went out and relayed the information to Lucy.

"September 16," she breathed.

"Yeah."

"I'm glad we have an actual date to look forward to."

"A sort of date, anyway. Dr. Carson said the ultrasound will make the date more accurate. It's starting to feel much more real now."

She laughed softly. "It sure is."

We booked an ultrasound appointment with the receptionist,

then got back into the car to head home.

"I was thinking I should get a new car," Lucy said suddenly as she started the ignition.

"You love this car."

"Putting a car seat in here would be tough with the two doors."

"There's always Sol's truck. Don't you seriously love this car?"

She cast me a look. "You're going to put the baby in Sol's truck? That thing could break down any second."

"But your car! Your dad gave you this car."

"It's a car, Maeve. Not a baby."

"I could get a car."

"You don't have a license."

"I could get a license."

"You could get a license."

"I could ask Levi to teach me how to drive. He's a good driver."

"And he loves you."

"What?"

Lucy feigned innocence. "Hm? I didn't say anything."

"He doesn't love me, Lucy."

"Suit yourself."

"He doesn't."

"Don't try and convince yourself you're not loved. What would be the point in doing that?"

"But Levi doesn't love me. And even if there was the slightest chance that he might, I've royally screwed that up now." I pointed to my stomach.

"Did Sol ever tell you about my accident?"

"A little."

"What did he say?"

"Only that you were in a motorcycle crash."

"Anything else?"

"No."

She sighed, flicking up her turn signal. "I'm going to show you something." She turned off the highway and we drove away from Rutherford. We sat in silence. After a half hour, she cut the engine on the side of a road. We got out of the car.

Her black hair blew around her face as she crossed the road. She went to a certain spot, then stood there for a moment. She dug her toes into the dirt, making circles with the tips of her shoes. There was a small stake driven into the grass where she stood. It looked like a makeshift cross and had old, dried flowers tied around it.

"Come here, Maeve," she said, so I went. "This is where the accident happened."

I nodded as if I knew. I didn't.

"It happened twelve years ago. I was with my boyfriend at the time and he was a real piece of work. We didn't do much good together, I'll tell you that much. Just a whole lot of drinking and drugs, trying our best to survive. We survived, sure, but we never did much living. He told me he loved me and I told him I wanted us to get married." The wind slightly muffled her voice.

"Growing up, that's all I wanted. I saw my mom and dad and how much they loved each other, and I wanted to grow up and be married like them. My boyfriend knew that and he kept telling me we would, we would, someday we would. Finally, he proposed. I was beyond happy, dreaming up what would be our perfect life together. I wanted to surprise him so the next day I went to his work. I found him sleeping with another woman. It just so happens they'd been together for a long time." She looked away and I thought of Gray.

"That's not a new story, of course. It happens to lots of people. But when it happened to me, I was… broken, and angry. I called my sister and told her everything. She said she would come get me. I was supposed to wait for her, but instead, I went back home and drank and got real high, and then I took his motorcycle out and went for a ride. I was messed up, and I got into an accident—a bad one. I ended up killing someone." She looked at me and tears were streaming down her face. "Turns out it was my sister. She was on her way to get me, and we were going down the same road. This road. When I lost control, I hit her with such force she died instantly. I should've been killed too—my body was broken in so many places—but I wasn't. The doctors called me a miracle. I didn't feel much like one."

I watched her kneel down in front of the small cross.

"My parents didn't want to press charges against me. They had already lost one daughter and couldn't handle the thought of losing another. In court, their lawyers convinced the judge I needed rehab, which I did. My body healed from the accident, except for the scars. I needed the scars. They reminded me." She took a wavering breath and I went and sat next to her. "I spent a lot of my life convincing myself I wasn't deserving of love. I had done too big of a bad thing, made too many mistakes. But the truth is, Maeve, I'll do more bad things, I'll make more mistakes, and I'll still be deserving of love.

"I've said this to Sol so many times: we can't let our past define us. I let mine for a long time. I woke up each day with the weight of my sister's death on my shoulders, and I told myself that's who I was: her murderer. Not her sister, but her murderer. That guilt was ultimately killing me. It took me years to choose a new definition for my life." She grasped my hand. "This baby does not define you."

I wiped a tear from her cheek and felt them seeping down my own.

"You are smart, and brave, and beautiful. That's your definition—not a seventeen-year-old pregnant girl. You have not royally screwed up the possibility of people loving you. Nothing could do that." She smiled, tears spilling into her lips. "My parents love me, even after what I did. Sol loves me."

"I love you."

266

Lucy nodded and brought my head to her chest. She nodded into my hair, and we got one another damp with our tears. "I love you, too, Maeve. I love you, too."

OVER THE NEXT FEW WEEKS, people at school started to realize I was going to have a baby. I wasn't the first girl to show up to school pregnant, but I hoped the gossip would die down sooner rather than later.

Levi and I ate our lunch in the hall, instead of the cafeteria. Well, he ate. I stared longingly at his food, wishing it didn't make me feel so ill. Although much to my relief, the morning sickness was beginning to subside a little.

"People have been asking me who the father is," Levi informed me, shoving a bite of sandwich quickly into his mouth.

I groaned. "What have you told them?"

"That it's none of their business."

"I'm sure they love that."

"They all think it's me."

Starting to laugh, I giggled, "That's what your mom thought! Didn't I tell you that?"

Levi's eyes were wide. "What are you talking about?"

"Your mom asked me if you were the father!" My ribs began to ache from the laughter.

"That's so awkward!"

"She was quite relieved when I told her you weren't."

"She actually asked you that?"

I laughed, "She sure did."

"She has no boundaries," he said laughing.

"She was being Nora. I wasn't offended, don't worry."

"I wish people didn't intrude."

I smiled at him. "They always will. Don't you remember their speculations about Ky?"

"Sadly."

"I know."

"Have you heard from Alice recently?"

"No, I haven't. Not really."

"We should go see her." Levi got up and threw away his garbage, grabbed his backpack and lent his hand my way.

"You mean right now?"

"Sure. Why not?"

I took his hand and he helped me get up. "What about class?"

Levi shrugged and tossed me a mischievous grin. "It's Friday."

"All right," I gave in easily. "But Mrs. Greene better not find out about us cutting this afternoon. She wouldn't be very happy with me."

"My parents wouldn't be either."

"Especially if you're cutting class with *moi*. Nora might think you'll get me pregnant all over again."

Levi couldn't stop laughing.

ALICE WAS PILING THINGS INTO the trunk of her car when we pulled into her driveway. I hadn't been to the house since before Ky died.

"Hey, Alice!" Levi called out. The weather was warming up quickly, so we'd rolled the windows down for the drive.

Alice seemed genuinely surprised to see us. "Oh," she said as we got out of Levi's car. "Hi. What are you two doing here?"

Levi looked at me, then at her. "We thought we'd drop by. Hadn't seen you in a while. Are you going somewhere?"

Cardboard boxes were strewn aimlessly around her car, some already stuffed into the small trunk. There were a lot of boxes and her car was fairly tiny. I wondered how she was going to fit it all in.

"I'm moving," she announced.

"Where?" asked Levi.

Alice sighed, leaning her hip against the side of her vehicle. I was struck again by the exhaustion that permeated her face, stretching against her taut skin, seeping out of every pore. "I don't know," she said finally. "I don't know where I'll go. But I can't stay here any longer."

"What's happened, Alice?" I asked. "Is there news about Jared?"

She had lost a lot of weight and looked unhealthily skinny. "This morning the police found him a few towns away. Detective Haddon thinks he'll plead guilty because of the letter—it's pretty incriminating evidence. She thinks he'll get eight years in prison."

"That's it?"

Levi took my arm.

"I want him away for life," I explained to both of them. "He should be convicted of murder. She died because of him!"

Alice shook her head. "That will never happen."

"Some justice will be served," Levi offered.

"That's right," Alice smiled sadly. "Some justice."

"Where are you going to move?" I asked. "And why are you leaving before he's sentenced?"

She lifted her shoulders, then let them fall. "I can't be here any longer, Maeve. Not near this house, not near him. I think I'll go to Hawaii, maybe, or perhaps California. Somewhere warm."

"You should go to Iceland. Ky always wanted to visit there."

"I forgot about that. She did want to go there, didn't she?"

I nodded.

"Maybe that will be my first stop."

"You don't have to leave," Levi told Alice. "You could stay."

Alice reached out and grazed Levi's cheek softly with her knuckles. "What do I have here in Rutherford, Levi? Nothing. Only the reputation as the mother whose child committed suicide. And as soon as the media releases what happened today, I'll be the mother whose boyfriend was sexually assaulting her baby girl. I need to leave here and reinvent myself. Be someone new. Or if not new, try to be the person Ky always knew I could be."

"But Ky grew up here. This was her home…" I whimpered.

"Not a very safe home, was it, Maeve?"

"Tell me you'll talk to someone, Alice. Please talk to someone or your grief and guilt will swallow you whole. Please promise me."

"I will. I promise." She squeezed my hand. "Detective Haddon will give the letter back soon."

"Thank you," I told her.

Levi leaned in and wrapped his arms around us both, and the three of us huddled together in a clumpy cluster of broken but mending hearts, the anguish thick and palpable. We stood there for awhile and I think Alice was crying.

"It's up to us now," Levi said. "We won't forget her, Alice. I want you to know that. We loved her—"

"Love her," I corrected.

Levi smiled softly at me. "Love her. We always will. Nothing could change that."

"I'll miss you both," Alice told us. "You were kind to me."

"Not as kind as I should've been," I admitted.

"Maeve," Alice kissed my hairline. "Pain is hard. It's what you do with your pain that matters. You were kind." She released us, then leaned down to put another box inside of her trunk. "I'm off to do something with my pain. I think I'll start with Iceland."

We helped her pack the rest of her things, the sun shining bright and spring-like down upon us.

TWENTY-SEVEN

"ARE YOU READY FOR THIS?" asked Levi.

"I'm not sure," I told him honestly. "I don't think so."

"Do you want to wait a little longer?"

"No. I don't know if I'll ever be ready. Let's go, okay?"

My belly had started to show, as I was nearing the eighteen-week mark in my second trimester. I pulled the seatbelt over myself and laid my head against the seat.

"You all right?"

"Tired."

We pulled out of the driveway and I immediately rolled down the window. I seemed to constantly be boiling hot.

"I made a CD for the drive," Levi said after awhile.

I laughed. "You did?"

"I did. This is a road trip. A mix CD is like the fundamental law of road trips."

"Right."

Levi lifted his soft drink and motioned me to do the same. I did. "Here's to adventures," he said as a toast. He tipped his bottle against mine.

"To adventures," I echoed softly.

"I haven't been on one in a long time. This feels good."

"Your life is an adventure, Levi."

"Not true."

"Sure is."

He rolled his eyes, but I could see his goofy smile appear across his face as he popped the CD into the stereo. He rolled his window down and started to belt out the song. He sang loudly, his voice cracking, and I couldn't hold the laughter in.

He continued to sing and I kept laughing at him. We both had terrible voices.

"Good mix CD," I told him, "I mean, really good. But I would like to make a formal request for our next adventure road trip."

"And that would be?"

"That the CD be made up solely of the one and only Levi Fisher and his... phenomenal voice."

"Let me think for a minute. Hmmm. No."

"Are you kidding me? That would be great!"

"More like tragic."

"I could sell a million copies, I'll bet. And if I sold each CD for only one dollar a piece, I could easily become a millionaire. I'll share with you, of course, the musical genius."

"You believe in me that much?" he teased.

"Levi Fisher," I said to him seriously. "I believe in you much more than that."

He smiled. "I'm glad the mix CD got the Maeve Parker stamp of approval."

"You make me sound very prestigious." I scoffed.

We exited out of Rutherford and headed toward the town of Sycamore. The town was about two and half hours from Rutherford.

"Thank you for taking me today."

"Any excuse for a road trip."

"You didn't have to do this though, and I appreciate it."

"You would do the same for me."

I nodded. "I would."

"I know you would. Even if you wouldn't, I'd still be coming along with you today."

"Why's that?"

"Because this is where I want to be."

"I wouldn't have wanted to go alone."

"Are you nervous?"

"I think so. I feel kind of sick, actually. You know, she might not be there. She could have moved away."

"But this is where Lucy saw her. Right?"

I nodded. "The peach house in Sycamore. It was the house Sage and I lived in before she met Sol. The three of us lived there until she left, and then it was just Sol and me. He lost his job that summer and we moved to Rutherford."

"I'm glad you moved," Levi said. "I'm glad I met you. I can't imagine if we'd never met."

"No, neither can I. Who knows what kind of person I would be?"

"Likewise."

"You'd be much better," I said, half-joking.

"I'll never agree with that."

"Your mom might."

We both burst out laughing.

"She loves you as if you were her daughter," Levi told me. "She talks about you all the time. Especially after that article you did for *The Dish*—the one you wrote for Ky."

"We could pretend. We could turn around and pretend it's Nora who's my mom, not Sage."

"And pretend you're my sister?" Levi wrinkled his nose in disgust. "No thanks."

"All right, all right. We'll keep going."

"I'm curious to meet this Sage. I wonder if she looks like you. Do you have any pictures of her?"

I shook my head. "I haven't the slightest idea of what she

looks like. I'm hoping instincts kick in. I should know my mom, shouldn't I? When I was a little girl I used to see her everywhere. It was never actually her of course, but it was nice to imagine."

"I'm sure you'll know her," Levi assured me. "You'll know her right away."

I WAS SEVEN-YEARS-OLD AGAIN, then eleven, then fifteen, and the sight of the peach house came into view. I had lived most of my life in the Sycamore house. It was where I shared my first kiss with a boy named Kirk, where I learned to ride the broken bike Sage brought me from the dump, where my life felt like it would always be.

"I painted that house," I informed Levi. We were sitting idle in the car, a few houses down. "Sage and I did. When I was like four or five-years-old. After my father died."

"It's very… bright."

I whispered a laugh. "It's how Sage wanted it. I can't believe the new owner didn't paint over the peach. I forgot how ugly it is. Sol never bothered to paint it, of course. Too much work, he said." I looked over at Levi. "I don't know if I can do this."

"You can," he took my hand and intertwined his fingers alongside mine. "I know you can."

"You won't leave me today… right?"

He shook his head. "Never."

"This is for Ky," I told him.

"And you."

"Yes, but right now it's better if I pretend it's all for Ky."

"She'd be proud of you."

"Would she?"

"She was always proud of you."

"Sage may not be here. I don't see a car in the driveway."

"Could be in the garage," Levi reasoned.

"Maybe there's a reason she didn't try to find me…" I let my voice wander and looked out at the other houses on the street. All of them a normal color, gray or white or brown, probably filled with families who hadn't splintered apart.

"Maeve, look at me."

I turned to gaze into his eyes; his tidal wave eyes.

"Don't talk yourself out of this. We're here. Let's go knock on the door."

I took a breath. It's something Mrs. Greene taught me. *Focus on your breathing*, she often said. *It will steady you. It will allow you to focus on something else, aside from what's happening around you.*

"Okay."

Levi got out of the car, then came around and opened my door for me. He took my hand and helped me out.

"Is the baby all right?" he asked.

"I think so. I think he's happy for me to stretch my legs. Hopefully Sage will let me use her bathroom."

As we walked closer to the house, I tried to remember how to take the deep breaths Mrs. Greene kept advising. I saw the screen door—the same one I had stood behind every afternoon, waiting for Sage to come home.

So she had come home, after all. She just hadn't come home to me.

Levi opened the screen entrance and knocked on the front door. I gladly let him take the reins. Once he knocked, we both took two steps back and waited on the front porch. My palms were sweaty. I wiped them on my pants in case Sage shook my hand. Is that what a mother would do after not seeing her daughter for ten years? Shake her hand? I wiped my hands on my pants again.

The front door opened. It wasn't Sage. It was an older woman. She stared at us through the screen. She was maybe in her sixties and was very small, but didn't appear frail. Her hair was whitish-gray, pulled back into a messy braid that cascaded over her right shoulder. Her hair was long.

"Hello there," she said in a nonplussed way.

I blinked. "Do you live here?"

She smiled. She was very pretty, a few wrinkles dancing across her skin, wrinkles you could only describe as laugh lines. "I do."

"We must have the wrong house," I told her. "Sorry to bother you."

We turned to go, but she opened the screen door and took a step toward us. "It's not often I get young people showing up on my front porch." I thought about informing her that we weren't there to visit her, exactly, instead we were looking for a tall, willowy woman who had refused to allow me to call her Mom, but then I wondered if perhaps this lady had dementia and maybe she thought we were someone else entirely, which got me thinking she was most likely still too young to have dementia, but perhaps anyone could have dementia—and was dementia something you could catch during pregnancy? I've digressed.

"Have you lived here long?" Levi was asking the woman.

"Not very. Moved in a few months ago, actually. The rent is good."

"I used to live here," I told her.

"Is that so?"

I nodded.

"Is that why you're here? To visit your old home?"

I considered telling her about Sage but decided against it. Too complicated to deposit on a virtual stranger. "Yeah," I finally said. "Just wanted to see it again."

"How long did you live here?"

"For most of my life, basically. We moved last summer. My mom and I painted the house this color. I'm surprised you didn't paint over it."

"That was one of the things that initially drew me to the house. I loved the color. It was very unusual."

"That's one word for it."

The woman laughed. It felt like she was hesitant about something, the way she looked at Levi and me. "You could… come inside… if you'd like to see the house again. I don't mind. As long as you're not armed and dangerous." I couldn't tell if she was joking.

I looked down at my stomach. "Let me tell you, I can do a lot with this protruding belly. It's pretty savage. You should be cowering in fear."

She looked at me for a moment then laughed again. She opened the screen door. "Come inside."

The house hadn't changed a bit. Even some of the furniture was the same, and I remembered that Sol left a few pieces when we'd stopped renting it last August.

"It's the same," I told her.

She nodded. "Feel free to look around. I'm going to get some lemonade. You want some?"

Levi and I nodded. "Thank you," Levi said.

She disappeared down the hallway.

"I'm sorry," Levi told me. "I thought for sure Sage would be here."

"It's okay," I said to him tiredly. "We tried. That's what matters."

"We'll find her someday."

"Maybe so. I'm fine without her. I've made it this far."

"It doesn't make sense, though. Lucy saw her here."

"Lucy *thought* she saw her. She was clearly mistaken. It's not like she knew what Sage looked like."

"Yeah, I guess so."

The woman called out, "I've got lemonade in the kitchen!"

I nodded in the direction of the kitchen, and we walked down the hallway.

"Would you like to sit down?" she asked. She was sitting at the kitchen table, three sweating glasses of lemonade and a tray filled with shortbread cookies positioned beside her.

Levi and I each took a chair.

"What are your names?" She asked.

"Mine's Levi."

"Maeve."

"What lovely names. Your parents chose well." She smiled at us. "I'm Aubrey. When's your baby due, Maeve?"

"In September."

"Are you excited?"

"Yes," I told her honestly, "and terrified, too."

Aubrey laughed. "That's entirely normal, my dear."

I took a long, cool sip, and it slid down my weary throat.

"Are you retired, Aubrey?" Levi asked.

"Not officially, but I've stopped working. I used to be a hairdresser. My hands are too shaky to do that now. I had my own salon and everything. It was a lovely way to meet people. Are you both in school?"

Levi nodded. "We're both in eleventh grade."

"How's that?"

"It's all right, I guess. I don't like school that much, but Maeve is a good student."

"Sometimes," I said. Aubrey laughed. "I don't mind it. I like English."

"So did I. Especially reading all those books they assigned," said Aubrey. "I love reading."

I nodded. "Me too."

"Not me," Levi said.

I bet Aubrey would have patted his hand had she known him better. You could tell she liked him a lot, but that wasn't a real surprise to me. He generally had that effect on people.

"Would I be able to use your bathroom?" I asked her.

"Of course," she breezed. "I'm sure you know where it is."

I grinned. "I do." I easily found my way and could hear Levi and Aubrey talking to one another through the paper-thin walls.

"I want to be a kind person," I told my baby, who seemed to

agree. There were kind people left in this world. It was an easy thing I often chose to forget. I washed my hands quickly and could feel my stomach grumbling with hunger.

I opened the bathroom door and walked back to the kitchen. "What are you two doing in here?" I asked jokingly.

Levi was staring at me, his expression unreadable.

"I could hear you all the way in the bathroom," I laughed. I looked at Aubrey and realized she was standing beside another woman. The woman was lithe, her braid matching that of Aubrey's. Grocery sacks were piled high on the counter.

"I'd like you to meet my daughter," Aubrey told Levi and me. Her hand was set gently on the woman's forearm.

I looked at the woman for a long time and reached for Levi. He found me, clumsily wrapping his fingers against my goose-prickled flesh. I was fairly sure my heart had discontinued its regular pumping of blood because the air felt stale and there was pressure in my head.

I was staring at Aubrey's daughter.

Or more accurately, I was staring at her floppy hat.

TWENTY-EIGHT

"MAEVE," THE WOMAN SAID.

I didn't speak.

She was taller than me, but I still felt as though I was looking into a mirror.

"My," she said smiling. "Look at you."

I focused on taking another breath. I watched my chest cavity rise and fall, rise and fall, rise and fall. Levi moved his fingers from my wrist to my hand. I stared at her—the woman who held me safe within her womb for nine full months then brought me out into this dazzling world; the woman who caught me fireflies and sang me songs and wrote me poetry. I didn't say anything, just continued to breathe and stare at her. Levi broke the uncomfortable silence and introduced himself.

"I know who you are, Levi," Sage said to him.

"You do?" He was surprised, obviously.

"Yes."

"That's right," I finally spoke. "You know all about us. About me, and Levi, and even Ky! Probably about this baby, too. Why didn't you talk to me when you called?"

Sage placed her hand firmly on the countertop. She was still graceful and long-legged, picturesque and delicate like a wildflower or a ballerina.

"I didn't feel it was my right."

I blinked.

Levi circled his thumb gently along my hand.

I breathed. "Where have you been?"

She clutched her arms tight against her chest. "Many places."

"Do you have other kids?"

"No."

"Do you think about me?"

"Every day."

"And yet you never came home."

"It wasn't my place to call home. Not anymore."

A beat.

"Was it mine?"

"Yes. Of course. You had friends—you had security. I didn't want to rip you away from all of that."

I choked back my disbelief. "Right. Why are you here?"

"In this house?"

I nodded.

"I found Aubrey a couple of years ago. She's my mother."

"Your grandmother," Aubrey said. She'd already figured it out, of course, perhaps as soon as she saw me on the front porch. I looked at her and saw the same blue-green eyes that decorated the face of Sage. That decorated mine.

"When I saw the house was up for rent last August, I took it. It was the only place that felt like I might belong. Aubrey moved in a few months later."

"Why didn't you come back for me?"

She didn't say anything.

"You told me you were going to come back. You promised me." My tone bordered on whiny, but I didn't care. I wanted to tell her exactly what she missed, hand her a written list of all the things she hadn't been there for, but for some reason, I didn't. I suspected she already knew. Instead, quietly, I said, "You missed everything." I searched her face, those blue-green eyes staring back into mine. "Why didn't you come back for me?"

Sage tilted her head. "I wanted to. Every day, I wanted to. But Maeve, you have to know, I wasn't a good mother. I'm not a good mother."

"Yes, I'm well aware of that."

Sadly, she smiled. "I know you are. And I know that's not an excuse. I'm years too late."

A light breeze blew through the open window in the kitchen, swirling memories all around us. "Did you manage to figure out who you are?" I asked.

Her eyes were sad and full of disappointment. "That was such a poor explanation for leaving you. Once I had been gone for awhile, I was riddled with guilt. I convinced myself that you wouldn't accept me if I came back." She closed her eyes. "I became quite good at lying to myself."

"There's a lot that has happened, Sage."

She opened her eyes and nodded as if she already knew what I meant.

"I'm not… I'm not seven anymore."

"No, you're not. You're seventeen years, three months and nineteen days."

I laughed softly, despite my grief. "I suppose I am."

She came closer to me. She reached out to touch my cheek, her fingers skimming the surface of my skin. "You're such a good girl, Maeve. And so pretty." I think she was memorizing me then, trying to commit the feel of my face so she couldn't forget. "I'm sorry I've disappointed you."

She let her hand fall back down.

"I've disappointed myself." I took a deep breath, about to tell her every poor decision I'd made—so many piled up onto the next—and I'd convince her that I wasn't really good, that maybe I never was.

"Your friend Lucy came and saw me," she said, barging in through my thoughts. "I had been calling Sol for awhile—to check in and see what you were like. I was always so curious to find out what interested you. Then one day Lucy came to the house," Sage smiled. "She kept telling me what an amazing girl you are. I didn't doubt that, not for a moment. She told me how much I was missing." Her eyes searched me, begging for some sort of understanding. "I knew you'd be amazing, but I didn't know if I would be amazing for you. If you were so amazing without me, then maybe if I came back I would mess everything up. I was scared, Maeve. I wanted to come see you but I didn't know if you'd want me. I've let you down for a long time. It was the only thing I was truly successful at."

"Did you complete your list?"

She blinked.

"Your list," I repeated. "The one you carried around in your pocket."

"I didn't complete it, no. Well, I went back to Aubrey. I didn't do any of the others. It was a stupid list."

"It was a way for you to dream."

Sage smiled softly at me. She'd hardly aged, at least not that I could see. She looked the same way she'd looked when she took me to the carnival. "That's right," she laughed to herself, soft and far away and nostalgic. "I desperately wanted to dream."

"I have so many questions," I told her.

"As do I."

"I don't trust you."

She didn't say anything.

"I would never leave my baby like you left me."

She took a step forward and I dropped Levi's hand. She wrapped her arms around me. I stiffened immediately, but after a moment relaxed, and I felt my palms rest softly against her back. I could feel her breathing—rhythmic, slow, right there against me. It was awkward, and yet exactly the place I wanted to be.

Leaning closer, placing my lips to her ear, I said to her, "We are not defined by our past, by our regrets, or by the choices we might have made." I shifted back and there were tears in those blue-green eyes. "Lucy told me that."

"She's right," Sage whispered. "I hope you believe her."

"I do," I said.

I do.

AUBREY AND SAGE MADE US sandwiches because it was past five o'clock in the afternoon and we were all hungry.

"Will grilled cheese be sufficient?" Aubrey asked.

I nodded. "Levi loves cheese."

"I really do," Levi said. "I really love cheese. I would be miserable if I were lactose intolerant."

I shook my head. "That would be the worst."

Sage laughed. "Can you imagine a life without ice cream?"

"Absolutely not," I told her. "I can't imagine it."

"Or cheese," Levi said. "I cannot imagine a life without cheese."

"That would be the worst," I said again.

We ate our grilled cheese sandwiches outside on the front porch because the sun was shining and spring was in full swing. There were four white wicker chairs with a small white wicker table, and it was there that we sat.

"Thank you," I told Aubrey.

"Good manners." Sage winked at me.

"I didn't learn them from Sol," I said, laughing.

"No," Sage mused. "I bet you didn't. How has he been?"

"Ever since Lucy came along he's been doing great. He started getting better when Ky killed herself—I think because he felt bad for me, or something. But he's stopped drinking now, or at least he's trying harder than I've ever seen. I don't think you could find one speck of alcohol in the house. He's taking himself seriously."

"Really."

I nodded.

"That's a real feat. Lucy must be Wonder Woman."

"No, but she is a wonderful person. Don't you think, Levi?"

Levi nodded, his cheeks large with sandwich.

Sage smiled. "I got that impression when she came here. Did she move in?"

I shook my head. "They love each other, though. I haven't seen Sol this happy since the early days with you."

"The early days, huh? Is that what you call them? Makes me feel old."

"You're not old."

"You are."

I laughed. "Am I?"

Sage reached out and skimmed my cheek with her fingertips. "Old and young, all at the same time. Sol loves Lucy?"

"Yes."

"And Lucy loves Sol?"

"She does."

"And do you love the boy who's the daddy of your baby?"

I sighed, looking down at my half eaten grilled cheese. Levi didn't say anything. "Did you love my father?"

Sage looked out at the houses across from us, distant and close, all at the same time. "I did," she said after awhile. "I loved him very much. I was your age, you know, yours and Levis', and your dad wanted to marry me. Make a life together, he said." Sage looked back over at Levi and I. "I was going to be a dancer. A ballerina. Or so I wanted. I was going to go to New York City and dance until my feet bled. Your father wanted to stay here in Sycamore and be a family—the kind that went to church and had Sunday pot roast for lunch. The idea of that made me feel like I was suffocating."

Sage didn't say anything for a while.

"Go on," Aubrey encouraged.

Sage looked at me again. "Your dad's name was Jed. Jedediah Bronson Parker was his full name and he was a kind boy, Maeve. I regularly told him he was an artist because he could build the most beautiful furniture you ever saw. He carved intricate pictures into tables and chairs, and his hands always felt rough when he held me. Like sawdust. He wanted a quiet, simple life, and I wanted flashy lights and adventure. But I loved him, and he loved me. And he loved you, Maeve. Believe me, he loved you." She laughed softly, remembering. "The day you were born he looked at you and wrapped your hand around his finger. He told me you were the prettiest thing he had seen in his life. You have his nose."

"Do you miss him?"

"I do. He was a good man. He didn't deserve the life I gave him."

I thought of the boy sitting in a white wicker chair beside me.

Aubrey said, "Sage, you can't think like that. You gave him a beautiful baby girl who he loved with all his heart. He had a good life, even if it was short."

Sage smiled wistfully. "Sol loved you, too, Maeve. He was harder than your dad. Tougher." She breathed a laugh. "What am I saying? He was the opposite of Jed in every way. That's why I brought him home. I thought I could try to reinvent myself, I suppose. But Sol loved you. Loves you."

"Did you love Sol?"

Sage sighed. "In a different way than I loved your father. I was young with Jed, and I felt naive and uncomplicated. But with Sol I was jaded, and more grown up; I think looking to disappear from the grief I felt after Jed's death. It was love, but it wasn't lasting."

We quietly ate our sandwiches and listened to the cicadas sing.

"It's getting late," Aubrey said.

"We should go," Levi told me.

"We should go," I replied.

"My mom wanted us home before the sun set. She doesn't want me driving far after dark."

Sage looked at me. "Maeve… I could take you back in a few hours. We could talk for a little longer." She struck me as shy. "If you wanted."

I glanced at Levi.

"Do you want that?" he asked.

"Just to talk?" I asked Sage.

She nodded.

"You won't try and… make me sleep over or anything?"

"No."

"I have to be home before midnight," I lied.

"You will."

"All right."

Levi said to Sage, "Sage, can I ask you something?"

"Sure, Levi."

"You'll promise me you won't leave again? You'll promise that to Maeve? She deserves a mom who will be there for her."

"I know she does."

"So you'll promise us you're not leaving again?"

Sage looked at me, her eyes an abstract painting, just as I remembered them. "I promise."

"We'll see," I said.

"HOW ARE YOU DOING?" LEVI asked as we walked down the street to his car.

I took a limp breath and leaned against the passenger door. "Tired," I replied.

"I bet. That was a long day. Are you okay to stay here for a few more hours? You can come home with me if you want."

"I guess Sage wants to talk."

"You can ask her your questions."

I nodded again. "Thank you for bringing me."

He leaned his arm against the side of the car and looked at the houses across from us. "Not only did you find your mother, but you found your grandmother, too."

"I didn't know she existed."

"She knew about you."

"I think you're right."

"How do you feel?"

I turned my body so I was facing him. "Tell me something, Levi. Have I wasted my life being angry?"

Levi looked at me. "What do you mean?"

"I've been angry at Sage my whole life, it feels. This underlying sense of betrayal and loathing was always there inside of me. I blamed her for all of the bad in my life... like if she had been there, none of it would have happened. I've been angry at Sol for getting drunk, and angry at Ky for killing herself, and angry at Jared for making her do it. Angry at Alice for loving him, and Gray for leaving, and you for being relentless with your friendship. Some days I'm angry at this unborn baby. But most of all, I've been angry at myself for blaming everything on everyone else." I leaned my head on his shoulder. "I'm tired. I don't want to be angry anymore. I could choose to be mad at Aubrey, and definitely at Sage, but..." I let out a sigh that felt as though it had been rattling around in my ribcage for a long time. "I'm tired, Levi."

He held me against his chest, his cheek lying on my hair, the world turning fiery and orange around us, ablaze as the sun began to lower.

"You should go," I told him after a few minutes. "You'll be driving in the dark at this rate."

"I should go," he agreed. But instead he held my face within his hands and I looked up at him. "You're not an angry person,

Maeve. You're the best person I've ever known."

"I know that's not true. There are far better people out there."

"None that I care about as much as you."

I stared at the curve of his lips. They were pinky peach, but getting warmer and darker as the sun was leaving the sky.

"I'm having a baby," I told him. He pressed his lips against my forehead for a long time.

"I know."

"I'm seventeen-years-old and having a baby. You don't want to be stuck with me. I won't allow it."

"Being stuck with you…" he breathed a laugh. "It would be a pleasure to be stuck with you. I wouldn't be stuck at all. You must know that by now."

I pulled myself away from him. "You don't know what you're saying."

"I do. Maeve, I——"

"Don't say it."

"You knew what I was going to say?"

I nodded.

"Then you know I mean this. Every word of it."

I took a step away from him. "I care for you, Levi—more than I've cared for anyone before. You're my favorite person in this whole freaking world. When something sad or good or boring happens, you're the first person I want to tell. You're kind to me, and you believe that I am smart and capable——"

"You are smart and capable——"

"Let me finish. I can't tell you how much you mean to me. Truly. You are so… good. But this will never happen, you and I. No. You deserve more."

He reached to grab my wrist, but I tucked my arms against my chest.

"Don't do this, Maeve," he almost whimpered. "Don't make this decision for us."

"I'm having a baby! Which part of that don't you understand? What are you going to do—pretend to be the baby's father?" I shook my head ferociously. "No, Levi. I won't allow that. You have a life to live, and I will not be the one to drag you down or stand in your way."

"You have a life to live, too," he said quietly.

"I know I do. But it looks different than I originally thought."

"It doesn't have to."

"You're hopeful. And completely unrealistic. But you're optimistic and hopeful, and I am not."

"You can be. There are a thousand reasons to hope, Maeve. Why do you give up before it has begun?"

"I can't hope," I told him. "I'm far too scared."

Levi unlatched my arms and took my hands into his. "Of what?"

Tears streamed from me. "This baby. Letting you go. Not letting you go at all."

"Do you want to be a mother?"

I shook my head. "I love this baby. I mean, I think I do. I feel him inside of me and I know there's so much of me that has made so much of him. But my dreams are dying. Mrs. Greene tells me college is still perfectly attainable, but it's not. I'll never get there. I won't go to school or get a job or write anything worth reading. Instead, I'll have a baby and be a mother and live in that house with Sol for the rest of my life."

"I don't believe that," Levi said.

"Yeah, well, you've never been very practical."

He grinned. "That's true, but you're hardly one to think of the good."

"If you prepare for the worst, you can never be disappointed."

"And yet you've been disappointed so many times."

I bit my lip so hard it drew blood, and I allowed myself to fall against him again, feeling the weight of his arms circle around me. And I felt safe, and I felt protected, and even though I knew I could never let him love me, I allowed myself to think of the good for those few minutes. And I was loved.

TWENTY-NINE

AUBREY MADE POPCORN ON THE stove, and Sage and I sat in the living room on the couch, her feet tucked underneath her thighs; mine stretched out along the coffee table, both of us relaxed and comfortable.

"Do you like butter, Maeve?" Aubrey hollered from the kitchen.

Sage snorted at me. "Is that even a question?"

"Definitely not."

Aubrey rounded the corner and passed us each a big bowl of buttery popcorn. Sage and I thanked her. Aubrey sat on a chair across from us.

I turned to her. "How come you didn't do anything when Sage was pregnant with me?"

Aubrey thoughtfully chewed on a piece of popcorn. "Because I didn't know."

I looked at Sage.

"That's right," Sage said. "I ran away when I found out I was pregnant. I didn't tell Mom anything. Just left a note saying I was going away for awhile."

"You have a habit of leaving," I noted.

She ran a hand through her long hair. "Not a good one to

have. I'm learning to stay. It's a slow process."

"Were you sad when Sage left?" I asked Aubrey.

"Devastated," Aubrey said. "She was my girl. My husband and I called the police and filed a missing person report. We looked everywhere for her. The police couldn't find her, but they didn't look very hard because Jed had gone missing too. They put two and two together and told me Sage would come home when she wanted to come home."

"Your husband?"

Aubrey smiled. "Your grandfather. He passed away fifteen years ago from a heart attack. He would have loved you."

Sage said, "He was full of life, your grandfather. Dad never stopped smiling. I called Mom the year he died. You were two years old when she told me what happened. I was going to take you home to see Mom, but I was so saddened by his death that I stayed away longer. I wasn't a very reasonable person. I allowed my emotions to dictate my actions."

"So you married my dad?"

"That's right. We were married on my eighteenth birthday; the two of us in a courthouse. No one would have thought it was slightly romantic, but Jed made anything special. He was good at that."

"I wish I had been there," Aubrey said.

Sage nodded sadly. "I know. I'm sorry." She turned to me. "I thought I knew everything. I didn't."

"That reminds me of me."

"Don't repeat my mistakes," Sage said. She reached over and gently touched my knee. "You have so much life to live."

"Are you talking about the baby?"

"You're not a mistake, Maeve. I don't regret keeping you for anything. But I wish I had made different choices. Let me ask you something: Are you ready to be a mother?"

I let out a long breath. "I have no idea."

"There are other options, Maeve—"

"I know my options, but I'm almost eighteen weeks. It's too late now."

"I'm not talking about an abortion."

"I don't understand."

Aubrey leaned forward. "Maeve, I want you to know. We will support you with whatever you choose. If you allow us to."

I looked at Sage.

"Have you thought about adoption?" She asked.

"Adoption?"

"Only if you want," Sage said, "and only if you feel like it's the right decision for you."

"I never thought about it. Not really."

"There are couples out there who can't have babies," Aubrey told me.

"Is that what you both think I should do?"

Sage shook her head. "I'm not going to tell you what to do, Maeve. Not after disappearing for ten years. It's your choice, your life. But I hope you'll let me be a part of it."

"You already are," I told her. "Somehow you always were."

SAGE DROVE ME HOME AROUND a quarter to nine. I had the slightest suspicion Aubrey wanted to ask me to stay over, but I didn't want that. Not yet, anyway. Maybe someday; perhaps after seeing Sage stick around for awhile. I told her about Gray and Ky and Mrs. Greene. I tried to sum up what my life had been, but I knew a two and a half hour car ride would not suffice for the ten years I had lived without her.

"Are you angry with me, Maeve?" She asked halfway through the drive.

"I don't want to be," I told her honestly. "I was for most of my life. I blamed you for everything."

She was quiet.

"It was easy to blame you. At least it was easier than trying to deal with what I was feeling at the time." I looked at her. She seemed focused on the road, and I looked at her profile, her sloping nose, her full lips. "I'd like to try and let that go now. I've held onto it for far too long."

"Thank you for giving me a chance," she said after a few minutes.

"I'm not sure if I would call it a chance just yet. I still don't trust you."

"Thank you for giving me a *sort of* chance before giving me a *real* chance."

"Use it wisely," I counseled.

"Thank you for the advice." She smiled.

We rolled down the windows and let our hair whip across our cheeks, wild and spirited. I liked driving at nighttime, the way it felt like we were the only two people left alive in the world. I hadn't realized how much I'd longed for it to be only us again.

"Sol told me you're a writer," Sage said after awhile.

I nodded. "Kind of a writer."

"Kind of?"

"I've only written a few articles and a little bit of poetry. I'm not sure if that qualifies me as a real writer."

"Do you like writing?"

"I love it."

"Do you want to keep writing?"

"Yes, I do. I want to study it in college if I can."

"Then you're a real writer to me. Working at a newspaper is a big deal, Maeve. You should give yourself more credit."

"Mr. Morris—my boss—he's a kind man, and he gave me a chance."

"Those are the sort of people you always remember, huh?"

"They are."

"Are you looking at colleges?"

"Not specifically. I still have another year left. But Mrs. Greene thinks I have a good chance at graduating with honors if

I keep working hard."

"Maeve." She flicked on her turn signal and we entered into Rutherford. "That's incredible."

"Thank you."

Sage gave me a toothy grin. "I'm proud of you. Can I say that?"

I thought for a moment. I weighed it in my head. I decided yes. "All right. You can."

"Then I'll say it again. Maeve Olivia Parker, I am so proud of you."

I think she meant it.

"WON'T YOU COME IN?" I asked Sage when we pulled into my driveway a little after eleven-thirty.

"Don't you think that could be awkward?"

"Awkward?"

"With Sol."

I waved my hand. "You're both grown people. It'll be fine. Come on now. You've driven two and a half hours. Let's go inside. I'll get you a drink and some food."

Sol and Lucy weren't there when we went into the house.

"They must be out," I told Sage. "How hungry are you?"

"Not very. I should head back. It's late."

I pulled out vanilla ice cream and root beer and made us each a large root beer float.

"I used to make these for you every Saturday night in the summertime," Sage said, taking a giant sip.

"I remember."

"Do you remember a lot about what we did with one another?"

I nodded. "Mostly art projects."

Sage laughed loudly. "Oh—the art you and I would create together! Finger painting and pottery and bead making. We had such fun together. Those were the best days of my life when I look back."

"You had fun with me?"

"I did."

"It didn't feel like you were babysitting?"

Sage took another sip. "No, not at all. You were mine. That was the difference."

I sat next to her and took a sip of my float. "Do you think I'll feel that way?"

"With your baby? Sure. It won't be someone else's child. That baby will be your flesh and blood. You won't understand now—not until you hold that baby in your arms, and you look at him or her and see yourself in all of their features."

"It's weird to think about."

Sage laughed again. "I remember thinking that, too. But you'll understand in a few months. Does the father know?"

"Yes. But he left a few days after I told him."

"I'm sorry."

"It's all right. He wasn't who I thought he was, I guess."

"It's a real shame when that happens."

"I wanted him to love me. He told me he did, but the truth is we hardly knew one another. I never thought about getting pregnant or anything. In my head that was impossible."

Sage nodded. "But then it happened."

"It did. Not so impossible after all."

We were quiet, sipping our floats.

"Can I ask you something?"

"Sure."

"When you left on March 13, did you have a plan to come back?"

"I didn't have a plan that day, no. I was listening to all of my emotion and pain, and right then it felt easier to leave than keep going. At that point in my life, I'd left more times than I had stayed. I figured I would form a plan along the way. I didn't think I'd leave you forever. Maybe a month or so. Get my bearings straight or something."

"Were you ever going to come back?"

"When you turned eighteen."

"You were going to wait that long?"

"I figured if I waited until you were considered a legal adult, you wouldn't think I was swooping in and trying to be your mother. I knew I'd lost that right the day I walked out on you. Maeve, I'm sorry. I can't tell you how sorry I am. You don't have to forgive me. I don't expect that."

"You promised Levi you wouldn't leave."

"I'm not leaving unless you tell me to."

Sol and Lucy walked in, and Lucy was laughing.

"Maeve!" she cried happily when she saw me. "We missed you."

"I was gone for less than a day, Lucy."

Sol was staring at Sage. "I can't believe it," he said.

Sage stood up. "I understand if I'm not welcome here."

Lucy smiled at me, then turned to Sage. "Of course you're welcome here. I'm glad to see you again."

"We don't need you," Sol told Sage.

"I'm aware of that," Sage said. "I'm not trying to be needed."

"I needed you a long time ago," Sol said. "I thought you would come back to us, and I kept thinking everyday would be the day you'd come home."

Sage listened quietly.

"But you didn't. And I moved on." Sol wrapped his arm around Lucy's waist.

"I'm happy for you two," Sage said. "I honestly am. I'm sorry I hurt you, Sol. I've made some terrible mistakes and I wish more than anything that I could go back and undo them."

"You can't," Sol said.

"I know."

Lucy squeezed Sol's hand. "We've all made terrible mistakes

that we wish we could undo. Isn't that right, Sol?"

He was still staring at Sage. I wondered who he was seeing her as. A girl he once loved? A girl who once left him? Or perhaps the woman who stood in front of him now, the one whose dreams and desires didn't seem to have been met with anything remotely close to fulfillment. But this is all of us: we are people, and in that, we are many people; we are segments and slivers of one another, lovers and leavers, and incandescent dreamers. We hope for things far beyond our reach, and we are people, wildly flawed and yet deservedly loved people.

"That's right," Sol said.

Lucy looked over at me. "You got anymore root beer and ice cream?"

I grinned. "I sure do."

PRESENT DAY

THE BABY IS CRYING.

Not loudly, only a few soft cries that wake me up. I open my eyes and look to my right. Sage has her arms wrapped around the baby, nestled close and tight against her breast. She's whispering faint words I can't hear, humming a quiet tune, and I hear small coos come from the tiniest lips I have seen. The cries slowly begin to fade as Sage rocks the baby back to sleep.

Sage's hair is matted against her forehead. The rest of it is tucked into an unruly braid that runs down the side of her body. Mine must look the same way. Although worse, I imagine. Sage braided my hair in between the contractions, twisting the listless strands into a braid at the crown of my head like she had done when I was a young girl. Braiding herself into me once more. She was calm during the labor, allowing me to clench her hand every time the pain shot through my body. Which it had. Often.

The baby came early, and Lucy and Sol are away on their honeymoon. They're at the ocean. Lucy's sad she missed the birth, but she'll be okay. She's where she's supposed to be. They called me yesterday and Lucy kept saying, "It's pure bliss, Maeve. That's the only way to describe it. The sun is shining, but it's never too hot. And a breeze always rustles your hair so you're in this constant state of refreshment. Just... bliss. We'll take you here someday; you, me and Sol." You can hear the sunshine in her voice.

They got married two weeks ago today, at the edge of the forest. Lucy didn't stop smiling that entire day. Neither did Sol, for that matter. We hung strands of ribbon from the trees which had danced as the breeze ran against them. Lucy wore a simple white dress, and a headpiece made from the same ribbon we had hung on the trees, her hair long and flowing down her back. She had never looked more beautiful, which I kept thinking, and Sol kept saying. He wore a suit with a tie and Lucy told him he looked dashing. I agreed.

There were about twenty of us all together, including Lucy's parents and a few of her close friends. Lucy wanted it to be intimate. "Just the people I love the most," she had said. We went to the Fishers' house after the ceremony, and Nora cooked the best meal I've ever had. It was one of those days where nothing went wrong, where you looked out at the people among you and you saw that everyone was genuinely happy to be there, sitting there celebrating with one another. And you sat there wishing that sort of day would never end—or at least that you could keep that feeling for a little while longer. Sol continued smiling and holding Lucy's hand, his wedding ring prominent on his fourth finger. I never thought I'd see the day. But there are a lot of things I didn't think I would see, a lot of things I didn't think could be possible, and it turns out they are all very possible indeed.

Aubrey is out getting another coffee. She's exhausted. Sage keeps telling her she can go home, but Aubrey won't listen. Their stubbornness is cut from the same cloth. The same as mine, I suppose. Decidedly, it's not something I'll be ashamed of.

Sage looks over at me.

"You okay?" she whispers.

I nod.

"Tired?"

I nod again.

She laughs softly. "You were wonderful, Maeve."

There's a knock on the door and a woman comes in.

"Hi, Maeve. I'm Jess. I'll be looking after things today. How are you doing?"

"I'm all right."

"Is there anything I can do for you? Anything I can get?"

I shake my head. "I'm okay, thanks."

"Okay." Jess looks over at the baby asleep in Sage's arms. "I'll be back in a couple of minutes then."

She leaves the door open and a few moments later, Francine appears.

"Hey, Francine," I say when I see her.

She's staring at the baby. "Hi, honey. Are you doing okay?"

I nod.

"You're still sure about all of this?"

"I'm sure."

Francine comes over to my bed and takes hold of my hand. Her eyes never leave the baby. "They didn't tell me what gender."

I smile. "She's a girl."

"A girl," Francine breathes.

"A tiny, healthy girl. Six pounds, two ounces."

There's a knock on the door and Nora and Levi are here. Francine goes to hug Nora, and Levi comes over to me.

"Hello there, Maeve the Brave."

I laugh. "Where'd you come up with that one?"

"It's fitting."

I give him a look but he leans in and hugs me, his lips softly meeting my cheek. I close my eyes and wrap my hands along his shoulder blades, and he whispers in my ear, "You did good, Maeve girl. So good. I've never been more proud of you."

I look up at him, tears pooling in my eyes. I blink them back.

"And you look beautiful." He tugs the bottom of my braid gently.

"You're a terrible liar."

Nora says, "My turn!" Levi goes over to Sage and the baby, and Nora gives me a hug.

"How do you feel, honey?"

"I'm good, Nora. Thanks for coming."

"I wanted to be here. For you. For Francine."

I nod. "I'm glad you came."

Nora claps her hands, declaring, "Let's see this beautiful baby!" Sage gently places the baby into Nora's arms.

"It's a girl," I tell Nora.

"She's beautiful," Nora murmurs. "Absolutely beautiful."

"What's her name?" asks Levi.

Francine places her hand in mine and the tears that roll down her cheeks fall onto our clasped fingertips. "You name her, Maeve," Francine whispers. "You tell us what her name is."

I kiss Francine's hand, the tender spot in between her knuckles. "Kylie," I say to Levi. "Her name is Kylie."

He nods slowly and Nora places Kylie into my arms.

I look up at Francine who stares down at the baby. "What's her middle name, Francine?"

Francine smiles, her tears still falling silently. "Olivia."

"Kylie Olivia," I whisper to the little girl in my arms. I memorize this—the weight of her body against me, the soft rise and fall of her chest, and I picture her tiny lungs that are working inside of her, pushing breath in and out, exuding life. Exuding a future.

I kiss her forehead, then the bridge of her nose, in between her closed eyes.

She is soft as I hold her and I know she is not mine.

For this moment I think of what our life could look like together, a life with Sage and Aubrey, Lucy and Sol, and Levi...

a life where she could be built up by strong and stubborn women who fight and run, who write and hope, who might love her more than she ever thought she could be loved. I whisper my fingers against her dark, downy hair. I pushed and cried and birthed her into this world a few hours ago, and I know she is not mine. I love her so, and I would die for her if it meant she need not be hurt, and I would bleed for her if it meant she need not know grief, and I would give her away if it meant she grow up safe, and whole, and free.

I cry as I watch her sleep.

I know she is not mine.

Jess walks back in. "Ms. Sinclair," she says, "I've been looking for you. You're not supposed to be in here."

"I'm terribly sorry," Francine says and moves towards the door. "I didn't know."

I say to Jess, "It's okay. I want her to stay."

Jess looks surprised. "You do?"

I nod.

Jess says, "It's almost time, Maeve."

I nod again. Nora looks over at me with tears in her eyes, and says, "We'll give you some privacy. Come, Levi. Let's wait outside." He looks at me and I turn the sides of my lips up at him. Not a smile so much as a promise. He mouths something to me as they go out the door, but I'm not sure what he was trying to say. It's all right. We have time.

Sage asks, "Do you want me to leave?"

I shake my head. "No. Please stay."

"I'm sorry Sol and Lucy aren't here," Francine says to me.

"It will be okay."

"I'll love her," she says. "I already do. My heart feels swollen."

I look back down at Ky, and her eyes flutter open and seep into mine. I hold her closer to me and tell her, "I'll always love you. I promise you now, there will never be a day where I won't think about you, and never a day where I will doubt that you are loved." I kiss her again, breathing in the smell of her, drinking in the sight of her, shedding tears against the blanket which swaddles her safely in.

"If she ever asks you, will you tell her about me?"

Francine places her hand against my cheek. "Of course."

"And someday, but only if she wants to, she can come find me. She can always come find me."

Francine nods and kisses my hairline. "Yes," she whispers, "she can."

I look down at Ky again and I am still crying. I kiss her tiny face all over, praying she might remember the girl who loved her first. Sacredly, I place her into Francine's long awaiting arms.

"How long is the drive?" Sage asks.

"Three hours," Francine answers. "We won't go until tomorrow. But we'll stop by my mom's on the way so she can meet Kylie. Then we'll head to our new home."

"I'm sorry you had to move," I say.

Francine shakes her head. "Maeve, honey. Please don't apologize to me. You have given me the greatest gift I could possibly receive, and moving was the right thing to do. It's a new life we have."

"Yes," I say. "It is."

Jess comes up and says, "It's time to go, Francine. I'll take you to another room now."

Francine leans into me, and Ky is safe between us. Her two mothers. "Thank you, Maeve," she says.

I bend in and kiss her cheek. "Love her," I say.

"I do. I will."

Jess nods her head at me and escorts Francine from my room. I turn my head to Sage who is still standing to my right. She is looking at me. I shift over in the hospital bed and Sage comes and crawls in beside me. She wraps her arms around my neck and I lay down, my head resting on her shoulder.

I weep against her.

"You are safe," Sage whispers and I think my tears might drown us in this room. "And special, and important..." Her fingers clasp like a chain around me, and I know I am safe here beside her. We stay this way for a long time, this muddle of limbs and longing. After I don't know how long, she says, "Let's go home."

Lifting my exhausted head to see her watery eyes, I begin to count the speckles that are flecked like gold paint inside of her. I'll tell her this someday—when the sharpness within me has dulled to an ache, when my lungs can catch a full breath again. But I wonder if she's realized it on her own.

We are already home.

All of us.

ACKNOWLEDGEMENTS

I am grateful to each person—Mom, Dad, Papa, and so many more—who read this collection of words long before it came to be this novel. I remember getting copies printed and spiral-bound, handing them out to the people whose opinions I valued immensely. I would say to that person, "If you want to read this book, you must promise to give me your honest opinion." To each of you who read an early version: your encouragement and kind critique allowed it to become the book it is today.

Thank you to Olivia Bronson, Sarah Roessner, Mike Bronson, Nick Pegg, and Katherine Brown for allowing me to ask your opinions, for solving plot holes, and for being honest. Thank you for believing this would always come to fruition—even when it took years.

Thank you Annie Downs for calling me to say you had read my book on a plane and cried twice. You said, "It's John Green good," which gave me hope to continue trying.

I want to thank two very influential teachers—my grade twelve Writer's Craft teacher, Mr. Spree, and my Digital Storytelling Journalism professor, Christa Morrison. Both of you gave me courage.

Thank you to the (in)courage community for welcoming me in with wide-open arms four years ago.

Thank you Jesus for giving me words and stories and a life to the full.

And to anyone holding this book within your hands—I cannot thank you enough. You are holding my dream.

ABOUT THE AUTHOR

Aliza Latta is a twenty-something Canadian writer, journalist, and artist who is a huge fan of telling stories—whether through speech, written prose, or art. She writes about faith and young adulthood on her blog, *alizanaomi.com*. Her love is divided between fiction, Africa, and journalism, and someday hopes to combine all three. This is her first novel.

Find her on Twitter or Instagram as @alizalatta

74615589R00188

Made in the USA
Columbia, SC
06 August 2017